Beyond Tahiti

Beyond Tahiti

Bud Higgins

iUniverse, Inc.
Bloomington

Beyond Tahiti

iUniverse books may be ordered through booksellers or by contacting:

iUniverse
1663 Liberty Drive
Bloomington, IN 47403
www.iuniverse.com
1-800-Authors (1-800-288-4677)

ISBN: 978-1-4502-7297-1 (sc)
ISBN: 978-1-4502-7299-5 (ebook)
ISBN: 978-1-4502-7298-8 (dj)

Library of Congress Control Number: 2010918106

Printed in the United States of America

iUniverse rev. date: 1/26/2011

Even in friendship, the arrogance of man ... proves deadly.

Contents

Acknowledgments

First off, I'd like to thank my soul mate Paula. Without her love, support, and patience, this novel would have never been possible. Her wisdom and gracious nature have guided me through the sunniest of days, and the darkest of storms. You are forever a part of me.

I'd also like to thank all the members of my family, and the great friends and acquaintances I have managed to collect and enjoy over the years. I have learned much from all of you. An artist cannot exist without inspiration, and many times that inspiration comes from the people and experiences closest to them.

To Ursula K. Le Guin: Thank you (I "borrowed" the turtles). To Tom Wolfe and Ken Kesey, I too am a prankster!

Thank you, Gene Roddenberry, for giving us all hope for the future, and some really hot green women. The universe will forever be in your debt.

Big thanks to Captain Andy for his friendly support, and his military and technical expertise.

Athena, Salem, Tony, and Nathan: I love you, and I know that you are all out there!

Mystery Plant

Origin, Species and Artist: Unknown

Panama-Pacific International Exposition

San Francisco, California: 1915

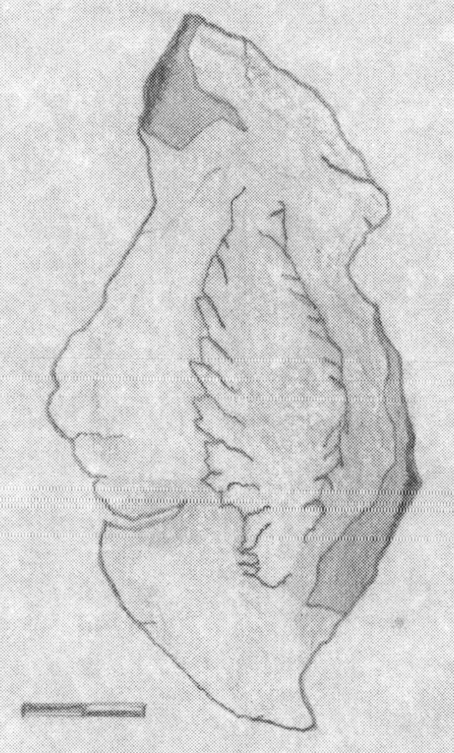

Mystery Island

Origin, Location and Artist: Unknown

Panama-Pacific International Exposition

San Francisco, California: 1915

Introduction

Meet Nathan Thomas Cole, a disillusioned product of the Gen-X tribe, a man who had it all but still lacked happiness. Nathan wakes up one day to find his greatest wish finally fulfilled. He has become the master of his own universe. There's one small problem: He is now the only resident of that universe. On this day, Nathan finds himself completely alone on a seemingly deserted tropical island, unsure of how he arrived there, how long he'd been there, or whether he was really there at all.

Now a nightmarish transcendence into mental and physical survival begins. Alternate realities begin to provide an ethereal landscape as unexplained events and scattered scenes from Nathan's life begin to play out in random sequence, forcing him to live in an ambiguous reality.

As Nathan's exile in paradise continues, the island seems to come alive. Is Nathan's subconscious coming out to play? Or has this mysterious island provided him with an exclusive key to his own lost past, unlocking the present, and careening him perilously forward into his own questionable future? If these events are only dreams, could they have the unconscious power to heal ... or could they kill? If they are real, how and why are they happening?

And what of the succulent and sweet purple berries, the "Paradise Berry," one of the island's few indigenous food sources ... What powerful and unanswered secrets do they possess?

Every minute brings a new experience for Nathan, as he encounters moments of tranquility and happiness ... and sometimes, moments of uncertainty and terror. Worst of all, he encounters his own true self.

As Nathan drifts on the edge of sanity, somewhere in this twisted menagerie of lost days and random realities, the real truth is exposed. Forever altering the course of Nathan's future ... and the future of mankind!

Chasing Dorothy

Chapter One

"These berries are sweet. I hope they're not dangerous."

Somewhere between Tahiti and my own passion for solitude and personal destruction, I became the last man in the universe—in my universe, that is. Was I arrogant enough to believe that I could sail around the world as the solo ringmaster of my own ego-filled, wind-powered circus? Or was I running away from something or someone so lost in time and memory that I questioned the validity of my own physical and spiritual existence? Did I leave behind friends, family, and pretty much all of a rancid society on just a whim? Or did the indelible truth that we're a flawed, greedy, uncompassionate species inhabiting and deliberately destroying a beautiful Eden finally drive me over the edge? Could I actually smell the discontent, mistrust, fear, and loathing that humanity had successfully decreed its common denominator, or did my motivations go much deeper than that? Maybe I learned to read people so well that verbal communication had become an inconvenience, a waste of my valued time, and consequently, no longer a priority. Maybe I had needed to get away so badly that my inevitable demise was sealed by my very own hand. It is possible that the perfect storm that brought me here to this deserted paradise was in itself the nameless shadow of a travel agent known as fate. If fate, and not a storm, brought me here ... then where was here, and when did I arrive?

Maybe I died? Maybe this is purgatory. Could this be Heaven or, I know this may sound crazy, someone's warped interpretation of Hell? So deliciously cruel, yet tastefully ironic ...

The new Hell ... clean, progressive, and well-thought-out! Complete with salad bar, valet parking, V.I.P. seating, full membership privileges, and a complimentary Armani suit! No burning pits of lava, no eternal suffering ... just eternity. Eternity with nothing but you and an overstuffed Goodwill bag of everything you've ever said, thought, or done. Continuously repeated scenes from a movie that will never end ... yet in some way already had.

Was this a happy ending? Did I sail off into the sunset or fall into the abyss? Had I been sentenced to forever relive scenarios that could never be changed while ceremoniously sipping on endless shots of coconut milk, loneliness, and tears?

Okay, I'm not dead. This is neither limbo nor the drive-thru window at Burger King. I merely crashed into an island on my way to the greatest mono-eccentric party of a lifetime: *Solitary confinement on Gilligan's Island.*

Let's put down the newspaper for a minute and try this one again. Maybe all this time it was me. Maybe the situation I found myself in had something to do with my interpretation of everyone else's actions, which was based on my own erroneously linear sensitivities, or lack of them. Did I have it all wrong? Was I not a compassionate light shining goodness and love on all whom I met and touched? Wasn't I the one who opened doors for little old ladies and was kind to animals? Did I not, even though I am notoriously cheap, give change to homeless guys so they could buy a beer? Perish the thought I was ever wrong ... just being facetious, of course. I was wrong at times, but I've always been a good person ... right? That counts for something. Doesn't it?

God loves me, I know he does! I'm one of his best, his finest ... a sterling example of humanity in its highest form. I don't know who or what God is, but if he's out there, I know he loves me. He showed me ... *he gave me this great island!*

Stop the presses: God rocks! Now if God could get me a refrigerator and a satellite dish, we'd be on. I'm gonna start prayin' ... I'm prayin' hard, hallelujah ... praise the Lord ... whoo-hoo, hallelujah, brothers and sisters, whooooo-hooooo!!!

Oops, no electricity. Add it to the list. Pray harder ... harder, HARDER! Yes sir! Hallelujah, Halle Berry, Chuck Berry, Buddy Hallelujah and the Crickets, halle-heck're-ya-doin', hallowed be thy name, yeah here it comes ... here it comes!

I CAN FEEL IT!

Yeah, oh yeah, oh my God, yes, yes, yes, yes, yes ... oh yeah, oh yeah, yeah ... whooooo ... *"I'll have what she's having!"!* Oh yeah ... yeahhhhh!!! Oh yeah ... whooooo!

And while you're at it, add a Ferrari and a flat-screen ... yes, my brothers and sisters, sixty inches of pure plasmic love, courtesy of the Big Man himself!!!

**DOES GOD CHARGE FOR DELIVERY?
I LEFT MY WALLET AT HOME ... OOPS!**

How long have I been here? When did I arrive at this fortress of solitude with palm trees? Oops again! I failed the *Robinson Crusoe* test. I haven't kept track of the days and nights. That's all right; I don't have a calendar anyway. If you're gonna keep track, you gotta do it right. Can't keep track of the days and nights without a calendar!

This island is big, real big. Hope there aren't any cannibals. Wait a minute, where's my boat? Did I even have a boat? There must be some wreckage somewhere, if not, how did I get here? Put on to-do list: *Search for boat!* Should I search for cannibals, too? Naw; if they're here ... I don't wanna know about it.

BACK TO THE STORM

I thought there was a storm, but now I don't know. It's an awfully nice day today, yes sir it definitely is a nice day today. Look, up in the sky ... no it's not a bird or a plane; it's my intrepid solar friend ... the sun! I like the sun, *I hope he likes me.* Wait a minute, I'm talking to myself, and the dialogue is really creeping me out!

Man, there goes that weird brain feeling too; you know the one I'm talking about. That spacey, sick feeling you get in your head when you consciously try to imagine just how big the universe really is ... when it began and where it finally ends ... when you attempt to foolishly muddle through the insane process of calculating the numerical parameters of infinity. Bull ... you can't define infinity; it's still going on! Does infinity even know what it is, let alone where it's going to end? It probably doesn't even know when it began! It probably doesn't flipping know it even exists! Wow, feels weird, doesn't it? Weeeird! Infinity has no clue, and neither do we ...

WHEEEEEEEEEEEEEEEEEEEEEEEEEEEEEEEEEEEEEEEE EEEEEEEEEE!!!

You know what? Screw infinity! Screw the exact date it began, 'cuz frankly, I don't give a flying flip when or where it's gonna end!

STILL THE QUESTION REMAINS

How did I get here? When did I get here? Why am I here? Where is here? Okay ... slow down. Let's take this one from the beginning ... one more time!!!

HOW DID I GET HERE?
WHEN DID I GET HERE?
WHY AM I HERE?
WHERE IS HERE?

I guess the best place to start is the last thing I remember, right? Problem is ... I can't remember the last thing I remembered. There is a serious disconnect, a malfunction at the junction, a crack in time, a rip in the universe, a hitch in my giddy-up. Where do I begin? I could start from the ending and go back, but that's like trying to drive out of the garage with the door down. I could wait for the answers to present themselves at a later date, but that's like trying to get laid by osmosis or frying an egg on a Jell-O ice cube, absolutely futile. I could end up waiting forever. Forever is a long time ... a long time, and I don't know how much time I've got. If I could save time in a bottle ... can you save time in a bottle? I've heard it in a song. You can send a message in a bottle. I've heard that in a song too. As a matter of fact, I've seen it in the movies! The lone castaway lost on an uncharted and deserted tropical island ... hey, that's me! Now all I need is a bottle, a pen, and a piece of paper, and I can send a note. *Help, I'm stuck on an island and I don't know where I am ... save me!* Crap, that won't work ... outta luck again. Pray harder, Nathan, harder! No, I've got to search. But before I can even begin to locate the proverbial needle, I have to find the haystack. But how do you find a haystack on a deserted tropical island? I got it, Nathan you're a flippin' genius ... find the farm, yes, find the flippin' farm! That's where you find haystacks right? Or did all those years of watching reruns of Green Acres teach you nothing at all. *"Farm livin' is the life for me ..."* Oops ... no farms on this island, what now?

Don't tell me the answer is blowin' in the wind ... oh, and by the way ...

I'M HUNGRY!

I can't remember the first time I had the mysterious island berries. Small, succulent, purple, and sweet almost to the point of seduction ... I was hooked from the very first taste. They were of a species I had never seen before. Yet somehow, even alone on this lost island, I shed my natural distrust of the unknown and indulged myself in this true alien delicacy. Besides, what choice did I have? It wasn't like there were hot dog vendors popping out of clamshells or pizza guys offering me a slice at every turn of a palm tree! The berries became my salvation. A tasty distraction from the solitude I had once so desperately desired and now vehemently despised. They, like the sun, had become my drafted friends. They gave completely of themselves with no restraint, and no regret. My exotic edible friends would soon show their lush mind-painting effects, and mold the revolving-door realities of my accidental island exile.

This morning was no different. I watched the sun rise as if for the very first time. I went to the field where the berries grew, my field of dreams. Its surreal landscape was hauntingly reminiscent of the Technicolor poppy field in *The Wizard of Oz*. I wondered if my subconscious mind had made more than just a coincidental connection between my Paradise Berries and the mystical poppies that had whisked Dorothy and her motley crew away to the world of sleep and virtual dreams. Had I possibly visited the vaunted Emerald City before and not remembered? Days and nights on this island had a strange and reoccurring habit of becoming lost soldiers. Like shooting stars hitchhiking across the night sky, momentarily seen, and then lost ... *forever.*

WEIRD DREAMS

Strangely enough, my dreams have recently taken on an overwhelmingly powerful new sense of reality. They leave invisible footprints in the unconscious sands of time and space, footprints that lead neither to nor from any tangible hope of resolution regarding my present circumstance. Yet I feel the footprints are desperately trying to show me something. Something I have missed or possibly ... something I have done. I sleep at odd times of the day and night, and don't really remember entering any state of slumber. Is it the berries? I can't stay away from them. Are they addictive? What are they really doing to me? They are the most plentiful source of food on the island. I need them. C'mon, man, they're only freaking berries! Has my slow decline into solitary island madness finally begun? Is this the beginning of my mental end? The obvious lack of proper diet and human contact must certainly be speeding me toward complete intellectual collapse. *Madman in Paradise: The Life and Times of Nathaniel Thomas Cole,* kinda has a nice ring to it. Would be better though if it was someone else. Think I'll wait for the movie.

Maybe I am the last man on earth. But if I was, how would I know it? How could I be positively sure? Remember, I'm stuck out here on this deserted island. It is deserted, isn't it? I know I'm lonely, very lonely, but isn't this what I was hoping for the whole time ... the complete and total absence of human contact and the pathetic drama that comes with it? This definitely puts a new spin on being careful what you wish for. Wait a minute, maybe I wished myself here. Is that possible? I mean, if you try really, really hard, can you do that?

Maybe somewhere along the line I actually was chasing Dorothy through the poppy field, and this is all a dream, a psychotic byproduct of wishful thinking, an extension of my own innermost thoughts and personal fantasies. A living tribute to years and years of collected fear and sub-conscious anxiety running amok under the powerful cloud of slumber brought about by excessive stress and mental fatigue ... or is something else running the show?

"The beast smiles gingerly at the gate as the beauty beckons him to enter her forbidden enchanted world, the winged unicorn glides gently across the river ... and Alice and friends are crashing in Wonderland."

Yes folks, this indeed must be a dream. Soon I will awaken to the egregious sounds of morning radio, and shower in the familiar presence of my unrelenting contempt of a selfish and uncaring humanity ... one whom I totally despised but was freely an accredited card carrying member of ... or maybe I really did wish myself here ... but where is here?

I'll be more careful what I wish for next time ... if there is a next time.

Reflections
"1974"

Despite the uncertainties of my present situation, there are still quarantined memories forever illuminated in the directionless core of my so-called mind. They provide miniscule clues about my existence, but no answers as to my future. My name is a great start. I know that I am Nathaniel Thomas Cole, date of birth December 7, 1974 in San Mateo, California, thirty-three years to the day of the attack on Pearl Harbor. Gerald Ford was president. We were still reeling from one heck of a backyard barbecue in a far-off land called Vietnam. The Oakland A's won the World Series, and the Miami Dolphins won the Super Bowl. Muscle cars were king and gas was around forty-eight cents a gallon. You could even get an ice cream cone for ten cents ... double scoop! *Happy Days* debuted on ABC, and disco was right around the corner. We had already landed a man on the moon. Through a clandestine agreement between NASA and certain unnamed shadows of private industry and the underground scientific community, we also launched the friendship probe Luna-1 straight into the heart of the Pergasas A-73 system.

Luna took with her facts about Earth's technology, art, science, sociology, and trivia. It also carried an advanced cryogenic chamber filled with samples of living organisms. Rumors would later circulate that Luna also held a suspended-animation chamber with who-knows-what in it. All this science and technology was blasted into space in the feeble human hope that there would be someone or something on the other end to receive it.

Having joined the sunlit world in early December, I was automatically tagged a Sagittarius. According to Ms. Linda Goodman, I'm a *"showman and an entertainer, full of life and energy."* I'm an idealist, full of hope, ready to change the world at the drop of a dime. I'm a "brutally honest advisor," whatever that means. I love activity and hate to be locked in a box. I see straight to the heart of the matter and the truth, hence the archer. Whoo-hoo, whip out your big arrow, sailor! I'm a philosopher, an adventurer, and a free spirit. *I think, therefore I roam.* Maybe that's what got me here ... maybe I thought, and then I roamed! But to where did I roam? And when did I roam? What day of the week is this, anyway? Fine, they can keep their tarot cards, shrunken heads, voodoo dolls, and fortune cookies. Can someone please just tell me where I am? I can't even remember where I've been. On top of that, I seem to have left my wallet at home ...

Oh well. I really don't think money's gonna do me much good here anyway. This island probably doesn't have an ATM ... or a 7–Eleven!

Sirens

Chapter Two

***"I would drink the sweet wine from her soul …
and she from mine."***

The beauty of life can only be measured by one's personal perception of its value at any precise moment. On this beautiful morning I was experiencing such a moment, a moment of beauty, and the precise value of its undeclared contents. The angelic terra-incognita goddess of land I called my island was being showered with warm and comforting love-light by my intrepid solar friend the sun. At this moment, this crossroad of appreciation, happiness, and epiphany, I set aside my confusion and bewilderment. I was actually feeling pretty good. The disillusioned state of consciousness I had so selfishly hoarded to eagerly feed my personal contempt and self-loathing had not completely disappeared. It had simply been bitch-slapped to the curb to await its inevitable reawakening down the road.

I CALLED MY ISLAND "TERRA-DONNA"

There may have been a meaning in that name somewhere, but to me it just sounded nice. It was reminiscent of some late-night black-and-white movie I had watched as a kid hidden under the covers at 4:30 in the morning … I never did sleep well. Though I know I've explored Terra-Donna many times, my recollections of those journeys remain dim and without context. I remembered an inlet on the southwest part of the island, where fresh water from the upper elevations flowed down to the ocean. I recall vaguely having been on the higher ground visible from my lair. I remember the Paradise Berries growing in abundance. That was today's quest. My mission, if I chose to accept it: Climb the mountain, find the berries, and eat, Nathan ... eat. It was a beautiful morning, rich with the promise of new and exciting adventures to come. So what was wrong? Something must have happened the last time I went up there, whenever that was. What have I missed? Did I see something? Was there a giant one-eyed monster waiting for me to fulfill his minimum daily requirement of castaway? Maybe there were aliens? Naw, if they were here, they'd have gotten me by now ... I'm the only game in town. Whatever was bothering me would have to wait to present itself once again at the proper time, the proper place.

MAYBE I'LL JUST STAY HOME

Mission postponed for the moment. Instead I would feast upon my dwindling stash of Paradise Berries and coconut milk in my southern abode. There would be time later in the day for discovery and adventure, but this morning belonged exclusively to my mysterious edible friends ... and my constant, trustworthy companion known as the sun.

I WAS HUNGRY, IT WAS TIME TO EAT

SALEM

Salem Kimura waited patiently outside Carlo's apartment. A light rain fell on a gray Tuesday morning. She remembered many mornings like this from growing up in San Francisco. Wisps of heavenly mist swept through a gentle, ethereal landscape. Yet the mist carried with it an almost deafening silence, a hypnotic silence demanding that only the angelic music of its celestial tears be heard. But the intermittent sweep of windshield wipers returned Salem to a more practical train of thought. Reality beckoned. Was it to early to ring Carlo's doorbell ... was he even up yet?

The lab was shut down that morning for routine maintenance. Carlo had requested late-night telemetry logs from the Excalibur satellite probe sometime that day. He had mentioned picking them up himself, but Salem wanted to do this. It was almost 7:00. He must be up; he really wanted to see these reports. But did he want to see her? Even the slightest hint of rejection from Carlo would be an emotional catastrophe for Salem. The issue wasn't their long-established working relationship ... it was what he didn't know. Even though Salem, many times the object of other men's affection, had diligently pushed aside her innermost thoughts and feelings about him, she was losing the war, slowly, painfully. This was only compounded by the fact that she had equally strong feelings for Carlo's best friend and co-worker, Nathan. But the presence of Nathan's beautiful wife, Athena, and the seemingly picture-perfect romance the two of them shared made it easier for her to keep her feelings contained behind a wall of professionalism and restraint.

Still, the question lingered. Should she look into the window of his first-floor apartment, or should she wait? No matter what her resolution, time would soon take the uncomfortable reality Salem had come to hate and love so well, and turn it into a slow, sickening tailspin of unexpected betrayal and disbelief.

WHEN WORLDS COLLIDE
LIVES CHANGE
AND THE FUTURE
IS FOREVER
ALTERED

In the ensuing moments, four fragile lives would intersect, setting off a tragic chain of events that would epitomize the frailty, unstable reality, and savage contradiction of the human condition. As Salem morphed into the gentle patter of raindrops upon the soft glass windshield, the rain stopped ... but the storm was just beginning!

ATHENA

Athena appeared at Carlo's door. She rang the doorbell and almost immediately Carlo answered. Her entrance into his hallway seemed almost by script, it came with no hesitation or extended greeting. This had happened before ... many times before. Salem's mind and soul went numb. She tried in vain to reason away the scenario that played out before her. Athena kissed Carlo and hypnotically fell into his arms before the door was even closed.

Blind shock turned to a clear sense of betrayal. But who was betraying whom? Some of the betrayers didn't even know who they were betraying, that was Salem's dilemma. And some knew exactly, but didn't seem to care ... that was *Athena's* deceit.

Nathan had said yesterday that Athena was meeting with a client early the next morning. Poor Nathan, he didn't know. He couldn't have seen this one coming. This was the ultimate act of intimate terrorism. A betrayal built on lies, not love. Inevitably the mighty waves of truth would pummel the shores of deception and expose those hideous lies with a force equaling that of the passion fueling this clandestine and sickening double-cross.

But what direction would the wave come from? When would it strike? Nathan and Carlo were far too close, and Nathan far too smart, for this theater of the absurd to reach the second act ... but it had. And when the curtain rose on the third act, unceremoniously revealing the forbidden truth, what would be the initial fallout ... and the long, sobering rain of collateral damage? It's often been said *"the more you have, the more you have to lose."* This ensemble cast had everything to lose.

This was Athena's fault. It had to be. Her gypsy-blue eyes and mythical-goddess aura made her an unearthly, sensuous icon, a virtual siren, able to ravage and exploit the unsuspecting soul of the men who were at her beckon call. Athena's betrayal would destroy Nathan; his emotional state, fragile on a good day, would shatter and sink against the rocks of Athena's deception. Salem searched for clarity. One thing stood out, crystal-clear and non-negotiable. She would be the messenger. She alone had the power to stop the siren and smash the clouded windows sealing the house of lies. *She was the power of truth.*

NATHAN

Athena was a florist. She sold flowers in town. She was good, real good. She was a true artist, crafting wondrous arrangements and bouquets with such magic and attention to detail that people came from miles around to admire and buy. People just couldn't get enough. That morning she was meeting early with a client and I had the day off, my lab being shut down for a day of routine calibration and maintenance.

The morning seemed a little off, though. I felt a twinge of unfamiliar anxiety somewhere deep down inside, but I could not figure out why. I should have been happy. I had the day off, house to myself, a fridge full of beer, and I was getting paid. All the makings of a great day … or so I thought.

I wasn't expecting company that morning, especially at 7:20 A.M., when anyone in their right mind would have just stayed in bed and enjoyed an uneventful picture gray dawn … and I definitely wasn't expecting Salem.

Being a man, I claim no feminine intuition, whatever intuition I had that day slipped quietly out the back door. Salem's presence was unexpected. She had always been predictable and consistent. But at this moment, standing cold, shivering, and wet outside my door, the woman I had come to know as a close friend and trusted co-worker morphed mysteriously into a provocative stranger, recognizable yet strangely foreign. I could sense she was at critical mass, but why? What strange course of events delivered her to me in this condition? What would happen if the red zone was exceeded and meltdown occurred? Would we both be safe in the eye of the storm, or would we be blown into the mysterious abyss of her internal suffering? I had no rational way of explaining what I was feeling at that moment, but I seemed to know exactly where we were going. Our eyes met for a brief, eternal second. Her lost stare pierced my soul like light through a prism, radiant white light expanding chromatically, immersing my mind and body with mysterious, erotic fear and sensuous feminine warmth. Fear and warmth like this could only come from a woman. As I stood there trying desperately to translate the situation, she walked in ... and closed the door.

Behind this silent encroachment was a message, but I wasn't able to decipher it. Therefore the message became a mystery, and the mystery became intriguing and seductive. The fear was still there, but it did not scare me. Instead, it invited me into a new world of guilt and pleasure that words could not possibly describe. Thoughts and desires of my inner core manipulated all logic and common sense, turning safety into danger without even questioning the consequence of those actions. This unexceptional drizzly morning had taken a quick turn down a dangerous and unforeseen road. Now I could only hold on for the ride.

Salem wore a light silk blouse with ruffled sleeves and plunging neckline. Black knee-high boots and a dark leather mini-skirt finished the look: biker chic meets Victoria's Secret. Her warm vanilla perfume permeated the air and intensified with her mood. In a moment as intoxicating as a pint of blackberry brandy, I realized this was as far away from dull white lab coats and encrypted equations as we could ever get. Salem was a seductive mix of Japanese and Brazilian. Her father was a well-known sculptor. Her mother, a model and popular San Francisco art dealer, drove the family bus. She had molded Salem's attitude and values, and pretty much put Salem's father on the map of the art world's trendy elite. I suddenly realized that in the course of the mundane work world, we tend only to see the uniform or the tasks achieved. In a world of goals, profit, and paper, the true value and passion of the individual becomes victim, not priority. Suddenly I was seeing Salem for the very first time. I understood her passion, not for cold numbers or spatial calculus, but for the true passion indigenous to her bloodline and her very soul. This burned deep and would not be denied—not today.

Without a word, Salem took my hand and walked me to the back of the house, my soul floating on a trail of warm perfume and feminine aura. We arrived at the heated atrium that led to the backyard garden. Athena and I had converted one of the bedrooms into an indoor sanctum for her exotic fruit and plants. We were very proud of it, our secret garden of plumeria and silk. We made love there frequently, enjoying wine and the celestial nightlights. It felt like Salem was carrying Athena with her, carrying a secret neither was willing to expose by conventional means, but yearned to share nonetheless.

There was no ritual pause between entering the garden and Salem's kiss. No deep longing glance in the eyes or loving peck on the cheek, just fire. Fire inside that assured me that we were not just clock-punching drones or government-sponsored puppets ... we were real. Deep inside both of us laid the secret of the heavens and beyond. We were the universe, and the universe was us. This was not sex, revenge, or impulsive behavior ... *this was an awakening.* I would jump off the page and join her body in one moment that would last forever. Salem tasted good, really good. I tasted her soft lips and sweet skin, and I also tasted her soul. I would drink from her soul, drink from the pool of her very being, until she became me ... until we became one.

ONE POOL OF LIFE ... ONE COMPLETE BEING

I could feel the blood surging through her body, circular in its everyday task yet waiting to merge. Her mind spoke through her fingers and kisses. Her message was still a mystery, but she was not shy of passion. Her legs wrapped around mine, holding on like a silent Asian snake squeezing its prey with dominance and desire ... guiding me to the lair of Venus, no turning back. At that brief moment, I felt guilt *and* I felt pleasure. Both hit with equal intensity, not canceling the other out, but opening up a rip in the universe I desperately hoped we would slip through and never return. The power of this garden, this garden of plumeria and silk, and the mystery of Salem's visit, took over, taking us both far away from any logic or emotion. There was no model, map, or precedent for this firestorm of desperate confusion and erotic passion. This should not be, but was. *This cannot be* ... but is!

We'd hit a Neverland of physical bliss, and were each stripped of our own identity and ego. We were one ... at least for this unexpected moment.

As the gates of unearthly pleasure quietly closed and the universe returned to its cold chaotic state, Salem's body melted away from mine and crumbled sensuously into a subtle cloud of angelic memory. A fleeting reality that should never have been, whose very existence was doomed from the start, was now over. The ships that had passed in the night now sailed onward towards a lost eternity. As Salem slowly dissolved into the garden of plumeria and silk, I turned back to reality, only to realize that ...

WE MAY NOT HAVE BEEN ALONE

The sun, an unpredictable usher in my lost theater of exiled dreams, has made his entrance once again. Where have I just been? Who was I with? What did I do? I feel the worst sense of solitude and loss I've ever experienced. They were here, here with me. I touched them, tasted them ... smelled them, and now they're gone ... lost. Lost in an abyss of what was but would never again be. I feel I'm the transparent attendant of a tollbooth guarding the infinite road to nowhere, taking quarters from passers-by with eyes that look straight through me. They are lost, and so am I. They drive and I watch. As I reluctantly let the sun infiltrate my tropical island cinema, I wonder ...

WILL THIS EVER END?

My eyes are on fire, my head is throbbing and my feet and hands feel numb. I can hardly move. Where am I and where have I been? And if I have been gone, how long have I been gone? I'm back on the island ... or still on the island. Something feels strange, it feels like someone is watching me ... watching me from the garden. But that can't be: no one on this island but us chickens. It's past midday now, what happened to my morning? I was planning on going to the upper elevations today. I'd better

get started if I want to be back before dark. I truly have been looking forward to this. I will once again ascend Terra-Donnas' looming and mysterious mountains to confront the questions that I cannot answer. For the sake of my own fortitude and sanity, something on this island has to be confirmed as tangible and true …

FOR WITHOUT TRUTH …THERE CAN BE NO LIES

Invasion

Chapter Three

"For years, the quiet upper echelons of the political, scientific, and military communities had suspected there was intelligent life in neighboring system Pergasas A-73 ... they were right."

The great cities of Earth, once bastions of culture, life, and commerce, had become cesspools of violence and insanity. The horrific Pergasan attacks left the remnants of humanity drowning in a sea of fear and desperation, preying upon its own for survival. These were the new dark ages ... of man.

Humanity, with all its resourcefulness and technology, had been forever altered by a force it had known nothing about ... but would never forget.

Colonel Scott looked concerned, and rightfully so. This wasn't the first time he'd seen a blip on the orbital scanner, nor was it the first time that he'd tracked an object from deep space. But this particular time, things were different. This object wasn't a falling satellite or returning station shuttle. This blip on the screen had been a long time coming, and it came from a long, long way away. Adding salt to the soup, this wasn't one of ours. As a matter of fact, this blip was a mysterious scientific reply to an equally mysterious scientific question launched from Earth many years earlier.

THE QUESTION: "ARE YOU OUT THERE?"

THE ANSWER: SOMETHING WAS!

Though the tracking station at Moffett Field Naval Air Station in California was not the highest carrot in the military the chain of command, it proved to be the most important that afternoon. From NORAD to Washington DC, China to Jamaica, Hawaii to Russia and far beyond, Colonel Roger Scott bore the burden of mankind's fate on his well-seasoned shoulders. Of all the experts in the world, it would be his decision and his decision alone as to whether or not the alien craft could enter the planet's upper atmosphere, hopefully providing Earth and all its inhabitants the first tangible contact with an alien race.

How would Scott make that decision? If there was no evidence of a clear and present danger, why stand in the way of history? But what of lessons learned from man's violent past, legends such as the Trojan horse, which keenly reminded him that *what is perceived to be often isn't ...* and misperceptions sometimes bore tragic and irreversible consequences.

STILL THEY WERE HERE ... WHY?

Wasn't this a reply to our friendly Luna-1 probe, launched years earlier, having successfully reached the Pergasas A-73 system? But what of the fate of Luna-Two, launched years later, which had mysteriously disappeared shortly after entering that very same system? Was this a matter of faith, science, or a little of both? Now one quiet, solitary human being would personally open up humanity's front door to unknown strangers waiting in the dark.

By the time the alien probe was roughly halfway between the moon and Earth, every living, breathing member of the military and scientific community was on high alert. The civilian population had slowly been let in on the secret months earlier, only after years of speculation, conspiracy theories, and multiple cover-ups, generating anticipation on a planetary level. Every geek, freak, and sheik had something to say about the upcoming event, and in typical fashion the human community banded together to let the universe know it was ready ... one way or another.

THE BIG QUESTION ... WAS COLONEL SCOTT READY?

"Update, Lieutenant Stevens," Colonel Scott said calmly.

"International space station has visual contact, sir, eta for atmospheric entry and projected course on your screen."

Though Colonel Scott was the king on this intricate global chessboard, the command post at the tracking station was modest and understaffed. But we were electronically plugged into the pulse of the world ... and the world into us. It almost felt like being in the broadcasting booth on Super Bowl Sunday ... just add aliens! Having designed the navigational and support CPUs for the ill-fated Luna-Two, as well as the diagnostic monitoring devices for the command post, Carlo Roselli and I were invited to participate at the behest of Colonel Scott and the U.S. government. Also on hand were five military radar specialists and two communications experts. Though this technically was a scientific event, all of the military personnel were armed and there were several special-ops sharpshooters posted outside the rigid steel door of the command post.

Rounding out the party was Niles Aundros, special liaison from NASA. Unlike the chiseled, clean-cut military professionals that manned their assigned posts with calm precision, Aundros paced the room like a psychotic midwife, nervously rubbing his palms together and sweating profusely from his brow. His retro white seersucker suit and loud pastel tie provided a colorful distraction from the glowing green screens and drab military attire. He was the antithesis of Colonel Scott and his crew, a spinning road flare in the uncertainty and darkness of outer space, warning us that at any moment the coin could drop the wrong way with potentially cataclysmic results. Carlo was totally onto him. In classic Roselli form, he subtly got my attention, the same way he'd been doing it since high school: whispering a secret conversation.

"Our NASA guy's a nervous Nellie," he quipped, attempting verbal Morse code on the down low.

"They've been on pins and needles since we lost Luna-2, Carlo," I replied patiently. "Mr. Aundros and crew would definitely prefer it if we rolled up the red carpet up on this one."

"I take it he's not the trusting type."

"All the deep tracking we're using is their new system. I think he's here to make sure we don't press the wrong buttons. But the final say is still in the hands of the military."

"Hell of a time for a test drive."

"Keep the faith, brother. They're using our parts."

"That's what worries me," Carlo laughed.

"Keep it up, man. You won't be invited to the next company picnic."

"Oh, and miss all the stale chips and warm mayonnaise?" he joyfully replied, remembering his gastronomic soiree at the last picnic. Carlo had been sick as a dog for at least a week after that. I, on the other hand, was merely hung over. But those were miniscule details that faded into obscurity as the events of our close encounter began to unfold like a snowball in the Alps, slowly picking up speed ... eventually becoming a raging avalanche.

The words of impending truth now resounded throughout the room. "Sixty seconds to exospheric contact sir," said the young naval officer.

Colonel Scott was silent for a moment before responding. "Maintain post, lieutenant," he said, knowing full well the clock was ticking and no amount of conventional training or experience would help in this, his final decision.

Suddenly I remembered something my late father had told me a long time ago. He was involved in *"Operation Crossroads,"* the early A-bomb tests in the Pacific atolls. He had also been an electronic engineer, a witness to the dawn of man's scientific and technological awakening.

"Technology will eventually be mankind's downfall, Nathan. But for now, it's all one big party."

NOT LONG AFTER THAT HE COMMITTED SUICIDE ... leaving me to ponder the exact meaning of those words and what they meant to him ... and what they eventually would mean to me.

"Sir, the president's on standby, protocol unchanged."

"Thank you, major," the colonel calmly replied.

"Colonel Scott, we have confirmation from station Thule, Greenland. Thirty seconds until upper atmospheric contact."

"Showtime," Carlo quietly mused. "What do you think the old man's gonna decide?"

"My guess," I replied, "is that we'll be eating homemade alien stew by dinnertime, provided they give us the recipe."

"Assuming we open the front door, of course."

"I think that's a given, Carlo. We've got way too much into this one, man. Don't forget, it's not just the government and the military that are splitting up the pie. There's a lot of private interest involved. Screw tanks and guns brother, business is where the real power comes in.

And then the words came. They were the words the world had waited for, waited for with as much anticipation as apprehension ... words that opened a door to the universe that had never been opened before. They were words that transcended geographical borders, religious beliefs, parliamentary procedure, chains of command, office politics, racism, hedonism, fundamentalism, and socialism. They were words backed by no marching bands, fanfare, or emotion ... just plain simple words ... words that would change the history and course of mankind.

"All sisters checking in, sir ... projected touchdown somewhere in the Marshall Island chain ... we have contact."

THE DOOR HAD BEEN OPENED ...

"Colonel, Seventh Fleet is heading towards the area. Fighters have been dispatched for intercept and all regional commanders have been alerted. We do have a sub in the area. If the probe doesn't change course, they will be our first contact."

"I take it the sub commander is aware of the situation?"

"He is, sir. They're taking appropriate actions. We're handing off to Command Pacific. General Gordon sends his personal regards and says there will be a little bonus on our next paychecks. The president is also coming on line, sir."

"Thank you, lieutenant. It's amazing what you can get for an extra sixty seconds worth of work," Scott said. For the first time that afternoon, Colonel Scott smiled. The tension seemed to literally roll off of his body ... and out of the room. But that was on the surface, it still felt like there was a window left open in the house of cards, and though the breeze was light, there were still many questions to be answered. But for the moment, everybody shared a brief sigh of relief.

AND THEN IT HAPPENED
SIMPLE WORDS AT FIRST
BENIGN
UNSPECTACULAR WORDS
BUT THEY WERE THE FIRST SIGN
THAT SOMETHING WAS WRONG
THEY WERE THE FIRST SIGN ...
OF CHANGE

"Colonel Scott!"

"Major?"

"We're picking up unusual activity on the alien craft, sir."

"What kind of activity?"

"It's deploying several panels of some kind, sir."

"Panels ... communications maybe ... landing device?"

"Don't know, sir."

"Colonel, I'm also reading a change in operational status!"

"Maintain surveillance lieutenant, get me Command Pacific!"

"Colonel Scott!"

"Lieutenant?"

"Sir, the probe appears to be splitting up!"

"Confirmed sir, the probe is splitting up," the young major quickly added.

"Where are the fighters?"

"Not even close, sir. They won't be in visual range for ten minutes."

"Sir, the probe has completed separation. There are now seven separate craft. They've split up and are heading in different directions!"

"Seven craft ... seven continents, lieutenant; I want to know their exact locations, now!"

"General Gordon on priority channel, sir."

"Put him on."

"Channel's gone black, colonel."

"Uni-link's down, sir. It appears we've lost all communications!"

"Get it back Stevens! Go to emergency frequencies if you have to."

"Trying, sir ... nothing, no response!"

"Run a bullet, major."

"Diagnostic's clean, sir. We're fully operational."

"Sir, we should be completely functional."

"Get me a land line out."

"All lines are dead, sir. It appears we've been cut off."

"Mr. Aundros, please go outside and get a radio from one of the guards."

"What?" NASA liaison Aundros replied, confused and frightened, almost in a state of shock.

"Mr. Cole."

"Got it," I replied semi-reluctantly, almost in the same state of shock.

This was the moment nobody saw coming. There had been questions about the probe for months, and lack of knowledge had lead to rumors and misconceptions. But the calmer scientific minds that prevailed dismissed any chance of deception or hidden agenda by our galactic counterparts. They were simply responding to a warm, openhearted welcome from a friendly

neighbor. This was the simple beginning to the greatest tragedy mankind had ever faced.

One of the military guards entered the room and handed his radio over to Colonel Scott. Turning on his own radio, Colonel Scott attempted to get the two units to communicate with each other at point-blank range. Only static prevailed.

The colonel reflected on the results of his impromptu test. "We're in a locked, fortified, concrete-and-steel room with two fully functional radios one foot apart and they don't work worth a crap," he observed sternly. "What the hell's going on?"

"Some kind of blanket corruption, sir," Lieutenant Stevens began. "From what I can tell, it's taken out all electronic communication … everything, online, satellite, and terrestrial."

The room that had previously been alive with optimism and electronic chatter was slowly spinning into a den of uncertainty and fear as the lieutenant added more bad news.

"Our computers are now completely down, sir. We can't even run startup or diagnostic programs."

"Does that mean what I think it means?" Carlo asked, fully knowing the answer.

"It means, as the lieutenant so keenly pointed out, that we are completely cut off," the colonel replied sternly.

There was a brief moment of silence. The realization of technology's role in the evolutionary path of twenty-first century man menacingly smiled from the dark corners of futility like an unwanted joker pulled from the harsh deck of fate. But it was more than man's technology circling in the cold waters of doom. Something else had just entered the water, someone or something with a mission; an agenda … a purpose that at this point remained a complete and total mystery. Man would now wait as the sardonic laughter from the punch line of a distant and shadowy joke rang through the soul of a civilization teetering on the edge of destruction.

Emerging from the back of the control room, Niles Aundros looked like he had just seen a ghost, his normally flushed cheeks now almost the color of his cheap white suit.

"What's going on, colonel?" Aundros asked in a tepid voice.

After a brief pause, the colonel answered in a restrained tone.

"That's what we're trying to find out, Mr. Aundros."

"I demand to know what is going on out there!" Aundros frantically announced. *"I demand to know what is going on. You are the military! Where are all your people, where are they, Colonel Scott? Where are they, where are your people?"*

Suddenly, the room went completely black and hauntingly silent, as if in some strange way telling the beleaguered NASA liaison that there was still more to come. The timing was ironically perfect for Colonel Scott's calm reply to Aundros' outburst.

"Where are your people, Mr. Aundros?" he politely asked. *"Where are yours?"*

Almost immediately, the backup generators kicked in. "At least something's working," Colonel Scott remarked with a mild mix of exasperation and strained humor. "All right, people. Go through your systems. I want every contingency utilized, no stone unturned ... we need to know what's going on out there!" he ordered. Turning his attention to the back of the room he began to address his agitated spectator. *"As for your question, Mr. Aundros..."*

AND THEN SOMETHING WENT HORRIBLY WRONG!

The room suddenly felt different. The situation had already caused a significant amount of sensory overload, but the strangeness of this fresh new vibe was terrifying and odd ... and it was coming from Mr. Aundros. It crept in like a silent ninja virus, innocuous yet distinct. Like someone quietly opening up your shower door while your back was turned, but not sticking around to introduce themselves. It wasn't a continuation of Aundros's somewhat disjointed rant or terminal paranoia, or his bad suit and tie. He appeared bewildered and confused. Suddenly, his face began to contort with shock and pain. His expression took on the horrified look of a man suddenly aware he was about to die, but unsure why. A primal scream seemed to radiate from his inner core, more animal than human. Its nightmarish declaration provided the grisly soundtrack of a man being blown up and torn apart from the inside. The scream methodically turned into a wet symphony of imploding arteries, veins, and vocal chords ... morbidly fading into a sick diminuendo of his last tortured moments. He bled profusely from the sockets of his eyes, a testament to the destructive power of his unknown attacker. His body convulsed violently as his skin began to split open, sending fluid and tissue flying across the room. Blood gushed and sprayed from his body like a fire hydrant hit by a drunk driver. The blood was black and thick as syrup. His agony was over almost as quickly as it had begun. His body crumpled into a crimson pile of unrecognizable remains, his white suit a torn and bloodied canvas ... reminiscent of a mad painter's nightmarish last work.

All common sense and logic disappeared into the abyss as the process soon repeated itself on several of the remaining military staff, as well as Colonel Scott. The room became a bloodbath of surreal horror that even the darkest mind could not construe. There were no words for this horror. No verbs, adjectives, or colorful metaphors that could ever paint an accurate picture of the sheer terror that manifested itself in that compressed electronic dungeon of death.

I HAVE TO GET OUT
I HAVE TO GET OUT
THE DOOR
THE DOOR
RUN ...
GET OUT!!!

Nothing in life is really certain. We'd like it to be, but it just isn't. Yeah, you can have it "your way" at Burger King, or score a hundred-thousand-mile warranty on your power train. You can insure everything down to your discarded toenails, but in the grand scheme of things ... humanity has very little coverage.

The universe creates its own order. It doesn't haggle in back rooms or debate in neighborhood bars. Its actions are delegated by powers and wisdom much greater than its lowly inhabitants. And on this day, the universe negated all previous agreements

and promises with said inhabitants. It kicked out the delicate legs of the table supporting the frail universal chess set of logic and reason ... scattering its pieces like a police raid on a seedy bordello. Kings, queens, knights, and pawns all lay bleeding on its killing floor, begging for their lives to no avail ...

THE PERGASANS HAD ARRIVED!

Leaving the command center carnage, I entered a world that was not the same one I had left a few hours earlier. As evening crept in, darkness and smoke merged effortlessly into an acrid, nightmarish landscape. Something unexplainable and horrible had happened. At that point in time the only thing one could be sure of was that the world had just been turned upside down. There had been an attack, a horrible one, but the buildings and manmade structures remained intact.

The people were another story altogether. Bodies lay everywhere; in the halls, parking lot, and on the sidewalk. The bodies were soaked in blood, their distorted faces showing a horror they had never expected and could not understand. The adjacent freeway had become an arena of death and pain. Cars and people haphazardly cluttered its unforgiving asphalt. A helicopter lay on its side scorched and burning, its crew still trapped inside. A sobbing young mother clutched her dead child as she asked the universe, "Why ... why?" It was surreal beyond surreal, a nightmare I desperately tried to wake up from ... but the nightmare was real, and there was no waking up!

Whatever happened had happened quickly and without warning. The rain of horror was an obvious and deliberate act carried out with extreme prejudice and no mercy. Was this the beginning of the end ... or merely the beginning?

I HAD TO GET HOME!

My trip through the back streets and dark alleys of town was an outsider's tour of Hell. Though I hadn't been sentenced, I was amongst the guilty ... for I had survived. It was one thing witnessing the horror and devastation back at the command post. It was another to see it on my very own block.

I'd lived in the same house, on the same street, since I was born. I'd watched the town change in the slow dance of progress and time. I'd seen children grow, and the aged die. I played baseball in the street, and soccer in the park … tasted ice cream in June and my first kiss at fourteen. But what lay before me as I turned right on South Circle Drive, the same right I'd taken a hundred million times before, was neither nightmare nor reality. For in the life I had grown into so comfortably as cautious optimist, there was no place to put this, no words to describe it. I was not here … I was not anywhere. My soul was neither elevated nor disparaged. It was in spiritual limbo and so was the world. Most of all … 1138 South Circle Drive.

Night had now conquered day. But this was the beginning of a night that would never end … a night where shadows and death morphed into a slow hideous dance of horror and disbelief. There was an eerie silence as smoke and ash permeated the air. A full moon ceremoniously lit a stage littered with scattered bodies, wrecked cars, and life destroyed. An invisible thief had lifted a simple link out of the chain of life. An angry bully kicked over the first domino … someone opened up the window and blew down the house of cards. But who had actually been here? Who was the thief, the bully or the wind? Approaching my house I had a strange feeling I was in another universe … maybe this was a dream. The radio static that accompanied me on my arduous journey home now seemed to be the only thing alive, a strange source of comfort. For on this night on South Circle Drive, there was no movement, no sound. No dogs barking in their backyards, no children playing in front, just silence … and the sound of death. Pulling into the driveway, I knew what I would find. I could feel it. Even as kids, Athena and I had an invisible spiritual link, one that even through time and distance apart had never been broken. But on this night it was gone … and so was Athena.

She lay in the corner of the kitchen, unrecognizable. Her sandy blonde hair, that had once reflected the morning sun with such feminine radiance and beauty, was now matted and stained with the mysterious black blood. Her body was no longer intact, her electric gypsy-blue eyes ...

There was nothing to hold on to, no Athena to kiss goodbye. I prayed that it had happened quickly, but to whom to pray? If there was a God, surely he must have seen this coming. He could have stopped it! But I wasn't mad at God, I was mad at the universe. But my anger was trivial compared to the hollow and consuming heartbreak of the day's events. There was no going back and nothing to look forward to. Shadows were dancing on the wall, but there was no light to serenade them. I felt hot, disoriented, and lightheaded. My father was at the table drinking whiskey and smoking his Pall Malls. His eyes looked sad. His mouth didn't move, yet I heard his words ...

"Technology was mankind's downfall, Nathan.
Now the party's over, son ... now the parties over."

I thought of Athena. How I yearned to bathe in the warmth of her gypsy-blue eyes, but she was gone ... and it felt like I was drowning in my own blood. The fight had become personal, but futile. Are these the last final moments ... of my frail human existence?

IT WAS GETTING DARK ...VERY DARK

Reflections
"On The Bus"

KESEY LAY SIDEWAYS
ON THE KITCHEN FLOOR
SMOKING A JOINT ...
PAINTING MIRROR REFLECTIONS OF HIS SOUL
ON ITS SMOOTH HORIZONTAL SURFACE

An anonymous tree grew straight through the timeless

PRANKSTER BUS

Sequestered into eternal dry dock per Captain Kesey's orders

WHILE THE SMITHSONIAN
AND THE WORLD
WONDERED ...
AND WAITED

Mountain Girl and the surviving Pranksters understood ...

DID WE?

The Village

Chapter Four

"Either you're on the bus ..."

This was one of those mornings when a cup of coffee really tasted good. I appreciated its warm, rich flavor and wonderful smell. In some strange way, on this crisp and beautiful dawn, it was almost like an awakening. Like the first time ... my very first cup of coffee.

WE DRINK TOO MUCH COFFEE YOU KNOW

We claim it as an entitlement, a given ... part of our daily ritual. We have lost our appreciation for this tiny little speed bean. Just as we've lost our appreciation for the simplest wonders that occur in and around us every day and night. Every hour, every minute, and every lost second, we blindly proceed with the false hope that just around the corner all our eternal questions will be answered ... and every wish, desire, and dream gratuitously fulfilled. I had always appreciated the simple things and the simplest acts of the human experience. But I got lost, derailed by the secret enemies of my own *"self-state,"* the power of personal ego, and the not-so-secret expectations of others.

But on a morning like this, in the village, in my wonderful home ... everything fell into perspective. While the world outside revolved and churned, the world inside remained steady and calm ... picture-perfect moments frozen in time and hung in the gallery of dreams and perfection. My beautiful wife Athena sat across the table from me. The sun radiating sensuously upon her sandy blonde hair and reflecting in her gypsy-blue eyes confirmed with absolute impunity the phrase ...

AND GOD CREATED WOMAN

FOR ONLY GOD COULD CREATE A CREATURE OF SUCH HEAVENLY WARMTH AND BEAUTY

It's the second Saturday of the month, *"Freebie Day,"* as Athena and I called it ... our come-as-you-are, do-what-you-want day. We established a long time ago that no matter what, rain, shine, work or otherwise, Sunday would always be our day together. But that second Saturday of the month, *"Freebie Day,"* was ours to do with what we wanted. One of those silly things that young couples do in the beginning to hopefully keep the marriage fresh and exciting down the road ... *we're so blessed to have crystal balls!*

On these much-anticipated days, Athena usually shopped or took in a chick flick with her girlfriends, while Carlo and I played tennis or rented bad action flicks and ate crappy food, unceremoniously sharing the side effects of said culinary delights with our significant others later that night ... oops! Life is good. But this *"Freebie Day"* was to be a special one ... real special!!!

ON THIS MUCH-ANTICIPATED DAY
CARLO AND I
MADE PLANS
SPECIAL PLANS ...
REAL SPECIAL PLANS!!!

CARLO

Though Carlo Roselli and I had been best friends since high school, there was still a lot I did not know about him. He was the kind of guy you took for granted. His free spirit and easygoing demeanor made you feel like you'd known him for years, even if you had just met him. He could make you laugh without trying, and if you really needed him, he was always there. He would give you the shirt off his back or the last dime in his pocket.

But in the final analysis, it was all smoke and mirrors, and even the mirrors presented a distorted view of the man. Once the smoke cleared, you were left with more questions than answers. But that was your problem, not his. Carlo just rolled on in the same direction, at the same speed, barely acknowledging his own presence in the universe, seemingly oblivious of his impact on others. I was cool with that, as I kept my circle of friends very small. Even though at times Carlo was a mystery to me, I trusted him ... *and on this day, I would need to trust him!*

The beauty of my relationship with Athena was that we were totally honest with each other. She never lied to me, and I reciprocated. We had no secrets or skeletons in the closet. We had known each other since childhood, and though there were some gaps over the years in terms of physical presence, we were always connected. It wasn't cosmic or spiritual, or written in the stars or etched in stone somewhere on some *forgotten island* ... we were just meant to be together, and that would never change, in this life or the next ... at least that's what I believed. But today, the sheer white fabric of virgin truth would inherit a little stain ... a tiny, harmless blotch on the cosmic order of universal karma, nothing to get one's panties in a twist over, just a silly little guy thing. The stain would become me and Carlo's little secret. It would start with me meeting a rather colorful group of his friends from another life, a seldom-seen clan that he had met at a Grateful Dead concert years earlier. And though they rarely got together, when they did, the stories that Carlo would tell me became the sordid tales of debauchery and fun that legends were made of. They usually involved a lot of sex, drugs, and rock 'n' roll. When I say drugs, I don't mean stuff like heroin or cocaine. There were really only two: marijuana and LSD.

I'VE NEVER BEEN A DRUGGIE
I SMOKED A LITTLE WEED
IN HIGH SCHOOL AND COLLEGE

NOW I'M STRICTLY A BEER-AND-WINE GUY
BUT BEFORE I LEAVE THIS PLANET
I'M GONNA DO ACID
AT LEAST ONCE!

SAN MATEO HIGH SCHOOL ... *SOME YEARS EARLIER*☺

A harmless afternoon in the library doing research for a history paper ... when suddenly I noticed an interesting book with the coolest psychedelic cover I had ever seen.

THE ELECTRIC KOOL-AID ACID TEST
TOM WOLFE
FREAKED ON THE ACID TEST

"AN ASTONISHING BOOK ... IT IS TO THE HIPPIE MOVEMENT WHAT NORMAN MAILER'S THE ARMIES OF THE NIGHT *WAS TO THE VIETNAM PROTEST MOVEMENT."*

—C. D. B. Bryan, *New York Times Book Review*

THE UNSPOKEN THING

"How to tell it ... the current fantasy ... I never heard any of the Pranksters use the word religious to describe the mental atmosphere they shared after the bus trip and the strange days in Big Sur. In fact, they avoided putting it into words. And yet—"
— Tom Wolfe, *The Electric Kool-Aid Acid Test*

HOW IT ALL STARTED

From the moment I began my romp through the pages of Wolfe's masterpiece, I was hooked. I would never be the same clumsy teen I had been minutes before. I had found my calling, my place in the universe ... my people. But who were these people ... *these pranksters?*

They were a group of wild characters tripping around San Francisco (and pretty much the rest of the country) in a psychedelic 1939 International Harvester bus in the mid-1960's. They took acid, played music, partied with the Dead, Hell's Angels, Bill Graham, and Allen Ginsberg, et cetera, et cetera! They embraced the psychedelic culture as a cast and crew of the most colorful crazies to ever share time and space with humanity. They *"tootled the multitudes"* and made life miserable for anyone wearing *"black shiny FBI shoes."* They were originals, freely navigating the waters of strung-out hippies, anti-war protesters, and an intolerant *establishment* that on the surface thrived on archaic agendas and outdated values, yet underneath it all ... yearned to shed its own self-imposed bondage. To me, the Pranksters were not the "counterculture," they were *the culture!*

IT ALL SEEMED SO FUN!

At the helm of this rolling psychedelic circus was well-known author Ken Kesey, fresh off the success of two stellar novels, *One Flew Over The Cuckoo's Nest* (1962) and *Sometimes a Great Notion* (1964). He and his acid cronies lived by their own rules. They didn't retreat to communes or rush off to Canada. In their own way, they embraced America with all its freedom and culture ... and then they hit the road and turned it all upside down. Even their counterculture *"counterpart"* of the time, Harvard professor, Timothy Leary *("Turn on, tune in, drop out")* ran for cover when they made the trip out east to meet him, hiding out in his opulent, upstate New York mansion until they left!

Reading Wolfe's book in the library that day opened up a new chapter in my life. No ... I didn't rush out and take acid (although I did smoke my fair share of pot) but in the ensuing days, I developed a greater appreciation of the human spirit.

TO NOT ONLY BE PHYSICALLY FREE ...
BUT MENTALLY FREE AS WELL!

THAT WAS THEN ... AND THIS IS NOW

AGENDA:
PART ONE: Meet Carlo's friends.
PART TWO: The concert!

According to Carlo, *"The Group"* would swing by his house at noon. The ringleader was a cat named Captain Tony. Nobody seemed to know his last name, not even Carlo. Then there was Danny, a tanned, muscular Hawaiian dude with a great Hollywood smile; he was Captain Tony's best friend and lieutenant. Next came Weed, resident pot concierge extraordinaire, and his partner in crime, Spinner Jones, hanging tight as the funky black dude that deejayed with a vengeance ... and a lot of classic tunes! His claim to fame was that he'd banged more chicks than Wilt Chamberlain ... even though he couldn't dribble a basketball worth a s---.

On the female side there was Gina. She was Asian with long, dark hair and a killer body. Casey was some kind of high school or college track star. She had what Carlo described as a playful personality and *"smiling green eyes."* Carlo suspected everybody to be in their mid-twenties to early thirties, except Tony, who seemed a little older. Captain Tony and his spaced invaders were the modern-day embodiment of the Merry Pranksters. Cruising around in a painted bus, smoking weed, dropping acid, having sex, going to concerts, and doing who knows what else. Monday through Friday, they could have been doctors, nurses, lawyers, or accountants for all anybody knew and frankly ... I didn't want to know!!!

THE PLAN:

We would make the pilgrimage north to the Cow Palace to see a band I had never heard of, and along the way, we would take acid ... lots of it!

FINALLY
I WILL LOOK AT MY SUBCONSCIOUS
IN THE MIRROR
TAKE OFF MY EGO
PUT ON A DAY-GLO TIE
AND TALK TO GOD …
TOLL-FREE

(And pray Athena wouldn't find out. If anyone asks, Carlo and I were playing miniature golf.)

We were just finishing our beers when the bus pulled up. Captain Tony's cosmic coach was, to say the least, impressive. It was the visual equivalent of the Partridge Family bus on five hits of 4-Way acid and twenty Red Bulls! An intergalactic schoolyard throwback to the sixties, fueled by imagination, drugs, and good old fashioned gasoline … a psychedelic steel-and-rubber mind-blow careening through the asphalt universe at warp speed … acknowledging only the green lights.

It was everything I had imagined, and personally, I was more than ready to roll up for the *Mystery Tour!!!*

CARLO INTRODUCED ME
TO CAPTAIN TONY
WHO IN TURN
INTRODUCED ME
TO HIS INTREPID CREW

The inside of Tony's urban starship was its own private world. Windows from the middle of the bus to the very back were blacked out. With the exception of the rear bench, all the middle seats had also been taken out. In that space, Tony and company had installed a small kitchen complete with a fully stocked bar and plasma TV. Gina and Casey sat together on the rear bench. Everyone else gravitated toward the front, except Hawaiian Danny. He was unwrapping something from the ship's galley.

Taking command at the wheel, Captain Tony announced it was time to hit it! The party was on. As we rolled down the road, he lit up a joint. Passing it around, Captain Tony colorfully recalled previous misadventures of him and his intrepid crew. The weed kicked in, and I began sizing up the good captain as his yarns of past glory shot deep into my brain.

Tony himself was not an imposing man, but there was a larger-than-life Hollywood sense about him. His long dark-flowing hair, motocross boots, white skin-tight tee-top with black leather vest, classic blue jeans and free-spirited good nature immediately put him on my top-ten list of people I wanted to be. Goodbye, Tom Cruise ... hello, Captain Tony.

Soon Danny emerged from the galley with a small tray of chocolate-covered macadamia nuts. Upon offering them, he made it a point to let everybody know that *"His nuts were special!"* The girls giggled and I chuckled at the innuendo, not knowing at the time the true meaning of his words. They tasted good ... real good! Common reality became surreal as the urban universe outside the bus windows smiled upon us while we drove by at light speed.

WHERE WERE WE GOING?

Who cares, the world was happy ... I could feel it! Everybody loved us, they were smiling and waving ... they were happy we were having fun! We drove on for miles, smoking and drinking, indulging in a communal love-fest the likes of which I had never seen before. The weed seemed really strong, or maybe I was just totally into the moment. I was getting heavy vibes from Casey. Undeniable and warm, they rocked me to the core. She stared seductively from the back of the bus as Gina caressed and kissed her, both of them giggling like two giddy schoolgirls on a sugar high. Her smiling green eyes seared straight through my soul and beyond. My deepest inner thoughts and emotions began to slowly spread like warm butter across this mobile psychedelic landscape. Though I had just kissed Athena goodbye a few hours earlier, she suddenly disappeared from memory, like she had never been there in the first place. I turned to meet Casey's eyes … she let me know the door was open … I just had to step inside … but first …

"Tony!" I said.

"Nate!" Tony replied.

"When are we doing the nasty?"

"What nasty's that, Nate?"

"The acid, man, when are we gonna do the acid?"

"The acid?"

"Yeah, the acid … when are we doing it?"

"Didn't Danny tell you?"

"Tell me what?"

"You're on, brother; you bought your ticket wayyyyy back there … just hold on for the ride, man!

"I told you my nuts were special," Danny said.

WOAHHHHHHHHHHHHHHHHHHFREAKINGGGG GGGGGGGGGGGGCRAZYYYYYYYYYYYYYY YYYMANNNNNNNNNNNNNNNNNNN!!!!!!!!!!!!!!!!!!!

IT WAS ON …AND SO WAS I

No wonder the weed felt so strong! All right, things are good. I can deal with this. Whatever you do, don't fight it. You are about to join the vaunted legions of the greatest cosmic warriors of history. You will sit amongst such immortals as Kesey, Leary, Lennon, and … Tony (whatever his last name was).

But at that moment, the person I really wanted to sit amongst was Casey. I don't know if I was coming on to the acid or if it was just my imagination, but I could smell her warm perfume and taste her lips upon me, though we sat many rows apart. Her eyes were now tearing through me like a laser through a paper plate. I turned to meet her challenge and stopped dead in my tracks as I realized the laser was emanating from both she and Gina. At that precise moment, in that exact time and space on board Captain Tony's psychedelic interstate torpedo, nothing else existed except Casey, Gina, and the short walk it would take to close the distance between us. But that walk never happened ... I just arrived, and nothing else in the universe existed.

As the outside world melted into oblivion, my inside world became warm and strange. A flowing rush of excitement and elation surged through my body as I approached the goddesses' den, embracing my senses like an electric vice grip. Casey and Gina were both tripping; I knew that without asking ... this knowledge was our unspoken password to a brave new world of forbidden pleasure. Gina stood up. Gently brushing her body by mine, she closed a makeshift partition that separated us from the rest of the universe ...

LEAVING US TO CREATE OUR OWN COSMIC ORDER!

Though Gina mildly participated, she then left to co-pilot the interstellar groove train to wherever, as I made full-on love to Casey. The effects of the LSD took me to a previously undiscovered erotic-emotional well, one whose waters ran deep and pure, fulfilling every need and desire way beyond expectation. Casey's physical and spiritual presence sent me to a new level of consciousness I had never experienced before. I could easily chase those feelings for the rest of my life.

Opening the makeshift partition and exiting our electric-macadamia-passion-cocoon, my reintroduction into the real world (though I was still quite high) was the sight of Gina nesting comfortably in pilot Tony's lap ... that explained a lot.

"We were about ready to send a search party back there, Nate," Tony chimed, winking and sending a sly smile in Gina's direction.

"I kept him safe, Tone," Gina said.

"Do I have any say in this?" Casey asked, seductively approaching the cosmic cockpit. Her demeanor suggested she was not quite ready to let the magic go, and for what it was worth ... neither was I! We were both, at least in spirit, still in the back of the bus. Gina understood.

Tony replied, "Turn it loose, sister!" all the while beaming from ear to ear.

"Nathan rocked," she said seductively.

"Ouuuuu," Tony chirped with enthusiasm. "We all's got us a rock star on board," he quipped, once again eyeballing Gina, sending her secret messages only they understood.

Gina smiled and countered, quietly raising two fingers into the air and pointing at Tony, letting everybody know there were two rock stars on board.

THE VIBE WAS COMMUNAL, BUT NOT IN AN OUTDATED HIPPIE SENSE ... IT JUST FELT GOOOOOOOOOD!

WEED PASSED A JOINT TO SPINNER
SPINNER PASSED THE JOINT TO DANNY
DANNY PASSED THE JOINT TO CASEY
CASEY PASSED THE JOINT TO ME
I PASSED THE JOINT TO CARLO
CARLO PASSED THE JOINT TO GINA
GINA PASSED THE JOINT TO TONY

AS WE CROSSED THE GOLDEN GATE BRIDGE, OUR SOULS COLLECTIVELY LEFT THE BUS AND DANCED UPON THE COOL WATERS OF SAN FRANCISO BAY ... AND THE TRIP CONTINUED!

NEXT STOP ... THE COW PALACE

Time now disappeared into an LSD-fueled vacuum. As our intergalactic journey to rock 'n' roll nirvana concluded, the hangar-shaped Goliath known as the Cow Palace appeared on the horizon, gyrating slowly like a Jell-O mold in a small earthquake. Cars in the massive parking lot hummed and purred like kittens on a warm rug, all sharing a secret communication understood only by those of us in our enlightened, mold-induced state. The happy, sunny skies of the village traded places with the dark, foreboding clouds standing guard over the monstrous, brooding structure. I was still wondering if there were cows here, but I was pretty sure we were just going to see a band.

As if jumping off a magic cloud, Captain Tony parked his Crayola starship with military precision, taking care not to scratch the neighboring steel kittens still purring with secret contentment. Tony shut off the engine. Taking a long deep drag off a newly lit joint, he turned to happily address his troops.

"WE ARE HERE"
WERE HIS ONLY WORDS
IT WAS ALL HE NEEDED TO SAY
THE TROOPS UNDERSTOOD
THE CROWD WENT CRAZY

It took time to pack up and head in. The pilgrimage itself would be an adventure. The acid and marijuana made for a circus-like departure from reality. Mundane mainstream events had become live theater. And though we had paid to see the band, the electric images of humanity in motion provided the best entertainment I had ever seen. It seemed like hours before we found our seats, and even hours more until the band started. But then, suddenly, the hours felt like seconds.

THE TRIP WAS NOW IN FULL GEAR ... AND NOTHING WAS WHAT IT SEEMED

A CRAZED SEA OF HUMANITY CHURNED AND BOBBED LIKE PING-PONG BALLS ON A ROLLING WAVE

...

All right!!!
YEAHHHHHHHHHHHHHHHHHHHH!!!
I said, all right!!!
YEAHHHHHHHHHHHHHHHHHHHH!!!

Ladies and gentlemen!!!

OUYEAHHHHHHHHHHHHHHHHHHHHH
HHHHHHHHHHHHHH!!!
Ladies and gentlemen!!!
YEAHHHHHHHHHHHHHHHHHHHHHHHHHH
HHHHHHHHHHHHHHHHH!!!
Who's in the house!!!?
WHOOOOOOOOOOOOOOOOOOOOOOOOOO
OOOOOOOOOO!!!
Who's in the house!!!?
WHOOOOOOOOOOOOOOOOOOOOOOOOOO
OOOOOOOOOO!!!
Who's in the house!!!?
YEAHHHHHHHHHHHHHHHHHHHHHHHHHHHHHHH
HHHHHHHHHHH!!!
OUAHHHHIIHHHHHOUUUUUUUUUUUUUUUUUUUU
UUUUUUUU!!!
GIVE IT UP FOR … YEAHHHHHH!!!!!!!!!!!
!!!!!!!!!!!!!
GIVE IT UP FOR … YEAHHHHHH!!!!!!!!!!!!
!!!!!!!!!!!
GIVE IT UP FOR … YEAHHHHHH!!!!!!!!!!!!
!!!!!!!!!!!
LADIES AND GENTLEMEN … GIVE IT UP FOR …
THE GRAPEFRUIT UNDERGROUND!!!
OUAHHHHHHHHYEAHHHHHHHHHYEA
HHHHHHHHHHHHHHHHHHHHHHHHHHHHHHHH
HHHHHHHHHHHHHHHHHHHH!!!

THE BAND WAS HERE
IT WAS ALL THEY NEEDED TO SAY
THE TROOPS UNDERSTOOD
THE CROWD
WENT CRAZY

"ONE TWO THREE FOUR …" GUITARS, DRUMS, BASS, KEYS … "ONE TWO THREE FOUR …" BOOM! It was on. The band ran the room, and the great orb of human energy ran the crowd,

generously spilling into our brains like jet fuel from a beer bong. I didn't know the band or the music, *but I felt their groove …* and it felt good. Spinner was grooving too, almost propelling himself magically over the excited crowd. Eventually, people began to sit back and chill. Weed started distributing joints like the Red Cross in Somalia. Gina gently tapped my arm. As I turned to respond, she handed me a small stack of paper cups.

"Take one and pass the rest down," she whispered.

I didn't know what was going on, but I knew Tony was up to something.

I DIDN'T HAVE TO WAIT LONG FOR MY ANSWER

Down the assembly line, delivered personally by Gina, came a large yellow canteen with a big smiley face painted on both sides.

"What's this?" I asked.

"A full day's supply of vitamin C," Gina joyfully replied.

"I'm still trippin' on door number one," I said, now realizing the true contents of the yellow HAPPY JUG.

With that, Gina provocatively touched her lips to my ear. "I wanna take you higher," she seductively whispered.

Hendrix would have been proud I thought, carefully filling my cup with Tony's orange-juice-and-acid elixir. I was really thirsty.

The house music blared on when the band finally took a break. Casey was flying. While the crowd took a brief interlude from the supersonic decibel carnage of the Grapefruit Underground, she mounted me like a test pilot on a rocking chair. I could feel the heat through her clothes, but round two would have to wait till we got back to the bus. As high as I was, this was a little too public! For now, second base would have to do.

The band eventually came back and launched into what I was told was one of their greatest hits, just as I began opening door number two. Slowly levitating in my chair, I got a 360-degree view of the cosmic circus I had so eagerly volunteered myself for. A large white rabbit appeared on the edge of the stage and began eating the frenzied post-teen crazies clambering to get an inch closer or snag a free guitar pick from their sweat-drenched heroes. The rabbit tore off their heads, and blood shot straight into the air, shimmering down in shiny droplets like July 4th fireworks at the county fair. A large alien took the stage, playing saxophone like Bill Clinton in his cool sunglasses. *This is crazy,* I thought. I needed to get control of my mind ... it was getting way out of hand. But the fun continued.

Unseen sound and churning humanity were reaching an eerie pudding of critical mass. I was on an audiovisual roller coaster blasting through the vibrating community of cluttered carbon units at warp speed. The walls started to melt, as slow molten paint glowed fluorescent and unchallenged, ominously dripping to the ground ... then back up to the sky. My watch became incredibly heavy, weighing down my arm like an invisible cement block, blurting out time from different zones in strange and foreign languages ... cursing at me profusely. The band was playing at seventy-eight RPMs ... twisting and swaying like rabid weebles, wobbling uncontrollably but not falling down.

CASEY
I CAN FEEL HER TOUCH
HER LIPS
HER EYES
SHE IS INSIDE OF ME
SHE IS OUTSIDE OF ME
SHE IS EVERYWHERE
SHE IS NOWHERE

AM I REALLY ON THIS BEACH?

The sun is warm, and it feels like I have been here forever. My friends have come to visit. The occasion is special, but I don't know what it is. Perhaps it is my birthday. Everybody seems so happy. A light tropical breeze beckons, and the sounds of exotic birds embrace my ears. A Jamaican steel-drum band fills the air with island charm and the drinks ... the drinks are electric. But

the berries … the berries are special, an island delicacy, rare and indigenous, exclusive to this lost and uncharted paradise. My friends laugh, my friends smile, my friends toast! They toast to the good life and to the beauty amongst us. We are safe here on our island sanctuary. Our happiness prevails. We will never leave, for our boat lies pummeled and crushed … sunken in the secret channel.

IS THIS WHAT I'VE BEEN LOOKING FOR?

Tony and crew were glued to their seats, their blank stares faithfully trained on the band … eyes hardly blinking, never moving. They seemed to be on a frequency all their own, completely connected to their collective consciousnesses as a group … WOW!!!

Suddenly I had to pee … I mean, *really* pee. My last orange-juice-and-acid cocktail was a little too much for the levee, and I had to find the magic ceramic cathedral before it broke. I turned to Tony and crew. But they were gone, physically there, but mentally snowboarding down the slopes of mystical bliss. Their eyes were focused on the band, their minds askew in the combine harvester of synthesized indulgence … from "Owsley" with love.

KESEY WOULD HAVE BEEN PROUD!

Climbing over my frozen Popsicle friends, I traversed the back hallways and went down several levels. Slowly the sounds of people and music faded away as the tunnel like corridors became foreboding and cold. Where was I? I spotted a door. I felt a strong urge to open it. The door itself seemed odd. It didn't fit in with the decor. A sense of spirituality and power emanated from its mysterious labyrinth … almost as if it was living, or maybe, something alive was behind it.

Determining what was real was suddenly important. But reality was merely a starting point that had no beginning, its final destination an ending that had no conclusion. I was full-on tripping, and the fact that I could still be back in my seat watching the band with my fellow "cosmic cowboys" was not far from my mind. But if I delved too deep into that thought, I ran the risk of losing it completely. I could not afford to do that ... better just stay in and go with it. *"Remember, Nathan ... you wanted this! Open the scary door to the beyond, Nathan, you have no choice ... the hallway behind you is now gone."*

THE DOOR WAS THE ONLY WAY BACK!

Entering the church, the essence of candles and antiquity enveloped my senses like a warm tropical storm. Light and shadows danced a peculiar waltz of mystery and silence. Every cryptic sound echoed against the faded cathedral walls and high vaulted ceilings. Intricate stained glass windows yearned for the companionship of a passing sun to unleash their ceremonious color and beauty. But on this day ... darkness was all the heavens offered.

I felt a presence, someone or something familiar, but it wasn't physical ... and it was way beyond reach. It was neither here nor there, yet it enveloped every corner of the room as if it had been there forever ... as if we had been there forever.

"I'm sorry Nathan ... I'm sorry." The voice was soft and feminine.

My eyes followed the voice. Followed it to the cross ... the cross with Athena suspended upon its wooden frame, her sandy blonde hair draped across her raised shoulders. Her electric gypsy-blue eyes were gone, replaced by hollow sockets of darkness. Twin rivers of dried blood cascaded casually down her pale breasts. Her chest was torn and burnt as if lightning had made a direct strike at her heart.

A DESECRATED ANGEL HANGING IN A GALLERY OF PAIN, LIKE AN ABSTRACT PORTRAIT OF LOVE AND DEATH ... PAINTED METHODICALLY WITH HER OWN TORMENTED BLOOD

The essence of warm vanilla spice once again permeated my senses as Salem took my hand and led me into a slow dance powered by music only she heard, her arms caressing my body, her warm, sweet lips brushing my ear.

"Thank you, Nathan ... thank you," she said.

Suddenly, the room changed. Athena, Salem, and the cathedral disappeared, replaced by shadows of large mysterious aliens and a background halo of white light. For a second, I heard voices that confused me. Voices *en masse* ... voices from the past, conversations that I vaguely remembered haphazardly thrown together into a maniacal symphony of who I was and where I'd been. Abruptly, they stopped ... and there was silence. And then a solo voice sounded. A human voice ... telepathic, soft, and articulate ... directed solely at me.

"Good afternoon, Mr. Cole," the gentle voice said. "Did you enjoy your rock 'n' roll concert? Those four gentlemen play their instruments quite well, don't they? Do you play an instrument, Mr. Cole? Wait a minute, perhaps you're a singer. You *are* a singer, aren't you Mr. Cole? I bet you are probably quite good. Could you possibly sing us a song, Mr. Cole? Perhaps something on the lighter side, a simple ballad maybe ... yes, Mr. Cole, a simple ballad ... that would be nice."

IS SOMETHING WRONG MR. COLE?

(What about my friends?)

"Oh yes, your friends, a point of reference, Mr. Cole, that's all, a simple point of reference, something to help you answer some of those questions that as of late have disturbed and confused you. The truth can sometimes be a mystery, Mr. Cole, as I'm sure you are painfully aware. Sometimes the elusive nature of truth is such because we have made it that. The frail *oiseau des verite* has flown away, Mr. Cole, back to its gilded cage. Your wife is lovely, Mr. Cole, such beautiful gypsy-blue eyes. I wonder what the last thing they saw was, Mr. Cole. Was it you? Her last tender breath, her last mortal thoughts ... were you a part of those thoughts, Mr. Cole? I hear the wings, Mr. Cole. The cage door is closing. The bird will stay prisoner, because it is back where it belongs. Your mind is the cage, Mr. Cole, and no matter how desperately hard you try to hide the key, it is you that is locked in. Your people nearly killed us all, Mr. Cole, but you ... you killed your wife ... *you killed Athena!"*

As the mysterious aliens haunting words reverberated in my head, I was back in the cathedral. The eyeless but still moving corpse of Athena stands before me, my body frozen as she caresses and kisses me, her thick blood flowing into my mouth and down my throat. My hands rest on her soft breasts. The trickling red flow warms my fingers as I touch them. The sheer horror of the situation could not change the fact that I still loved her. I closed my eyes and bathed in her death ... as I felt new life. Salem joined in as the room slowly began to spin. Suddenly, the deafening sound of thunder rocked the cathedral. The intricate stained glass windows that yearned for the company of a warm, compassionate sun shattered with explosive force as all light and life dissipated into the dark abyss.

The bus is going faster and faster, but there is no road. We are going to crash, but there's nothing to crash into. And who is driving? Tony and his crew are gone ... and the bus is dissolving into a million grains of sand as the gentle lapping of waves on the beach serenade my return ... but from where?

Have I just learned the secret of my mysterious island exile? Or have I been dealt a blank card from a trick deck in a game of chance that I could never possibly win?

My solar friend is no help. He is the quintessential witness who will never talk. Warm and reliable, he is always there, always on time, but never willing to share what he has seen ... if he has seen anything at all.

I feel the presence of people, but I know that I am alone ... yet they were here, I know they were. Or maybe I was there. Or maybe we intersected at some cosmic filling station not on

the grid or anyone's map. Worst of all, I feel the presence of a woman, mysterious and warm. I have just touched her, kissed her … but where is she? Maybe she's on the island. Maybe she lives here … yes, maybe she lives here!

IT'S NOT TOO LATE IN THE DAY. I THINK I'LL GO LOOK FOR HER

BUT FIRST … I AM HUNGRY!

Reflections
"Twinkle Twinkle"

Twinkle, twinkle, little star,
How I wonder what you are.
Up above the world so high,
Like a diamond in the sky.
Twinkle, twinkle, little star,
How I wonder what you are.

HOW MAN IN HIS EARLY DAYS
MUST HAVE GAZED UP AT THE STARS
AND WONDERED ...
WONDERED WITH A MIND FREE AND CLEAR
QUESTIONING
WITHOUT SCIENCE
OR TECHNOLOGY

Just reaching out ...

WITH THE EYES OF A GALAXY CHILD

Galaxy Child

Chapter Five

"Beware the brothers of light"

"Never try to reason the prejudice out of a man. It was not reasoned into him, and cannot be reasoned out."
—Sydney Smith (1771–1845)

"Would you like a fresh towel, Nathan?" Jade asked in a warm, comforting voice.

I was just stepping out of the shower with the big question still ping-ponging around in the back of my mind. *Was it improper of me to be standing around butt-naked in front of a Pergasan female? Did she even care? What would Athena think? Would she even care? Oh well, too late now.*

"Thank you, Jade, a fresh towel would be nice," I replied. *What the heck, she's the one who offered in the first place.*

There were no other Pergasan females of the Jade series in the room, so I did not have to reply with her full name and identification number. The Pergasan form of identification was simple and rather unique. First names were given out as a series, and last names were simply a number coinciding with their arrival on the planet. For example, if you happened to be given the name "George," then you would be part of the George series. If you ended up being the fifth George of the George series arriving on earth, your full name and identification number would be George-Five. As Pergasans did not employ the institution of marriage, this made things very easy for everybody: no need to change last names ... or numbers.

Of course, if you ended up being George-1,250,426, that would be quite a mouthful, and would make it a real bitch signing checks. Oh well, no plan is perfect!

I liked the name Jade. As a matter of fact, I really liked Jade! I hope Jade liked me. I think she did. She offered me a fresh towel ... while I was naked.

THE SIGNATURE OF A TRULY PERFECT ALIEN HOUSEKEEPER

The Pergasan presence on Earth was initially a pleasant addition to human existence. To the upper echelon of the political, military, and scientific communities, their arrival had been an exciting and highly anticipated event, the result of years of meticulous planning, research, and above all ... hope. Within a scant few years, the Pergasan race had made a smooth and successful transition into human society. In an interesting way, this had an unexpected *spin-off* effect on many levels of human culture. Tolerance and acceptance of opposing faiths and ideas was greeted with a new sense of purpose and compassion ... but not everybody bought into it.

Though large numbers of Pergasans effortlessly morphed into service and small-business positions, many bridged into more elite careers, becoming scientists, doctors, diplomats, and even politicians. Their advanced intelligence and benevolent agenda earned them the trust of humans, though not the cure-all to man's international woes and divisions, the undeniable example of successful human-Pergasan relations had a positive and hopeful effect on global communities. Pergasans themselves occasionally assuming the role of goodwill ambassadors during tricky political or multinational negotiations. The positive effects of the Pergasan presence on Earth did not stop there. The planet itself would become the beneficiary of the aliens' advanced technology. After witnessing the slow decimation of Earth's polar icecaps and dramatic changes in global climate conditions, the Pergasans partnered with various governments and scientific organizations to contain Earth's eco-crisis, and led planning for the safe "re-evolution" of man and planet. This further strengthened the bond between human and alien, and gave hope for a world revitalized by virtue of cooperation and trust.

Unfortunately, for all the talk of goodwill and great hope, the toxic blood of the human condition still continued to pump furiously and blindly ... like a runaway train in an arctic blizzard, desperately seeking home, but finding only despair and a repeated path of lost horizons. How can man possibly secure a glorious and peaceful future when he continuously builds his dreams and desires on the bloody soil and tainted convolutions of his own dark past?

The saying "too good to be true" found an all-too-familiar expression on the dancing heels of an age-old monster of nature's own creation. A monster that, without compassion or logic, continuously gorged itself upon the fresh green grass of human hope and progress, a monster we've come to know as ...

PREJUDICE

APPLES FALL VICTIM TO GRAVITY
SAND CASTLES TO THE MIGHTY SEA
AND DAY FALLS VICTIM TO NIGHT
BUT NONE FALLS VICTIM SO TAGICALLY
AS MAN FALLS VICTIIM ...
TO HIMSELF

Man will always question what is different or strange to him, foreign to what he believes in or understands. And sometimes he will fear the unusual. Intolerance, ignorance, pride, and confusion can turn fear into hate ... and hate can develop into *tragedy.*

The earthbound Pergasans had done nothing to elicit such fear or hate. They were exemplary ambassadors of caring and intellectual wealth, examples that humanity could greatly prosper by and learn from.

The typical physical appearance of a Pergasan was somewhat anomalous by human standards, and as such, prone to suspicion. They were tall ... very tall, and appeared to be reptilian, though with humanoid qualities of upright stance and manual dexterity. Pergasan hands and feet were covered by thick, black gloves and boots. A large retractable scorpion-like tail, complete with stinger, provided deadly protection, though they were rarely seen. Their most prominent physical trait was the tortoise-shell-like apparatus on their backs. Actually, there were two shells, split down the middle, green on top with silver trim. Various tubes and wires linked to the exterior units, which provided armor and environmental equalization ... in essence, the shells were a terrestrial space suit. They weren't an actual physical appendage but part of a life-support system allowing them to exist in Earth's alien environment.

The males were dark and foreboding, yet curiously engaging. The females were slightly shorter and lighter in body tone, and their demeanor seemed less intimidating. But they still carried the aura of a far superior race. The Pergasans' Vader-esque helmets, a part of their environmental adaptation, gave little clue to what the aliens actually looked like. The helmets provided much-needed protection from our alien sun, many times closer to Earth than the Pergasan sun was to their home planet. The glowing red glare of their eyes was visible through the helmets, and only added to their mystique. If the eyes truly are the gateway to the soul, this was a major flaw. What was visible of their faces was dark green and reptilian looking. Yet they were warm-blooded, generous, and intelligent. The Pergasan culture that presented itself on Earth was marked by sophisticated ideology and an advanced sense of self. This contributed to the potential for fear and misunderstanding. Slowly, the stage was being set for a dangerous liaison!

A TRAGIC INTERSECTION OF CULTURE CLASH AND FUTURE SHOCK

A SICK UNRAVELING OF PROGRESS AND VICTORY THE UNFORTUNATE BEGINNING OF UNIVERSAL DEFEAT

AND IT ALL STARTED WITH A BEAUTIFUL IDEA

It is in man's nature to do what has never been done, to attain the unattainable and make possible the impossible. Wilbur and Orville, Lindbergh, Yeager, Gagarin ... all challenged the dragon and won, sometimes at great risk. Their wings enabled the rest of us to fly. Without flight, man's spirit cannot soar. It is that spirit that commands man to think the unthinkable, to push the envelope of logic, reason, science, technology, mortality, and fear. If a fish can live out of water and a flower can grow in the desert, why couldn't the genetic union of human and alien follow its logical course? This union would be humanity's greatest universal bridge, proving once and for all that man is not merely an effective agent of greed and destruction, but also a diligent guardian of the future.

Ten months, five days, four hours, seven minutes and thirty-one seconds after the cosmic cocktail of Pergasan egg and human sperm was mixed ...

THE UNIVERSE WITNESSED A MIRACLE!

BUT NOT ALL OF HUMANITY SAW IT THAT WAY

"Learn from me, if not by my precepts, at least by my example, how dangerous is the acquirement of knowledge and how much happier that man is who believes his native town to be the world, than he who aspires to become greater than his nature will allow."

— Mary Shelley, *Frankenstein*

If ignorance can be considered bliss, that bliss can be considered dangerous. For bliss can be construed not as a feeling, but as a simple, innocuous idea, a seemingly harmless motivation, perpetrated with little or no intelligence, and executed at the very worst moment possible. History has shown us that followers are as dangerous as kings ... and pessimists as dangerous as martyrs. History has also shown the pure advantages of intelligence. History has proven that commanders of great ships don't leave port in a hurricane, don't navigate without a sextant or map, and most important of all ... those commanders strive to have a crew that is trustworthy and loyal.

But the bulk of humanity is by nature not trustworthy or loyal. Nor does it consist of commanders and prophets. The majority of the earthbound flowers of man sway happily and freely upon the gentle breeze of bliss ... whether they know it or not. The ultimate act of ignorance is the belief of knowledge possessed, but not actually attained. It is through that ignorance that actions are blindly accrued. Decisions are made not based on education or experience, but more often than not based on fear and a lack of understanding. These actions carry grave and desperate repercussions. They distort history, beckoning the inevitable storms of intolerance and tragedy.

"Power is not a means, it is an end. One does not establish a dictatorship in order to safeguard a revolution; one makes the revolution in order to establish the dictatorship. The object of persecution is persecution. The object of torture is torture. The object of power is power."

—George Orwell

Power is fantasy ... and fantasy is power. Power and fantasy are fleeting. A car runs out of gas, a battery runs out of juice ... a man runs out of time. But an idea can live forever.

BUT EVEN THE GREATEST OF IDEAS
CAN BE STRUCK DOWN
BY A SWORD EMPOWERED
BY THE WRONG HAND
OR HANDS

Though they moved like shadows, they were known as the *"Brothers of Light,"* or the *"Enlightened Ones."* Their agenda was simple, their tactics destructive and deadly. The Pergasan presence on Earth posed a serious threat to the Brothers and their fanatic followers. The union of the two species was deemed sacrilege in the eyes of God, themselves, and all that was deemed holy. Hence their fight against the Pergasans would become a holy war.

At the Turner Institute of Science and Technology in Santa Cruz, California, a dark and sinister plot took form. This plot would not only change the course of history on planet Earth ... it would reach into the stars and far beyond. The plot's repercussions would savagely scatter the seeds of peace into the tumultuous winds of hatred and intolerance, forever quelling the hope that man and alien could co-exist peacefully ... for even though a miracle had been created, even a miracle could be destroyed.

The galaxy child hybrid made worldwide headlines. The institute that sheltered mother, child, and their scientific midwives gained worldwide recognition. Not since the original arrival of the first Pergasan *"Peace Ship"* had the human race greeted an event with such wonder and hope. Though threats and murmurs of resentment and fear underscored water cooler conversations and the Internet like the night after a bad episode of *American Idol,* there seemed to be no clear and present danger to the miracle child and the doctors and scientists of galactic glory. But even in the scientific community, ignorance can be bliss. Security at the facility had been greatly elevated and the surrounding areas of town set on limited lockdown. But the true danger lay inside, festering and plotting deep within the halls and rooms that sequestered the hopes and dreams of so many. The Brothers had successfully infiltrated the sensitive inner workings of the Turner Institute, as well as the ranks of local and state law enforcement. There was no place their bitter, tainted blood did not flow. For the sake of their own twisted agenda, the Brothers on the inside would eventually sacrifice their own lives.

On a picturesque Santa Cruz summer evening, five jet helicopters, armed with missiles, machine guns, firebombs, and grenades, strafed the Turner Institute. Terrorists on the inside released canisters of lethal sarin nerve gas, killing everyone instantly ... including the galaxy child.

The Pergasan elite—ambassadors, emissaries, scientists, clergy, and forward thinkers—waged formal complaints with Washington, the United Nations, the Vatican, and the scientific community. But the damage had been done. Soon after, the Pergasans were recalled. The aliens began an expedient exodus back to their home planet.

On the scorched earth of the former Turner Institute, a small monument appeared, expressing sadness for the lives of both Pergasans and humans unmercifully taken that day. The monument mourned the tragic desecration of a great dream by the dark and seemingly unexplainable side of pseudo-civilized man. The light of a great miracle had been extinguished, and in its place came sadness, despair, and the despondence of a hope that may never be resurrected. Yet one question remained ...

WOULD THE PERGASANS BE BACK?

The Station

Chapter Six

"You said no strings could secure you at the station ..."
—Jack Bruce/Pete Brown

"Suppose, just suppose," Brian said, "that when you die, you go straight to an assigned station. No heaven, no hell, no purgatory, no drive-thru window at the Burger King, and no long lines at the cosmic junkyard bank ... just your own assigned station."

***THE STATION:** *"A spiritual and/or cosmic re-enactment of a person's mortal life and times on Earth, or ...*

one hell of a hallucination!"

I am lonely. Even in the midst of all these people, I am lonely ... very lonely. I miss my home. I miss my wife. But where is home ... and where is my wife? Isn't this home? Aren't these my friends? Surely I know them; they seem to know me, at least some of them. Everyone and everything here seems to be a hazy remnant of something I left behind. The pieces seem to fit, but the puzzle is all wrong. I feel like I've made a right turn in the left-hand lane. Like I've boarded a plane with no knowledge of my destination, yet the pilots, flight attendants, and passengers all know my name and get particular joy out of telling me how much fun we're going to have when we get there. I was not expecting this, someone laced my beer ... put a time-rape drug in my Cosmo ... posed as an innocent Girl Scout and sold me hash brownies instead of Thin Mints. A strange feeling is piercing through my body and brain, like a sharp stick through a soft marshmallow. Have I impulsively jumped on the last train to nowhere, leaving my bags unattended and alone back at the station?

THE STATION ... IS THIS THE STATION?

And who is Brian? I've known a few Brians in my time, but this cat definitely isn't one of them. This dude has that weird English Australian kind of accent that tended to drive ignorant American ears like mine crazy trying to figure out exactly where they were from. Like does anybody even give a rat's ...? *(Try New Zealand, mate!)*

This party seems familiar to me. It should, I know the players, at least some of them ... but I don't know the house, or do I? The living room is real small, and I'm having lots of fun switching out stacked beer cans on the always too-short, too-close-to-the-sofa coffee table. You know ... the one on the mustard-colored, pizza-stained faux-Persian, mega-frayed, on-sale-at-K-Mart-Fourth-of-July-weekend luxury rug! Yeah, I know ... you've been there. Question ... when did I *arrive* ... did I come alone? Oops, I better shut up ... Brian's talking again!

NOW THAT I'VE GOT YOUR ATTENTION!

Brian is pontificating that the universe is only a figment of our imaginations, and that we are the universe ... and nothing else exists. Has Brian forgotten all about the station?

Someone politely asks, "But what's that up in the sky?"

THERE SHE IS!

I see her out of the corner of my eye, there she is ... now she's gone ... no, there she is again! I think I'm showing off for her, chillin' with my boys, playing beer games, posing and talkin' trash, lots of trash. Stupid stuff I can't even believe is coming out of my own mouth! How old am I? She's gone again. Was I too aggressive? Did my *"Look at Me Show"* shine the glaring spotlight on a cigarette-smoking, foulmouthed, arrogant, self-indulgent loser? Or did my Oscar-winning performance convince her I was a smooth, mysterious leading man sent by *angels* and *dragons* to rescue the fair maiden from her mundane life, eventually making passionate love to her in my eternal garden of plumeria and silk.

I think she just went to the can, which ain't half a bad idea right about now. The beers are gettin' to me and besides, I need a mirror. If she comes back, this mysterious leading man has got to be looking good. A man's gotta have game!

Problem ... why am I showing off? Why am I trying so desperately to win over this damsel? Don't we already know each other? Didn't we come to this party together just like we used to? What's happening? Now the sharp stick and the soft marshmallow are merging again. The right pieces and the wrong puzzle are at war once more, and my bags are forever lost back at the station ... along with my grip on this reality. Where's the bathroom? That's the key, *the bathroom!* Maybe in some strange way launching into a redundant and familiar ritual performed thousands or maybe even millions of times in my life within the confines of four small walls and a lightly scented box of Kleenex will help me to return. Or at least take me back to that familiar junction of what or who I am in this senseless nightmare. Maybe the simple act of taking a pee will get me out of here, break me free of this distorted Polaroid twilight zone, propel me around the sun at warp speed and take me home ... my real home. Where's the mirror? Gotta check myself out at least, if the pee don't work ... I still gotta rescue the fair maiden. All right, here we go. Whoa, something's wrong, real wrong! Man's looking good, real good ... a little too good, no lines under the eyes and about fifteen pounds less ... too good! It's me, but not the same me I remember this morning, if there was a morning.

My eyes are staring at a reflection that in itself is a question, but the question is lost, because the only possible answer still remains a question. That brings us back to the train ... destination unknown, bags at the station. But when did I pack? Where's Brian? Is he on this one too? Pilots and partygoers hold the map. They know where we're going, don't they ... don't they?!

SHE'S GONE
BUT ACCORDING TO BRIAN
NO ONE EVER LEAVES THE PARTY
THIS IS THE PARTY ...
THAT NEVER ENDS
"I WALKED INTO, SUCH A SAD TIME ... AT THE STATION."

ATHENA'S IN THE MIRROR

Athena's in the mirror, logic's out the window, and time ... time hangs in the balance, questioning the reality of its own existence. Can time be confused, vulnerable ... left cold, shivering and wet in the dark frigid night? Remember, time waits for no man. But at the station, time waits just like the rest of us. Time must take a number and hang out in line for the fresh, deli-thin-sliced, imported Swiss cheese on sale for $5.99 a pound. At the station, even time can run out of toilet paper at the worst possible moment. Time can get a parking ticket, step in doggie doo, or even get a nasty Cyclops-looking zit on prom night ... funny stuff, but would it be wise to make time mad? Would it be wise to make God mad? They're both questionable entities, at least in terms of physical form. But depending on whom you talk to, there does seem to be tangible traces of their existence. I don't know about you, but I personally have never met God, and I sure as s--- have never seen time! Yeah I've seen calendars, owned watches, used an alarm clock, and tried to impress old girlfriends by going at it all night ... but I have never *seen* time. "The times they are a-changin'": Bull! ***Things* change. *Time* doesn't, because in the final analysis ... *time does not exist,* at least in the realm of physical form.** Man created time. He created it so his checks would clear the next day. Cash is a thing, and having cash means we can buy things. We can't buy things with time, because we can't stuff time into our wallet ... or get it out of an ATM! In the end, we don't buy things on time with time;

we buy things on time with money. "Time is money," bull! Money is money ... ***TIME DOES NOT EXIST!***

EXCEPT AT THE STATION
WHERE TIME IS MORTAL
AND LONELY
SHIVERING
IN THE COLD
WET RAIN

But let's not make time or God mad, it's not good business. Besides, the one and only tangible conclusion I have been able to draw from this distorted mini-series cluster-chuck is that time might be my only friend. My friend that doesn't exist, that's only a paper trail of old calendars, cancelled checks and expensive watches ... time might be my only salvation, my last road to the truth ... if there is a truth.

"AT THE PARTY, SHE WAS KINDNESS
... IN THE HARD CROWD."

She's back, and so are the shadows. Something's changed, possibly a rift in the cosmic order of emotional timing. *Salem's* back, but something is different, I can feel it ... I can see it! Salem was my exotic princess of enchantment and mystery. But at this moment, I forget just when and where she entered my life ... and how she actually fit in. All I was sure of was that she had always been there. Salem's exotic eyes did all the carving. Unlike Athena's gypsy-blue windows to the soul that stopped at the heart, Salem looked through you, beyond you, straight into the next universe and past the boundaries of time itself. When her eyes weren't traversing the silent borders of spirituality and consciousness, they were set hard into the moment, freezing existence itself and everything in it. This moment was unexpected and confusing. Salem appeared as if out of nowhere. She entered the room looking straight at me, through me ... like we'd rewound the previous few scenes and started over with a different script. There was recognition, warmth, and a note of sadness that suddenly turned into a quick flash of warning and concern. She was moving straight towards me, oblivious to everyone and everything but us. The closer Salem came, the slower time seemed to move. Our semi-nostalgic, zombie-esque party guests were drifting hypnotically into a slow, macabre waltz. Glances and body language became long, uncomfortable acts of semi-conscious voyeurism and pseudo-narcotic thought reading.

Salem got us into this; Salem would have to get us out!

Sound had become incidental. The carnival-masked banter of a thousand unrehearsed, alcohol-fueled debates faded off into a soundtrack to nowhere. The shadows behind Salem seemed to move faster as the party moved slower ... darting through our four-walled cosmos with reckless abandon and ultimate freedom. In this eerie midnight-at-the-county-fair-of-confusion-and-chaos sequence, did the proverbial black horse on the white carousel hold the answer I so desperately sought? Or was this Salem's show, a last desperate attempt to shed the tremendous weight of a secret that rocked her to the core and shredded her very soul in its hideous attempt to break free?

That answer would come soon!

Salem's presence before me was powerful, demanding the captive audience of one that she had personally chosen. The shadowy whispers from the voyeur ghouls in the peanut gallery of carnival-masked party leeches faded slowly into the ever-brewing vat of gurgling silence ...

"SOMEONE LEFT THE CAKE OUT IN THE RAIN"

Her kiss was long, deep, and warm. I knew we'd been here before.

But like everything else in this candy-coated menagerie of paper shoes and broken glass ... I questioned even that.

"You look like you've just seen a ghost," she mused, holding the room quiet prisoner.

"And what does the ghost see?" I replied calmly, hoping she'd let the bats out of the cave and shed some revealing light on the present situation.

"Time," Salem effortlessly said, restraining her gaze not into the next universe, but directly to my humble front door of bewilderment and confusion.

"I didn't know you could see time," I countered suspiciously.

"You're going to see a lot of things, Nathan," she replied. "Walk in the garden?" she asked.

"Sure," I responded willingly.

All of a sudden it became clear to me. We had been here before. I knew this house ... and I knew this garden. Now the room was moving. The shadows on the wall were going crazy, chasing and dancing around like peyote-infested sugar junkies at a double feature's intermission. The bomb had ticked down to its final second. I had to clip the colored wire or all would be lost forever. Here lay the missing part of the equation, the stamped ticket to my accidental vacation in limbo. The holy grail of truth was flirting with promise ... I just had to decipher it!

As the shadows gravitated toward the back of the house, Salem asked, "Coming, Nate?"

I froze for a second, assessing the possibility of snipping the wrong wire.

She soothingly whispered, "You're not here to rescue me, Nathan ... you're here to see the truth."

As we entered the garden, the shadows disappeared; the room stopped moving ... Salem's voice was the only sound in the universe.

"You can see them now, Nate, really see them. Not as shadows or reflections, not as myth or lies, but for who and what they really are. Your wife and your best friend, your wingman and your soul mate ... they're lovers, Nathan ... they're lovers."

In a far corner of the garden, the intoxicated dancing shadows had become the embracing silhouettes of Carlo and Athena, locked in passionate fury and desire. Oh my god, this is what I've missed … missed it completely! It wasn't about Salem; it was about Athena, my wife … and Carlo. The day I knew, ***the day I found out!*** That's where she's been, that's what I've been looking for, Athena … ***Athena!***

Salem was gone. As for the party that never ended, it was time to go. The black horse had jumped the carousel, and the keg was warm. But I knew this time that I would be back. Back to finish what was started here, back to finish it … forever.

OR HAD I ALREADY DONE THAT?

"AS I WALKED OUT, FELT MY OWN NEED … JUST BEGINNING."

Reflections
"Vampires"

One day I woke up and the world had changed. I didn't recognize it anymore. Its people, once warm and accommodating, had suddenly become cold and indifferent. Like vampires in the mirror, their souls seemed to vanish from view, along with their humanity, replaced by self-absorption and intolerance. Not everyone had made the change. I still encountered a few gentle and good-natured souls during these strange and perplexing days, but they were few and far between. My basic perception of vampires in the mirror remained the same ... stoic, uncomfortable, and frightfully overwhelming.

MAN STRIVES TO ACHIEVE, TO BETTER HIMSELF AND PROSPER. BUT WHERE IS THE LINE DRAWN BETWEEN PROSPERITY AND COMPASSIONATE BANKRUPTCY?

It wasn't just people that had changed, it was life itself ... everything.

EVERYTHING HAD CHANGED!

But what the vampires couldn't comprehend was that once their souls had vanished from view ...

THE MIRRORS THEMSELVES WOULD SOON FOLLOW.

House of Frozen Angels

Book One

"There is a wisdom that is woe;
but there is a woe that is madness."
—Herman Melville, Moby-Dick

Many of the ships had gone, headed back to Pergasas, I presumed. A moderate contingent of the initial alien strike force stayed behind to secure Earth. Their orders were to eradicate any human survivors, whatever condition they were in, and to destroy the remnants of civilization. How had I survived this high-tech carnage? I did not know. The only thing I was sure of was that my surviving brethren had become the proverbial arcade ducks for unlimited target practice, a badge we were not honored to wear.

The Pergasans reminded me of what I had read about the ancient Roman Empire. They were a brilliant and sophisticated society, yet they were brutal, cold, and masochistic. But they wore it well ... very well.

Although the Pergasans' viral and physical attacks were quick and devastating, their follow-up had not been carried out with the skill and precision one might have expected. They had no sense of human tenacity. While the Pergasans attended to the disposal of human remains and the task of hunting down and killing any survivors, those humans that were alive and healthy took refuge and made plans.

They knew the gun stores, sporting goods outlets, armories, and police stations. Anywhere weapons could be found, they found them. Found them and hid them in bunkers, storm cellars, hidden rooms, and caves, along with canned goods, fuel, medicine and clothing. The warrior humans hid out in warehouses, office buildings, airports, and burned-out factories. Places where familiarity with structure and an open line of sight could level the playing field, at least a little bit. The Pergasans were indeed an advanced race, but they weren't bulletproof.

Our earliest studies of the Pergasas A-73 system had shown the Pergasan sun to be considerably farther away from their home planet than ours was to Earth. Though we suspected there to be intelligent life on Pergasas, their basic physiology would have to be dramatically different from ours. That turned out to be one of the few advantages the skeleton crew of humanity had left on its home court. The sun was an enemy to the Pergasans. Not only was its brilliant spectrum of light and prismatic color an annoyance to them, but its heat left them uncomfortable and drained. Their massive bodies constantly struggled with the debilitating effects of elevated body temperature, extreme sensitivity to light, and unfamiliarity with Earth's gravity.

THEY WON THE FIRST BATTLE ... BUT THERE WAS STILL A WAR!

The Pergasans may have had their work cut out for them in the daytime, but at night they were monsters. At dusk, you could see the change. For them, the party was just beginning. The cleanup crews were efficient and almost too tidy. The nightly death squads were terrifying and unforgiving. You could only wonder what madness fueled this kind of extreme hate and contempt for life. How could such hatred possibly exist, and what could have created it?

Most Pergasans could not communicate with humans. Only certain upper-level military officers and scientists had perfected a form of telepathic communication, which proved remarkably articulate and effective, though rarely used on man ... they preferred to kill not talk. They communicated between themselves through what sounded like short bursts of radio squall, compressing sentences and whole phrases into sounds only other Pergasans could understand.

My own observations led me to believe that the Pergasans had miscalculated serious key elements of their own compatibility with Earth's complex natural environment. Maybe they were just too stubborn and bullheaded to admit to these peripheral technical errors. It was truly hard to comprehend how a race so scientifically advanced could make such a glaring blunder. Regardless of why, the Pergasan invasion of Earth was an unforgiving task, challenging the aliens on every imaginable level. This was not going to be a walk in the park. They were going to have to fight for every inch of ground they had gained, and fight even harder to hold on to it. Their potential downfall might not only ride on the wheels of their physical limitations, but also on the runaway train powering their own ignorance and superego, not necessarily a club exclusive to humans any more. And one small detail remained ...

WE WEREN'T ALL DEAD!!!

For the time being, I would remain a shadow. Silently watching, patiently waiting.

And like a shadow, the sun would give me life ... and darkness would be my cover.

THE JILLIAN-KYLE INDUSTRIES SERIES 8 *"SMART-GIRL"*

In the days after the Pergasan attack, I stayed in hiding. My seclusion was interrupted only by necessity. Some days I would stray from my secret bunker to round up food and supplies. I was well aware that there were other survivors, but for the time being, I eluded any such contact with my anatomical brethren. I knew that one day I would be discovered, or would have to make contact. But the uncertainty of my present circumstance guided my instincts and told me to stay clear for the time being.

I had found an abandoned dairy facility on the outskirts of a town up north and claimed it as my fortress of solitude. Its location allowed me convenient, if sometimes dangerous, access to my home and former office. On the days I felt up to it, I would make clandestine journeys to those and other important locations to retrieve various personal items and necessities for my sanity and survival. On one such outing to my research lab I acquired the *"Silent Giant,"* a solar-and-gas-powered "super-cell" generator that made virtually no noise. The Silent Giant was worth its weight in diamonds, as I would find out later from monitoring ham and CB radio transmissions, as well as short-wave and other terrestrial broadcasts ... one more reason for my life of secrecy.

My world may not have been fashionable, but it was comfortable. I had my clothes, personal items, pictures, books, and music. I also had a small refrigerator, radios to keep track of the outside world, a killer bar, and a well-stocked pantry of canned foods and government grapefruit juice. I lived in a small rundown house about thirty-five yards away from the main facility. The open fields around the dairy plant allowed me to spot any potential danger. The house had two small bedrooms, a kitchen, bathroom, living/dining room, and a small attached garage. I knew eventually somebody or something would cross my path, but for now ... this was home.

I learned early on that the art of survival was like a virtual chess game, best approached on many different levels, with just as many strategies ... all played out to their ultimate conclusion. It wasn't just about food and water, fight-or-flight, kill-or-be-killed.

Survival was the mastery of mental prowess, the ability to cross the tightrope amidst a raging storm. Survival as an art required a finesse that I've never managed to define or articulate in a way a normal person could comprehend its delicate and immediate priorities. Even when not in the throes of an alien invasion, the human mind is in survival mode. It thrives on even the most basic of challenges, creatively propelling itself beyond to the next horizon of endeavor. It is forever bombarded with constant, demanding requirements of its own existence, selfishly positioning themselves at the front of the line to be fed first. Anger, greed, love, hate, jealousy, vengeance, pain, lust, and a host of other obnoxious neighbors endlessly banging at the door, begging for warmth and escape from the rain.

Survival boils down to that essential root element: need. Mental prowess puts that essential element into its proper order, and deals with it.

"Little do men perceive what solitude is, and how far it extendeth. For a crowd is not company, and faces but a gallery of pictures, and talk but a tinkling cymbal, where there is no love."

—Sir Francis Bacon

THOUGH I WAS DEVOID OF ANY HUMAN CONTACT ... I WAS NOT ENTIRELY ALONE!

Among my meager inventory of survival equipment, I had in my possession what might have been the best and most creative way of dealing with the byproducts of exile: five of the most beautiful women on the planet.

Athena, Salem, Chelsea, Lillian, and Jade were my post-apocalyptic goddess-android answers to one of man's greatest needs: companionship. Originally dubbed "Omega Mannequins," they were durable, reliable, fully-covered-under-warranty, to-die-for beautiful, and yes ... they were robots ... my *"Frozen Angels."*

"Smart Girls" were the result of a merger between two very different companies that had one thing in common.

The Jillian Angel Corporation was a leader in the manufacture of highly advanced robotic mannequins for upscale fashion houses, department stores, and boutiques.

Kyle Industries started out as a small robotics research and development firm, eventually getting contracts from NASA, the government, and various manufactures of transportation. Their claim to fame, "BOB-E," was basically an advanced crash-test dummy. BOB-E was a walking, talking dummy with highly advanced computer relay systems and physical structures capable of measuring human tolerance and reaction to almost any environmental or simulated situation. He was shot into space, thrown in the ocean, eaten by tigers, blown up, ripped up, frozen, smashed, thrown out of planes, and basically used and abused ... but the information he provided was priceless. Soon after that, Kyle's proprietary technology was stolen, and several foreign companies began producing their own version of BOB-E. A price war followed and Kyle's contracts were eventually dropped.

That was when Jillian Angel came calling. The "Smart Girl" idea having originally been hers. BOB-E was a technological wonder, a spawn of the macho mind, the ultimate G.I. Joe. Jillian's "Girls" had soft plastic, silky hair, delicate robotics, enchanting eyes, and everything in the right place. BOB-E had the advanced sensing and environmental reaction capabilities, superior CPU processing, speech capability, and micro-power equalization. BOB-E could also be thrown through a wall. Jillian's girls were ... girls.

Jillian's offer was seductive, her warrior-like business skills hard to resist. Soon Kyle Industries signed on the line ... and history was about to be made.

The first prototypes took about a year to complete. The finished product was introduced to the world a few months later. There were many improvements and upgrades added to the original units. Each new model came with its own distinct personality and intelligence. For an extra fee, you could download a completely different mind. I guess that was modern science's way of keeping the divorce rate down. The technology for the Smart Girls' superior mental and physical capabilities was called "H-BARR": Human-Based Automatic Reflex and Reaction.

H-BARR was a revolutionary marriage of machinery and science, giving the robots a lifelike human aspect previously deemed impossible. The more advanced units featured something called an "Orgone Field." It was a generator that produced an electrical envelope around the units, creating an almost lifelike energy. This electrical field, coupled with the use of synthetic pheromones and exotic scents, took the Smart Girls from the realm of machine and fantasy ... and straight into the world of reality.

The list of features went on and on, and so did the price. The cost of owning and maintaining one of these angelic plastic honeys was ... celestial. If you did have that kind of money lying around, you probably had at least one or two of the real thing.

Manufacturing and supply of these units was no picnic either. At a time when the global economy was in the absolute toilet, the Smart Girls were not exactly the smartest idea. The company folded less than a year after entering the world market.

So how did I have such an incredible in to this garden of unearthly delights? I designed the personality and language CPUs for the updated units, a variation of the ones we used in the Luna-Two project. Our bionic bunnies were a bonus bestowed upon us by Jillian and friends. My wife and many other men's better halves were not mortally overjoyed about our new concubines, so the Smart Girls became office wenches, doomed to forever inhabit the cold and lonely exile of backroom closets and outdoor storage units. They didn't get much use ... though they were a scream at holiday parties. But now, they were major players in my ongoing quest to survive and stay sane.

These plastic vixens were ironic reminders that once, not too long ago, humans had walked beautiful, healthy, and proud. Those same humans ruled the planet and gazed at the stars with wonder ... not fear.

This was a travel day. I hadn't seen any Pergasans for at least a week and I was feeling brave. Maybe they'd moved on permanently, that would be nice. I was still in the process of ramping up my arsenal, my surviving cousins having been quicker and more successful at relieving the local gun shops of their precious booty. There was a small, forgettable pawnshop in midtown. With any luck a weapon or two might remain there. It was worth a try. As I was getting ready to leave, I began having a strange feeling about my impending journey. As I started for town I was on higher alert than usual. When I hit midtown, I saw a few straggling human survivors. Most of them ran from me ... fear and uncertainty were a common denominator among those left behind. Some hid in the shadows, seeking cover in the burned out shops, twisted metal and broken glass. They appeared like ghosts. They had survived the Pergasans, but were leery of a fellow human.

The pawnshop was a bust. I was too late to find anything more than some old, dusty wedding bands and a plethora of ancient power tools. My heightened state of concern was bothering me, slowly opening up the door to the dark house of paranoia. Something didn't feel right. It was time to head back to my fortress of solitude and the stoic company of my synthetic wonder women.

Exiting the pawnshop with my new best friend, Mr. *"Louisville Slugger",* I realized I was being watched, watched by eyes much stronger than those of the human ghosts parading in the shadows. They were cool, silent ... quietly tracking every move I made. And they were close ... real close.

The warmth and presence of my mysterious stalker enveloped my senses. She was near ... I could feel it. But how did I know she was a she? Had all these lost months of being in survival mode fine-tuned my senses to such a high degree that I could sex my opponent without a clear visual? Or had my solitaire mental state blindly fallen victim to a simple case of wishful thinking?

As I turned from Fourth Avenue onto Main to head out of town, the doors of screaming paranoia and chasing shadows suddenly closed, and my mysterious stalker stepped out of the inner playground, straight onto the torn streets of reality.

She couldn't have been more than twenty feet away, staring me down like a scene from *High Noon*. But she carried no Winchester or Colt, just smiling green eyes and a soft, cheeky grin.

She looked healthy and clean ... a little too clean for a starving street tramp. She must have found a pod—a pack to run with. I had seen such gangs, but stayed away. Their actions were reminiscent of wild pack animals doing anything they could to survive. No quality of life, just constant desperation. Fighting and picking through the barren wasteland they once called home by day, scurrying and hiding from the Pergasan invaders by night. If she had found a pod, these guys were a class act or if nothing else ... very clean. As I spent a few moments sizing her up, I realized she wasn't doing that to me. She had done that long before. Her vibe was anything but inquisitive. It felt more like she was silently greeting me after a long observation. A powerful look of recognition flashed across her face. How long had she been watching me? Were there others? There had to be. Living alone out here was way too dangerous, especially for a beautiful young woman. Maybe this was a trap? But who would possibly give a rat's ass about me? The only things of value I had were a few old Beatles albums and twenty-five cans of government grapefruit juice. Maybe they knew about the generator? Naw, they'd have just killed me and taken that, no time or effort wasted there. Nope, I was merely one of a million displaced human souls waiting for whatever came next ... nothing special.

BUT SHE WAS SPECIAL!

Close up, she was absolutely stunning. Her wavy auburn hair framed a face of olive-toned perfection. I tried desperately to find some flaw, some hideous imperfection that could make sense of this angelic vision amidst the scorched landscape. I found none, but was happy to come up empty ... just a little confused. Her attire was pure motocross, without the helmet. She wore a tight green leather suit with knee-high dirtkickers, a thick red stripe going down both pant legs, stopping at the boot. The suit was zipped down halfway in the front. I figured the tight leather must have made her feel somewhat hot, but she didn't seem like it. Her demeanor was cool, like she had just downed a giant vanilla milkshake. She was about twenty-five, and had a subtle feline essence and the muscle tone of a natural athlete. She was all woman, but she looked like she could really kick ass!

It was hard to tear away from those eyes, but it was time to break the spell, time to pull back the sheets and find out who was really underneath. But at that moment, as if summoned by a much higher power, she turned and ran ... never looking back. I gave chase. I grew wings and pursued her through the quiet metropolis that once flourished with humanity, life, and unending dreams.

When an unknown man chases a lone woman down a deserted city street, fear is imminent. But in this case, there seemed to be no fear, only the odd feeling that she was teasing and taunting me in some obscure way. I couldn't see her face, but as she effortlessly left me in the dust, I could still feel her smiling green eyes and soft, cheeky grin. I broke off the chase, realizing deep down that soon ... we would meet again.

"I would rather trust a woman's instinct than a man's reason."
—Stanley Baldwin

"A woman is always a mystery: one must not be fooled by her face and her heart's inspiration."
—Edmondo De Amicis

The mysterious girl and the chase had left me tired and hungry. I would eat later. For now, a short nap was the only thing on the menu. I had always known that there were survivors, many of them. I saw them almost every day, but they always brought with them loss and despair. This girl came with her own world, a world much different from the present reality. I wanted to see that world, be let in ... become a part of it. The mystery of her very presence was more powerful than anything I had felt for a long time. My survival mode was merely a prolonged sentence of living death. Dying slowly, I still clung to alcohol and trinkets that only reinforced the fact that I was hanging on to a world that had already died. She was still with me, and I vowed to eventually find her. For now I would sleep. Slowly, I drifted off into a gentle afternoon slumber, my next stop ...

THE TWILIGHT ZONE

She was yelling, *"Run, don't look back! Just run!"* The primal urgency of her screams ripped through the air like M16 fire through cotton. Dorothy was trapped in the poppy field, but who was trying to catch her? Had the Cowardly Lion turned? Or had the gentle Tin Man gone on a homicidal rampage? I was confused ...

BUT I KNEW THAT DOROTHY WAS IN SERIOUS TROUBLE!

(Is this a dream?)

Having been a student of history, I had studied all kinds of atrocities. Being a human in the Pergasan occupation ... I was living through one. But what I would witness next was beyond the realm of sadism or insanity, far beyond the wicked threshold of violence and cruelty. As I broke out of my twisted theater of slumber and back into a surreal reality, the woman's screams intensified. She was still telling Dorothy to run. As I got to the window to see what was happening, my body froze ... and so did my soul.

There were only two of them, a mother and her young daughter, both terrified and running for their lives. The young girl was about twenty feet ahead of her anguished mother. The child was confused, not understanding what they were running from, only that the fear in her mother's voice was real, as was the danger. But I understood ... I understood all too well. I understood the primal depth and sheer terror in the mother's voice. I understood the source of that terror.

There were eight Pergasan demons chasing the two horrified females. The aliens could have easily taken them out with their weapons, but they smelled a kill. They wanted this to be up close and personal. This was the ultimate example of the unspeakable brutality and violence perpetrated by a race of alien invaders devoid of compassion. They were unholy physical manifestations of evil far beyond man's limited capability to imagine. The reasons for their human bloodlust were an unknown and haunting mystery.

The mother was exhausted and losing ground, still yelling for her daughter to keep running. She was sweating profusely, her breathing erratic and tense. The lead Pergasan was gaining on the fatigued mother when suddenly the woman tripped and fell to the ground. The terrified daughter stopped and turned around, her own horrified screams now mirroring the primal intensity of her mother's from only a few moments before. The alien beast loomed over the downed woman for a few seconds, staring blankly into his prey's eyes. He then catapulted his scorpion-like stinger into her mid section, slicing her skin like a sharp dagger through thin paper. The woman's last gaze fixed upon her daughter.

Her last words were "Mommy loves you."

The alien raised his stinger high into the air, his impaled victim lifeless and bloody. The Pergasan slammed the body to the ground, dragging it a short distance before releasing the woman's corpse.

The alien approached the child, now mute and frozen with fear. He towered over her silently, studying her as if she were the object of some insane, twisted science experiment. She looked back into the alien's eyes. She could not understand ... no human could. What was the root of their evil, the reason for their unspeakable bloodlust? Had we done something to them, maybe something we didn't know about? Was she like Jesus Christ, dying for mankind's own sins? Sins against a culture she had never even met? She certainly was no threat to them ... so why her?

WHY?

At that moment, something deep inside of me snapped. Like the skinny kid with the funny glasses striking back at the schoolyard bully. I don't know where it came from, but something screamed, *"No more, no freaking more ... this s--- stops now!"* I decided to go on the offensive. I would run no more ... hide no more. I would search for allies and fight. I would fight alone if I couldn't find others. Either way, I would fight!

Reality and reason suddenly became twin liabilities. I had to let them go, otherwise neither the girl nor I stood a chance. The meter was running and this taxi of death was about to deliver the young innocent to her final destination. I had few weapons, but what I did have I knew how to use. My arsenal of mayhem came compliments of several scattered sources found on fear-laced daylight journeys, but mainly one former meth lab I had fortuitously stumbled upon a few weeks earlier.

I don't remember leaving my resting place, I barely remember arming myself. But I do remember the loud sound and heavy kick of the Browning shotgun going off, hitting the alien predator square in the chest ... dropping him like a drunken sailor. "Now that I've got your attention" crept into my mind with the subtlety of a *Three Stooges* short ... but this was not the time for sarcasm. I ran to the girl, picked her up, and kept running ... the remaining Pergasans in hot pursuit. Now I'm not a particularly religious man, but at that moment I sincerely believed ...

IT WAS TIME TO TURN IT OVER TO A HIGHER POWER!

MAYBE TODAY I WASN'T GOING TO DIE!

At first I heard it, and then slowly I began to feel it. My focus was still intent and unwavering on the girl. Perhaps I was blinded by the urgency of my task, or the surreal nature of the present situation. But for a brief second, I stepped out of the dark ... and into the light.

When the Pergasans began falling like bowling pins on dollar-beer Wednesday night, I realized I was not alone. And that God, or whatever governing powers were in place, had pushed me aside for a cause much greater than I could ever have imagined. I returned to the moment, running, frantically clutching the girl ... she was cold, crying, and in shock. An innocent centered in the eye of an alien storm, she could not have possibly understood. I sheltered her in my arms, trying to convince her she was safe, preparing myself for the ensuing introduction to my mysterious battlefield saviors.

As the jet fighters screamed past me, taking out Pergasans like Tommy racking up points on the pinball machine, I felt like it was Fleet Week in San Francisco. The marines had landed, or somebody had. Frankly, I didn't give a s--- who they were ... I was just glad to see them. Behind the deafening roar of the fighters came the distinct sound of motorcycles, lots of them ... their entrance onto the field of battle was nothing short of spectacular and inspiring. But it was the leader of the pack that drew my attention. He was not an imposing man, neither was he scary. More like something straight out of Hollywood, a cross between *Easy Rider* and *Rambo.* His dark, wavy hair flowed long and free, catching the wind like a pair of wings. He wore a black-fringed leather vest with a large American flag sewn on the back. The flag itself was tattered and burned in some corners, haphazardly stitched on like something out of *Frankenstein.* Though the workmanship may have been sad, the message was proud. It told a story … though the ending was still a mystery. The two-wheeled warrior blew by me on his chopper, heading straight for one of the fighting Pergasans. His eyes were focused on a single, clear objective …

FIGHT OR DIE

What I would witness next was pure Hollywood, only without a script, cameras, or stuntmen. Just the brave remnants of humanity showing that for all of those whose spirit had been torn and crushed and for all of those whose hope had been lost … there still was a reason to fight!

THERE STILL WAS A CHANCE FOR HOPE

The sky above me had become a theater of war, and the landscape on which I stood bled. The mysterious hero vanished into a cloud of smoke and noise. I fought to make sense of the many realities playing out in front of me.

Each second brought a new challenge as I furiously ran through the house of a thousand rooms looking for safe haven. I was in the throes of a raging war, and clinging to me in desperate terror was a young shattered life, for which I was the sole guardian. I looked for sanctuary, but it was nowhere in sight. More Pergasans appeared, and just as many Harley-mounted warriors rose to meet them. It seemed my mysterious saviors had some experience in battling the alien terrors. They were doing well, and that was good. I made every attempt to shield the girl with my body. It was the only thing I could do.

For a moment, I looked up into the sky. I recognized F-18s and other military fighters pursuing the now-familiar yellow scorpion-tailed alien fighters. Even though the Pergasan ships were technologically superior to their human counterparts, the dogfight above seemed evenly matched. Perhaps it was home field advantage. Either way I was rooting for the locals ... go team!

Hand to hand, the warriors were no match for the looming giants. But the fearless biker troopers seemed to have a system, three humans to one alien. In addition to guns, my mysterious saviors were armed with small missiles, grenades, and other explosives. Those armaments combined with the battle in the sky created a sense of Armageddon; the world was on fire and blowing up around us. I'd seen and heard explosions on some of the best theater systems in the world, but nothing could have prepared me for the real thing. The percussion and heat adding special effects I was not familiar with and did not enjoy.

The young girl clutched desperately to my arm. I could feel her temperature slowly coming down, her body weakening by the minute. I feared she was going deeper into shock. My total attention was suddenly thrust back upon her.

THE BLOODY CHAOS THAT HAD RAGED AROUND US SUDDENLY AND MYSTERIOUSLY STOPPED. THE FAINT SOUND OF AIRBORNE FIGHTERS GOING AT IT OVER THE DISTRANT HILLS WAS THE ONLY AUDIBLE EVIDENCE OF A CONTINUING STRUGGLE.

For a brief moment, time stood still. The deafening choir of explosions and gunfire was silenced ... as if by heavenly intervention. My senses embraced this strange audible solace with genuine warmth and thankfulness, slowly tuning in to the subtle, ghostly soundtrack of wasted humanity and machinery shamelessly strewn out on the battlefield of blood and pain.

I HEARD
I WATCHED
I FELT

I ASKED WHY ...
FROM BATTLEGROUND
AND BLOODY SKY
THE GHOSTS OF WAR ...
JUST WALKED ON BY

Reality was once again taking a twisted turn. Nobody really knew where we were going ... except the mysterious stranger. He was the virtual center, the cornerstone, the very foundation that held this macabre theater of the damned together. We were at the crossroads and there was no turning back. Most of the bikes close to me were down, victims of explosions and fighter fire. I could still hear some of the jets off in the distance, sporadic gunfire suggesting the battle wasn't completely over. It was then that I heard him coming up directly behind me. I turned around as he passed me, his menacing sawed-off shotgun in his right hand. He was trying to fire it at something, but it was empty. He tossed the gun away but continued on his determined course.

The Pergasan that had killed the little girl's mother was on the ground but getting back up to fight. The mysterious hero aimed his all-American machine directly at the alien demon and drew a second shotgun from a holster. Without hesitation, he cocked the ominous sawed-off monster and took aim. But the ominous sawed-off monster jammed, and the mysterious hero was in peril, getting dangerously closer to a waiting, angry target ... but unwilling to break off his attack. He momentarily slowed his bike down, but did not change his course.

Heroes do what heroes do: they find resolution where there is none, and answers when answers don't pick up the phone.

The mysterious warrior reached into the pocket of his black-leather vest. Finding a lighter, he lit a piece of cloth dangling freely from the Harley's gas tank. Seconds from impact, he jumped. As the bike struck the Pergasan, there was a large flash of bright light. The alien lit up like a dried-out Christmas tree, its screams like nothing I'd ever heard before. I wanted it to end, yet I felt a morbid fascination about watching this soulless destroyer of humanity die a horrifying, painful death right before my eyes. It was strangely cleansing ...

BUT ALL GOOD PARTIES MUST COME TO AN END!

The alien's last death call faded as its body crumpled slowly onto the unhallowed earth of an unforgiving war zone ... the bloody battlefield was suddenly apologetic and calm.

TIME ...
LOST IN THE CONFUSION OF HATRED
AND VIOLENCE
STOOD SILENT
AND HAUNTINGLY STILL
THE DEAD ROSE
CONTINUING ON TO THEIR NEXT DESTINATION
THE LIVING ... WAITED

As the Pergasan succumbed to his well-deserved fate, an eerie silence once again prevailed. My attention returned to the mysterious hero as he rose unscathed from his tumble. His back faced us ... he was silently witnessing his evil foe's unceremonious demise. He could not have felt compassion or even a twinge of sadness for the downfall of his evil nemesis, that was a given, for his enemy was a harbinger of death to anything human, a stellar warlord sent on a mission with orders to do the unthinkable with extreme prejudice and absolutely no mercy. The universe had drawn a line in the sand, thrown out the rules, and issued a challenge for which all motivation and sense of purpose superseded common logic and compassion. What was the mysterious rider now thinking? One would have to have to read his eyes, face, and very mind to know at that exact moment.

This battle was not a new one for him. His reaction, or lack of it, showed me that he'd been here before, perhaps many times. I remember in one of Mark Twain's books Huck Finn said, "I could get used to a hot stove if I set on it long enough." Was this the hero's hot stove? Had he seen and been a part of so much death and destruction that he was now callous to the sensations attached to these horrific, bloody conflicts?

MY ANSWER CAME AS A TOTAL AND UNEXPECTED SURPRISE!

The mysterious hero slowly turned, zeroing directly in on me. His cold, hard stare imprinted my soul, burning into the imaginary walls of my mediocre human existence. For a second, I felt trapped. A hollow panic rose from my stomach and imprisoned my mind and body. I froze, not knowing what to do. He had saved the girl and me, but who really cared? Universal guidelines of human behavior were out the window at this point in time. I realized I didn't know this man, I didn't know any of them. They were killers ... not the reckless mold of a jealous husband in the right place at the wrong time. These guys were professionals! I came to the conclusion that I was at the mercy of the universe ... could I have possibly been the cause of all this? I should have just stayed in bed. My mind was racing.

Suddenly, without any fanfare or warning, the piercing stare of the mysterious hero turned soft and friendly, looking beyond me to his approaching comrades. He pulled out a small radio from his vest. For the first time I heard his voice.

"Attention, K-Mart shoppers, the party's over and the store is now closed. If you're still alive, check in. If you're dead ... forget about it. And hey ... good work everybody."

What? This mysterious hero, this killer standing knee deep in alien blood, this shotgun-toting machine, had a sense of humor? For some strange reason, don't ask me why, I didn't expect levity to be on the menu that afternoon. This was a day when the sun ran away; blood filled your shoes, and birthday cakes melted in the rain. A sense of humor ... man, I gotta get out of the house more often.

I was relieved at the change of tone but I temporarily stayed in my panic position as a few of his people walked past me toward him.

He spoke again. "You holdin' out for a raise, Danny?" He methodically quipped.

"Outta juice, bro," his comrade said, holding up an empty automatic rifle.

"We gotta take you shoppin', man," he replied. The two embraced and laughed, both flashing the Hawaiian "Hang Ten" sign, obviously happy and relieved that the other was all right.

"Check your radio, bro, I think it's cutting out," the friend commented.

Once again the hero's eyes met mine. The mysterious stranger made the first move, walking slowly toward the child and me, his friend falling in a step behind.

"Crazy freakin' cowboy," he said, warmly smiling. "Crazy cowboy taking on all those Pergasans by yourself, very brave but crazy, man, craaaaaazy." He introduced himself. "I'm Captain Tony."

He hadn't quite reached me yet. As I extended my arm to shake his hand and introduce myself, he spoke again before I could even get my first words out.

"I know, Nathan Thomas Cole," he coolly remarked. "We've been keepin' an eye on you, figured eventually you'd get in over your head."

He bent down and picked up his jammed shotgun, a momentary look of disgust crossing his face.

"By the way, how's the generator?" he smugly asked, somewhat comically restrained.

It was time to make my first verbal appearance in front of this heroic group of comedians. "Don't tell me I have a guardian angel?" I quickly retorted, congratulating myself on my smart, witty response.

"One of many," my new friend and savior replied, opening his arms wide to include his friends as my fellow guardians. "Come on," he said, "I'll introduce you to my motley ship of fools."

As we walked away from the Pergasan wreckage, I noticed a small group of people waiting for us about twenty feet away. Danny walked ahead to meet them as my thoughts shifted to the little girl still holding on tight to my hand. Though terrified, she kept up with us. Tony hadn't asked about her, but it was obvious he was keenly aware of her presence. I was hoping Tony's people would have a doctor to look after her, as shock was still a looming threat. The introductions started with his buddy from the field of battle.

"Nate, this is my right-hand man, hired gun extraordinaire and my very favorite Hawaiian, Danny Ohano."

"Right on, bro," Danny said, warmly smiling and shaking my hand. Tony turned to a tough-looking older Asian man wearing a very official-looking uniform.

"Next we have General Lee, resident weapons expert, chow mien guru, and faithful supplier of all that is evil and dangerous. Watch out, he is a real general."

"General," I said, bowing slightly in recognition of his obvious heritage ... oops.

The general bowed too as Tony said, "My bad, I forgot to tell you, the general doesn't speak English. And this ... this is Gina Lee," Tony sighed, "The general's lovely daughter."

Gina extended her hand to shake mine, but I kissed it like a hokey scene from an old movie. I suddenly realized it was a bad move; she was obviously Tony's girl. I felt embarrassed. I hoped I wasn't out of the club. Tony made a funny face and Gina laughed. All was well.

Gina's delicate frame and exotic beauty could not disguise the fact that she was tenacious and strong, and obviously a favorite of Tony's, as he was a favorite of hers. Her mysterious, dark eyes seemed to follow Tony like an afternoon shadow. He could sense Gina's acknowledgement, occasionally fixing his eyes upon hers, speaking in a secret language only they understood. The two of them were somehow connected both physically and spiritually. They had a secure, silent bond that could not be broken. Their souls were one, forever locked. I felt a slight twinge of envy, but I was happy for them.

Suddenly a soft female voice came from out of nowhere. I did not see her face, but in some strange way I knew her. Though I didn't know the voice, I knew that feeling when she was near. It was the kind of electricity you could feel throughout your whole body without getting hurt, a hot sensation in the brain bringing all of the senses to critical mass. As she approached from my blind side, the electricity went off the chart. As she turned to face me, I realized that this was the voice of my mysterious shadow ... the voice behind the fleeing angel.

"Are you going to introduce me, Tony, or do I have to do all the work myself?"

It was the girl from the pawnshop!

"Given half a chance dear," Tony replied in a wry tone, almost like they had been married for years.

"Hi, I'm Casey," she said, same smiling green eyes, same cheeky grin. "I believe we've met."

Up close, her presence was more intoxicating than before. Amongst the stench and brutal wreckage that lay scattered around us, I could not help but feel the exotic sensation and excitement reminiscent of one's very first crush. The contradiction of fantasy and reality caught me off guard for a second, but it felt good to give in and let down my defenses. For what it was worth, we had already shared stolen moments with each other.

"Try not to be so shy next time," Tony ordered, in an almost sibling-like manner. The consummate older brother protecting the promiscuous germ of a little sister, a relationship obviously built upon trust and powerful personal experience.

For a brief second I felt almost out of the club again. Tony's reaction to Casey hinted I might never have what they had. I quickly and desperately desired to be a part of their inner circle, to have experienced with them what they had experienced together. I was an inch, yet felt miles away from their secret world ... and I felt lost. The disparity of my hollow existence and a complete disconnect from anything human as I knew it had created a new Nathan Thomas Cole, one that needed to be deconstructed, and rebuilt to code, using only the finest of available parts. My lack of pride and self-esteem was pathetic. There was no reason for it. I had already formed a connection, and this was a juvenile reaction, perhaps based on months of living in the shadows of fear and countless hours of floating alone in a martini of insane reality that was one olive short of total madness ... a reality shaken and stirred with horror and death, courtesy of the Pergasans.

Tony and company brought life back to me. They were not battery-powered, computerized, or synthetic ... they were real, with real thoughts and real emotions. They loved, laughed, cried, dreamt, breathed, perspired, ate, drank, belched, farted, and basically reminded me that the tree I fell from was a community tree, the tree of man.

AND NO MAN IS AN ISLAND

As I wallowed in my neurotic evaluation of the moment, Tony chimed in, overriding my emotions and spastic hormones with a sober dose of reality.

"Who's the kid?" he asked inquisitively.

"Don't know, man. She and the mother came out of nowhere."

Tony leaned down to address the frightened girl. She held on tightly to my hand, trembling slightly and drawing closer to my body. Still leaning over, Tony backed up a little, reading the girl's body language and understanding the importance of space. Knees bent but not touching the ground, Tony was eventually at eye level with her, doing his best to project a calm, comforting manner.

He softly asked, "What's your name, hon?"

The little girl stayed silent and pulled even closer to me. It was obvious that through all the unimaginable horror this child had experienced, she knew I had tried to save her and her mother. Though nothing in her young mind could have possibly made any sense or logic out of this convoluted menagerie of events, at least one thing was clear ... she trusted me.

Tony stood up. Taking a few steps back, his gaze momentarily returned to mine.

"All right, she stays with you." Looking over at the girls, he said, "Gina, Casey, take them over to Doc Smiley. Have 'em thoroughly checked out and get some water in both of 'em please."

"I'll flag the field leaders and check out our casualty situation," Gina replied.

"Good, see if you can raise General Henderson, too. Find out where he is and what's going on, it's beginning to sound a little too quiet in those hills. Oh, and tell Doc they can bring the hospital truck out here after the general clears it, Mobile Ronnie's already on triage, I hope."

As Tony had noticed, the sound of jets and sporadic gunfire in the distant hills had ceased. More people were arriving on the battlefield, helping the wounded and quietly covering the dead. Violence and despair had now given way to organization and hope. Was this my new hope, too? Or had I blindly joined the human ants, bravely circumventing the vertical incline while carrying the Herculean breadcrumb on their bare backs ... falling to their death just inches from the top.

I personally wanted to stay on the field where everything had happened. This was my house, and I had almost died here. Tony had to understand this. I didn't mind being one of the ants. If I fell, I fell for good cause.

"If you don't mind, captain, I'd rather stay with you guys," I said, once more feeling foolishly brave and full of purpose. "I feel fine, and besides, I know the lay of the land. I'd be a lot more help to you guys out here."

"Suit yourself," Tony said, raising his hands in playful resignation.

Tony's response was comforting, being that he was in charge and I was somewhat challenging his battlefield wisdom while still a newcomer to the group ... be cool, Nathan!

It took a few minutes, but with the help of Gina and Casey, I convinced the young girl to go with them to see the doctor. For a time the girl would not let go of my hand, but she finally gave in to Casey, not only relinquishing her mental and physical bond with me, but accepting Casey as surrogate mother, or at least a big sister. Though trapped in the ultimate battle for survival, Gina and Casey seemed to have not forgotten the time-honored bloodline of whom and what they were at their core. They were girls, women, sisters, and mothers. They knew deep down that in the delicate balance of survival, love and compassion were as equally important and powerful as guns.

Now it seemed I had unwittingly stepped into on-the-job training. And in this company, there was no retirement plan or 401(k). No two weeks of vacation or paid sick leave. In this company, if you were lucky enough to make it to work in the morning, you were equally lucky just to get through lunch.

As the girls left for the hospital truck and the infamous Doc Smiley, Tony prepared for what was coming next.

"Danny, general, get a team together. Let's get these turtles into the soup."

"We don't have enough fuel for the barbecue, Tone," Danny replied.

"Drain some from the bikes."

"Bikes are almost dry, bro. We barely have enough to get back to town, let alone make a run for it if we have to."

"How about the armored vehicles, the cars?"

"Everybody's light, Tony. We weren't expecting all this. General Henderson's bringing in fuel tomorrow, lots of it, but it's en route and we gotta wait."

"All right, we'll throw the half-shells on the barbie tomorrow after the summit."

"What about the mother?" I asked hesitantly.

"We'll take care of her tomorrow night, as well as our own and the dead turtlenecks. We've got a little ritual, Nate. Nothin' fancy, but it serves a good purpose."

I was mildly intrigued by Tony's use of the word "ritual." Everything about him and his crew seemed deliciously shrouded in mystery. Maybe my imagination was overstepping reality a bit, but these guys brought magic and light back to a landscape that had been cold, dark, and lonely for way too long. Though we were dealing with death and suffering, seeing groups of people going about their assigned tasks and duties with urgency and reverence gave me hope. I felt a warm feeling in my stomach that for a brief second took me back to a time before the Pergasan presence, a time when a hard decision was paper or plastic, large or medium fries. My trip down memory lane was short, though. A young woman appeared from beyond the smoke and haze. She was dressed in army green and holding a radio that was different from Tony's. She walked straight and tight, almost like she was in formation, not like Tony's crew, who were attentive yet very loose. As she came closer I got the distinct impression she was a real army girl. She addressed Tony with a calm but stern tone.

"Tony."

"Yes, lieutenant?"

"General Henderson would like you and your people to stay here for the time being. We're going to do a sweep of the town, make sure there are no surprises. We'll flag you when it's secured. Are your wounded being attended to?"

"Yeah ... Gina, Casey, and Doc Smiley are on it. Excuse me, lieutenant." Tony politely paused before calling out the group. "Hey, has anyone seen or heard from Mobile Ronnie? I think my radio's gone poo-poo here."

"All the field leaders checked in, bro," Danny said. "We actually did pretty good."

"Kudos to our friends sportin' that wicked army green," Tony quipped.

"Thanks, Tony," the young lieutenant said, her demeanor softening a little.

"No, thank you, sister, you guys saved our butts out there. How long do we have you?

"We're your escort back into town, the general demanded it."

"Love that man ... love that man," Tony said, apparently happy to have the backup.

"You'll love him even more tomorrow," the lieutenant added with an almost childlike gleam in her eye. She was now in Tony's world, completely AWOL from her stiff army facade. She was sharing the moment with us and personally enjoying it. "It seems Christmas will be coming early this year. You won't be disappointed with what Santa's putting under the tree."

"I can't wait to open my presents," Tony replied, returning her beaming smile.

"Anyway, I have to get back to the plebes. Oh, by the way, Tony, we're not all army green anymore."

"How's that workin' out?"

"Well, if the marines would keep their hands more on their guns and less on my ass we might have a few extra shell-heads to throw on the spit."

"Some things never change, kid."

"I know what you mean, Tony. We'll be in touch."

"Be safe, girl."

"You too," She replied softly.

As the young lieutenant walked back through the smoke, I began to get a small sense of the new blueprint for survival. There was, at least for the moment, no army, navy, air force, or marines. They were now a coalition of specialists staying true to their training and expertise, but all flying under one flag, military and civilian alike. Rank was still respected, but teamwork and collaboration now set the tone for ultimate success. This was a plus for Tony. Though I had known him barely an hour, I could see that his freelance form of organization and leadership had a unique way of cutting effortlessly through rank, culture, politics, and basic social ambiguity. He raised the flag in the midst of the hurricane ... while everyone else ran for cover.

I was also curious about tomorrow, and what "Santa" was bringing for Tony and his crew. The group vibe through the afternoon had struck me as a little odd. The field had been turned into a horrific and bloody war zone. Yet the aftermath was approached with a quiet sense of order and efficiency. They seemed to know exactly what they had to do to get through this horrendous day. They had a system for everything, and followed it to the letter.

Though Tony was the obvious and ultimate leader of this extraordinary group of people, it was evident that they somehow represented, by sheer nerve of their actions, the new face of humanity, and the fact that no matter what the Pergasans did, mankind had a future ... these guys would make damn sure of it!!!

Danny approached Tony in what seemed to be the next part of the process. "Blackout, bro?" He asked.

"Too much goin' on," Tony replied. "Let's keep it down low, they know we're here, let's just keep it out of the papers, all right?"

"Right on."

"Danny, you and the girls are in charge for a few. Keep in touch with Lieutenant Fox. I wanna get back to town before sunset. I'm gonna take a little break from blood alley here ... I'll be close."

"Got it," Danny replied efficiently.

"Nathan," Tony said, suddenly looking a little drawn. "You got a place we can chill for a few? I gotta take a load off, man."

"Sure," I said quietly. "Follow me."

We started walking toward a small sheltered area close to the main road, farther away from my little house of alcohol and desolation. During his conversation with the lieutenant, I had begun to notice what I thought was fatigue in Tony's voice, not a surprise given the present circumstance. Now I noticed he was walking with a slight limp, favoring his left leg just a tiny bit. As we entered a small broken-down room off the main dairy production facility, I asked him if he was okay, the visual of him jumping off the speeding Harley still fresh in my mind.

"I'm all right," he replied, laughing at himself for his heroic but ludicrous behavior. "That wasn't one of my better landings."

We laughed softly, and then both fell quiet. Tony seemed fascinated by our temporary digs. The small, dilapidated building was literally a wooden shack, with one side almost completely open to a field that had once housed the dairy farms free-grazing cows and chickens. The wooden boards that made up the remaining walls had shrunk with weather and time. One could easily see between the large cracks, yet they significantly subdued the outside noise, almost like watching the neighbor's TV from your bedroom window. It was as if we had stepped into another world, leaving a frail, tattered door open to our previous destination.

Somewhere between my late morning chase with Casey and the gruesome Pergasan assault on the young mother and child, the skies had grown overcast and dark. The air was heavy with spent artillery and burning diesel. The surreal images of the day seared in my mind like a Picasso-esque nightmare on a torn canvas. As the sun descended in the hazy afternoon sky the landscape became even more foreboding. I could not help construing this as some kind of cosmic warning. In this vat of confusion, greater powers had to be in play. I could only wonder what the future held for all of us. We were on a road for which there had never been a map, and our destination was truly unknown. The feeling emanating from these decayed surroundings and the unmistakable presence of death reminded me of the Allman Brothers song *"Midnight Rider,"* it's ominous tone and brooding lyrics mirroring this haunting tapestry like a surreal morning dream. Tony too seemed to be off in his own world. He pulled out his radio and threw it on an old table. The box suddenly came to life with chatter. He picked it up and shook it, and the chatter cut in and out. Like Tony, the radio was probably damaged from the fall. Turning the radio down, he threw it back on the table, momentarily relishing the delicious blanket of silence. *"That's why I have an answering service,"* he said in mock disgust.

For a brief second our eyes met. Finding some rusty metal chairs, we both sat down. Tony seemed relieved to be off his bad leg. Somewhere in this temporary silence, I began to feel the beginning of something so lost in the convoluted context of our present situation I had forgotten it had ever actually existed ... *friendship.* Reaching into his vest, Tony retrieved two short, thin black cigars and handed me one. I thanked him. He offered me a light, and then he lit his, savoring that long first drag like it was an old friend he hadn't seen in years. I sat down across from him, enjoying my first puff with equal reverence.

"When you see the ghosts in the machine ..." Tony mused thoughtfully, observing an archaic milking device. "It amazes me how we used to live ... how we got to this point."

"We've lost our culture, our society in general, but we haven't lost our existence, Tony ... we'll only lose that with death," I commented.

"Look at you, the philosopher," Tony chimed, knowing he had me in an awkward position, smiling like the Cheshire Cat. "Is that what you do when you're not chasing pretty brunettes all over hell and creation?"

I could only shrug and answer with a silly smile. He had me on words, but then he gave it back to me ... maybe I had landed on my feet after all.

"You're right, Nate, right on it, brother. We have lost everything, everything that supports us on the outside. Money, status, power, politics, crap we never needed to begin with, the Pergasans got rid of for us. Depending on what side of the moral and philosophical pool you swim on, they might actually have done us a favor. Kind of ironic, isn't it? In some ways we've returned to a pure world, a world where humanity must live by its most basic instincts. There are no more flags or governments, no Vatican, no corporations or lending institutions. It's all about survival now, man. Canned beans and grapefruit juice have replaced greed and corruption on the menu ... and they're going to be the soup du jour for quite some time. There's no turning back, Nate. We can only go forward, or, as you so keenly observed ... we can die."

"I wasn't aware that complete eradication of a species was considered pure," I countered, skimming the dark waters of Tony's own philosophy, still careful not to color too far outside of the lines.

"The universe carves its own bird my man," he replied.

"I got you," I said, realizing that Tony had put a major spin on the conversation. It was getting late. There were things I needed to know ... it was time to ask.

"Back there, Danny mentioned a blackout ... radios?"

"Yeah, radio silence. We suspect that's how they're tracking us, killing us. Originally they jammed all our radio frequencies. But I guess they figured out that where there was the most radio transmission there was the most resistance. So now they let us squawk. But once you transmit, you gotta move … or stay and fight."

"Makes sense."

"Yeah, but that coin has two sides, brother, we've used their own logic to trap and kill 'em. It's risky business, but it has paid off. The one thing we don't know is whether they've got their own satellite infrastructure in place. If they do a larger attack on a carrier base or heavy fortification would be very dangerous, no element of surprise … we've got some guys at the Phoenix observatory working on that one now."

"Carrier base, heavy fortifications?"

"You'll find out about all that tomorrow … at the summit."

"The summit?" I asked, feeling the veil of secrecy surrounding Tony's presence lifting.

"Yeah, you *were* planning on attending, weren't you?" Tony facetiously asked.

"Didn't know I had an invite," I jested, now more curious than ever.

"I'll buy you a ticket, hottest seats in town," Tony replied.

Tony's crew was the largest and most diverse group of survivors I had seen since the Pergasan attacks. My follow-up question would take me beyond just their small pack.

"So uh … who is this General Henderson?" I unassumingly asked.

Tony seemed to understand I was in for the long haul. Taking a generous puff on his cigar, he kicked back as comfortably as was possible in his squeaky metal chair. Raising his eyes toward the heavens, his voice took on the familiar tone of someone taking a short stroll down memory lane, remembering how and why he ended up in this exact place, at this exact moment … having this exact conversation.

"General Tommy 'Tom-Tom' Henderson, Army Air Force, retired," Tony began. "Ex-Pentagon boy living the dream up in Lake Tahoe when the half-shells hit, he's the only soldier we know of so far that's been able to mobilize former military and civilian peacekeeping forces into a cohesive and organized group. You name it, man, if they're alive and functioning, he's been able to find 'em, or they've found him. He's a master of organization and mayhem. He came from a generation that didn't mess around. Negotiation in his world came from steel and raw nerve. He's got planes, tanks, fuel, medical supplies, and trained personnel to handle all of the above. Anything from nurses to snipers, anti-aircraft guns to hijacked government cheese, this cat is the Barnum and Bailey of traveling warfare. He's the perfect ringmaster who's got it all."

"How'd you hook up with him?"

"Officially, we haven't. Henderson sent his advance units in about four days ago. I meet him personally tonight. I'm telling ya, man, so much of the resistance right now is splintered and unorganized. Most of the information about the other groups is simply word of mouth, and usually it's inaccurate ... by the time you hear about these cats they're either dead or they never existed in the first place, urban legends. So far, the general's the only one that's been able to piece together a functioning communications network locally. That's how we got this thing goin'."

"How long have you guys been in town?"

"Couple of weeks; we hooked up with a group of locals that have been here from the beginning. They're not fightin', but they've been organizin', mainly staying in the shadows. That's how we found out about you."

"Why didn't they make contact with me?"

"They thought you were a little odd. That's why we sent Casey in ... she's good with the odd jobs."

"You consider me an odd job?"

"I consider you a crazy freakin' cowboy!"

"Oh sorry, I guess the sane people around here pass the time by driving flaming Harleys into seven-and-a-half-foot, human-hating, scorpion-tailed aliens!"

"Checkmate, bro. So why are you out here flyin' solo, Nate? What's the real reason?"

"You gotta ask?"

"I gotcha ... I know. These are strange days, brother. A man doesn't know who or what to trust. I wake up every day half expecting a stinger in my chest or a gun at my head."

"These people love you, Tony. They would die for you."

"It's not them I'm worried about ... it's the tribes that scare me."

"Tribes?" I asked cautiously. Another turn in the road I did not see coming.

"It seems, Nate, that most of what's left of humanity has joined the ranks of the cockroach, bro. Scurrying and hiding in dark corners, coming out only to feed on the vile fruit and rotting meat of a deceased civilization ... sick, scared, and lonely, some of them not even sure if they're dead or alive, just living everyday like diseased shadows. And *then* there are the tribes. Dangerous cockroaches en masse, killing and devouring everyone and everything in their path, leaving nothing but more death and destruction ... the human animal at its lowest."

"Have you come across any of these tribes?" I inquired, with tepid curiosity.

"No, and I hope I never do. But they're out there; brother ... they are out there. It's ironic that when man needs to unify the most, come together from the depths of horror and destruction and fight for a cause much larger than himself, he turns on his own kind. Killing and feeding on the very elements that unified could aid in survival, not hinder it. It's a sad thing, man ... really sad."

Tony's voice was once again the lead tenor in this sobering opera of clarity and perspective. You could tell the fight had taken its toll on him, yet he still remained the consummate hero. He had been out there, in the battle, struggling bravely to reach shore through a sea of blood and broken humanity. I, on the other hand, had stayed home, one of Tony's "diseased shadows." Though not sick, I had definitely experienced my fair share of scared and lonely. I could hear the disappointment and heartbreak in his words as he sadly pontificated about the present state of man's existence. I could sense his concern for the future, if there was to be a future at all. My next question seemed, to say the least, a little harsh and probing. True, Tony had given me the invite to this somewhat intimate meeting of the minds. And though I felt I had somehow known him forever, we had very little history in common ... short of lighting-up a Pergasan or two. But this was one of the things I really needed to know. I felt an honest answer from him would provide me with much-needed insight into the man and what kept him and his group together.

"Are you a killer?" I asked cautiously, ready to run for it if I had to.

"What do you mean?' Tony replied gently, composed but clearly somewhat surprised.

"Have you ever killed one of your own ... human?" I continued, still running with the caution flag out.

"A few," Tony answered with no change of tone ... almost too calm and unassuming given the gravity and content of the question.

"What happened?"

"We've had a few people come into the group that went from scared and running to full-fledged death junkies. They got hooked on the idea that they could run around and kill all in the name of survival, because their lives had been changed so dramatically ... that they would be protected by the group and there would be no consequence for their actions."

"How does that happen?" I asked, feeling myself getting completely drawn in by Tony's stark descriptions of humanity gone wild.

"It manifests itself like any other addiction," he somberly continued. "It starts off quiet and slow, and then turns into a freaking monster. First, they become kill junkies. Like starving kids ransacking the neighborhood candy store, their souls die as their killer instincts become rabid and hungry. And then they become power junkies, obsessed with possession and status. Anyone or anything that remotely questions their power or motivation becomes a dangerous threat in their minds. They want what you've got, they feel entitled, and they get restless and agitated if they can't have it. That's when they come at you. I've seen it happen more than once. It can become a deadly challenge. Personally, I don't like to fight. Fights are uncertain, injury imminent, and these are uncertain times. It's hard to survive injured. In answer to your question, if someone or something threatens the safety of you or the people you hold close, take the appropriate action at the time it happens. Second thoughts could get you killed. For most of us out here, it's not who we were or what we were about, it's about what we've had to become."

Tony's answer was seemingly textbook, given the insane nature of the present situation. Survival was the recipe of the day, and Tony's description of the "kill junkies" left a strong and clear picture in my mind of a danger I had not yet encountered. I worried about rogue people coming after me for food, or maybe even my generator, but kill junkies? The Pergasans were enough to worry about.

"Sounds almost like sport," I replied, envisioning rabid human-killing machines selling vacuum cleaners door to door.

"We're not the only culprits," Tony said, opening yet another door to his closet of secrets.

"What do you mean?" I inquired.

"That Pergasan you decided to party with has been on our dance card for quite a long time."

"Who was he … or it, or whatever he-it-she is … was?"

"He was a he. And he was one of the bad ones, not that there are any good ones, but he was just a little badder than the rest. He killed for sport … made it personal and very sadistic.

"Don't they all kill for sport?"

"I don't know, man. It seems …" Tony paused, seemingly contemplating a question that held even him in personal limbo. "It seems like they kill as their purpose. Almost like it's a job. Punch in, kill, break for lunch … come back from lunch, kill some more, punch out … go back to the ship, send in the next shift. It's methodical, routine … almost like clockwork."

"But for what purpose?"

"Don't know, man. I'd say for colonization, but there's urgency, almost a passion in their approach. That's where it gets confusing."

"Maybe for some reason they had to leave their own planet."

"Your guess is as good as mine. I mean, why would an intelligent, advanced race of beings attack and attempt to occupy a planet that they were so physically and environmentally out of alignment with?"

"How do you tell them apart?"

"Like us, they've all got their own little quirks, especially the officers and higher-ups. It's not an exact science; we've got a long way to go. It's just part of the process of gettin' into these mothers' world and hopefully either killing 'em or gettin' 'em the hell outta here."

"Speaking of quirks ..."

"I knew it ... I knew it, let me guess!"

"What?"

"You wanna know about the general."

"I already asked about the general."

"Not Henderson, fool ... Lee. You wanna know about General Lee. Everybody wants to know about General Lee."

"All right, tell me about General Lee," I replied, realizing that I *had* been curious about the stoic General, and very curious about his beautiful daughter, Gina. But I wanted to keep a little distance there. I'm sure Gina was of interest to many men, and these were dangerous times. I'm sure the both of them were well aware of that. Still, the subject might lighten the mood a little. General Lee was obviously a main player in Tony's world. Their seemingly odd yet symbiotic relationship added to the vivid colors of Tony's wild tribe. Noticing that his cigar was slowly dwindling, Tony gently looked into his vest pocket to take inventory. Satisfied with his present stock, he quickly glanced outside, and then reinserted himself into the conversation.

"It was in the early days after the first attack. Me and Danny and our fledgling core group were raiding a warehouse up in Sacramento."

"What'd you get?"

"Government cheese and canned grapefruit juice."

"Seems to be a lot of that going around," I said smugly, knowing full well Tony probably wasn't aware of the contents of my shabby pantry.

"Anyway," he continued, "as luck would have it, my peeps and his peeps both converged on the booty at the same time. Remember, at that point we didn't know each other. I'm tellin' ya, man, those cats were packin' heavy and trustin' nobody."

"There's a recipe for instant friendship."

"Brother, he had a crew of about a hundred people, and I mean they rolled up with tanks, missiles, grenade launchers, automatic rifles … They were runnin' fat!"

"What'd you have?"

"Seventeen guys, eight chicks, five M16s, a wheelbarrow full of pistols, no ammo, and eleven empty boxes of Wheat Thins."

The visual of Tony and Danny pushing a wheelbarrow full of pistols and empty Wheat Thin boxes was absolutely hysterical, taking into account their present status as serious and experienced warriors. I fought to keep my composure.

"What happened then?" I asked, biting my lip just trying to keep a straight face.

"The general suggested we saddle up and leave town before sunset. Gina translated of course. Ya see, he and his goons were on a serious mission, they had mobile refrigeration units, everything, man … and they weren't in a sharin' mood," Tony said, unaware of my rambling mental cinema.

"What'd you do?"

"I showed him the light."

"The light?"

"Well, actually, I made him a trade."

"You made him a trade?"

"Yeah, a trade. We became the best of friends after that."

"What did you give him? The Wheat Thin boxes?"

"I gave him a car."

"A car?"

"Yeah, a car. But not just any car, a very special car."

"What car?"

"The General."

"You mean a general's car, like an army jeep with a star on it?"

"No, I gave him a Charger with the number one on it!"

"A Charger with … the number one?" I was now wondering if we were talking about a car or an equation.

"Actually zero-one, right on the door."

"You mean a zero in front of a one … zero-one, on the car door?"

"Yeah, a Charger with a zero in front of a one ... on the door," Tony repeated, seemingly amazed I hadn't figured this one out yet.

"I give up," I began, slowly realizing how silly this whole thing was, finally brandishing the only crazy thing that came to my mind. "*The* General Lee?"

"Yeah, *the* General Lee."

"The General Lee as in *Dukes of Hazzard*?"

"You got it, the *Dukes of Hazzard* General Lee. Or at least one of 'em, but one of the good ones."

"You certainly have a way with people," I added, feigning subtle admiration.

"Funny how that works, huh ... I'm sure he could've just taken it if he had wanted to, but I don't think Gina would've let him."

"So let me get this straight," I asked, finding a whole new *thing* from Tony's world to muse over. "The general ... Lee, drives around in ... the General Lee?"

"Exactly, pretty ironic, isn't it?! But he's not a very good driver. Gina usually does the drivin' if we gotta get somewhere quick and in one piece. Don't tell him I said that, 'cuz he gets a little ... you know sensitive. Funny thing is the man can't drive a car for s---, but if you get him in a tank, I'm tellin' ya, brother, say goodbye to the competition."

The thought of the stone-faced, uniform-wearing tank demon getting all choked up about his bad driving was in itself a fairly odd thought, but I guess that pride manifests itself in as many ways as there are people. Tony's crew was indeed a complex and interesting tribe. I realized that if I were to stay with them, I would be an intern in their world for quite some time, if we had any time left. Nonetheless, I was genuinely interested in the true story of how they had all came together.

"The rest of these people, Tony, where'd they all come from?"

"Well, we took up a collection at the church of lost warriors and this is what we got. Pretty good, huh?" He laughed. "Actually, we all just kinda found each other."

"How long have you guys been running?"

"Running? Slow down, brother. We've been on the offensive. We're one travelin' can of whoop-ass, just a little short-staffed."

"And the summit?"

"This gig's been a long time comin', and I personally am lookin' forward to the guest list. It's gonna be good."

"Who's on the menu?"

"The A-list of humanity's last and best, bro, at least in this neck of the woods. Of course there's Henderson and his peeps. They came down from Fort Bragg, but locally grown we've got the Second Alliance."

"I haven't had the pleasure."

"Neither have I, but they've got some serious street cred. The Alliance is supposedly pretty organized. They're split up into geographic chapters, kinda like bikers ... and equally as tough. I'm tellin' ya, man, this is where it begins. This is where we put it all together for real."

"Is there a plan?"

"Not really, but once we connect the dots, fill in the gaps, and organize to the very best of our abilities, we'll devise and implement a strategy that will ensure our survival as a race. Rebuild our planet one stone ... one brick at a time."

"Sounds ambitious."

"These are ambitious times, brother ... ambitious and dangerous."

The simplicity and soul of Tony's words were encouraging, though the journey he described was daunting.

Through the span of a few more cigars and continued conversation, the afternoon train slowly pulled into the early evening station. I had learned a lot about Tony and his post-apocalyptic all-stars. Though there were still many questions, they would have to wait. There were no interruptions into our private world that afternoon, representative of an efficient and well-seasoned group of people. Danny, Casey, Gina, and General Lee were the nerve center of Tony's world, his core group. But there were others, equally as important, equally as efficient. Tony's troops quietly executed the imposing tasks at hand without complaint, with precision and finesse. Now it was time to return to the reality that had brought us all together here in the first place. Tony would be needed back in town, and I was suddenly faced with a decision that I feared could permanently get me kicked out of the club.

As we left the cozy, tattered world of our temporary shelter, I had one last question for Tony. "They call you captain ... army, marines?"

"Softball," he replied, looking straight into my eyes. "North Bay league, nobody asks anymore. Whoever or whatever you were before doesn't mean squat now, man. For all of us out here, it's not what we were about ... it's about what we've had to become."

"That's how you ended up like this?"

"Just fell into it, I guess."

"You do a great job."

"I haven't gotten a pink slip yet."

And with that, the meteoric ascent of Captain Tony was explained, an unassuming softball player rising to the occasion, battling human-hating space invaders while restoring truth, justice, and the American way ... wow.

It was getting darker as we stepped out onto the makeshift wrecking yard/morgue. Through the smoke and haze, we saw Danny and Casey approaching, both on their radios, deeply engaged in the choreography of a mass migration back into town. Danny finished first, clipping the radio back onto his belt as he approached Tony and I. Casey finished her conversation and followed a few feet behind Danny. Though his radio was turned down low, the past few minutes had brought much new activity to the airwaves, and Tony seemed aware of this. I knew the exodus was about to begin. I was hoping that Tony would ask me to join them. My very heart and soul yearned to hear his invite, a chance to spend the rest of my life as a bright flame burning steadily for the lives and souls of my new comrades, not a faint ember of my former self flickering alone and cold in the dark shadows of solitude, alcohol, and despair. But I wasn't ready to go yet. I needed one more night, one more night here. A night to stay in familiar surroundings, shabby and dark as they were, a night paying ritual to the last material anchors of a life I never had a chance to say goodbye to.

"Everybody's ready, bro," Danny said, looking toward the sky at a distant fighter plane coming our way, its screaming engines slowly getting louder. "The moment the first fighter passes over us, we'll have blanket protection back into town. But we gotta go now; they still have search-and-rescue teams up in the hills."

"What's up?" Tony asked.

"Henderson's crew did a great job out there, Tony. Mashed quite a few Pergasan fighters but uh … a few of his boys haven't come home from the dance yet."

Tony took a second to reflect. The art of war with the Pergasans had just been elevated dramatically, propelling itself into the next level during one of the most crucial times in human history. It was impossible to make plans based on any previous historical engagement. Hope was now as crucial an element as weaponry. Faith and bullets, courage and tanks, it all now shared a common ground, paired up in irony for an important and common cause.

Tony addressed his small group, slowly turning to me, his voice commanding, yet calm and friendly. "We hit 'em pretty hard. The Pergasans are gonna need at least a day or two to regroup, but one thing's for sure: They'll be back. You need to come with us, Nate. We're your only hope now."

"I appreciate that, Tone," I started, my words pouring past my heart like someone jumping a runaway train. "You'll never know how much. You've given me hope; you've given us all hope. But I'm staying here tonight, man. I love you guys, you saved my life but … for now, this is still my house. It's all I've got left. I have things I'm close to and I'm really not ready to abandon that … not yet."

I CAN'T BELIEVE IT!

I finally said it, but what had I said? In a heartbeat, I would have dropped everything to spend the rest of my life with these people. Did I really need to spend any more time wallowing in a past that was just a few old trinkets and pictures that meant nothing to anybody left alive except me? Though my heart had done the talking, my sense of logic was confused. I never asked for all of this. I didn't call up the Pergasan hotline and order a hot and fresh global invasion delivered to me in thirty minutes or less or it was free. I was merely a remnant, still clinging to the last memories of a life that that in some ways I had taken for granted, yet deeply cherished with all my heart. Yes, my sense of logic was confused. The comfort of the past had somehow made it bearable to live solitary, scared, and lonely. All things considered, I had been very lucky. This was the wake-up call I couldn't afford to miss! I just wanted ten more minutes of sleep in my own bed, before it all went away … forever.

TONYS RESPONSE WAS UNDERSTANDING AND COOL

"There's no debate, brother. I understand," Tony said warmly. "You know, Nate, you're just like the rest of us, ordinary people thrown into extraordinary circumstances. What you did out there today showed your true steel, man. For whatever reason, you did not let fear dictate your actions. Your actions dictated to fear. You're takin' a chance stayin' out here tonight, but I think you'll be all right."

Tony's words made feel proud. I was truly in the club now. Just one more night of private ritual, old music and memories, heavy drinking and maybe some time with my "stoic sisters of perpetual polymers," and I would be ready to continue my journey, not as a solitary survivor … but as a post-apocalyptic warrior.

Then Tony dropped the big one.

"Casey," he said. "I want you to stay with Nathan tonight. Keep an eye on him, just in case the mutant ninjas decide to come back and give him a hard time."

"Aye-aye, captain," Casey replied, her eyes a little greener, smile a little cheekier. This was an assignment she was not contesting in any way. Though I was temporarily in mental and physical suspension from what had to have been one of the craziest and most frightening days of my life, I had gotten an interesting vibe off Casey from moment one. She blew Captain Tony a kiss as she skipped past him.

"Yeah, don't make me pull your arm so hard next time," Tony muttered.

IT WAS GOING TO BE AN INTERESTING EVENING

CASEY

The sun was fading over the distant hills as the events of the day echoed and bounced off the walls of my shattered mind like bullets in a steel room. I was concerned about the little girl, concerned about Tony and his crew getting back to town safely, and concerned about when the turtlenecks would show up next. The battle had come to me. It was only a matter of time until my simple, secluded world would morph into the inevitable madness of the Pergasan Theater.

We were almost to the house when I suddenly realized Casey was no longer walking beside me. I stopped for a second, confused, and then was quickly relieved when I turned and saw her standing a few feet behind me. She slowly approached. As I looked into her radiant green eyes, my mind felt calm and quiet for the first time in quite a while.

"Your brain was too loud, I couldn't hear myself think," she said, raising her voice humorously, getting her point delicately across.

"Sorry," I said. "Sensory overload today."

"Get used to it. You can't hide forever, Nathan."

"What makes you so tough?" I replied, immediately questioning my words.

"Reality," she said, without skipping a beat.

"Whose reality?" I asked, well aware that I knew the answer.

"Ours, Nathan ... *ours*," She replied, with a calm sense of irony.

This was my first contact with a real woman since my self-imposed exile. Was she my guide to the next phase?

As we approached the front door, I suddenly stopped cold. Turning and looking into her soft, probing gaze, I realized the spell was still there. Even after the chase, she had never quite left me. Up close, I couldn't look away from her beauty. The space between us no longer existed. Giving in, I parked my soul … and threw away the keys.

"Nathan," Casey asked, her voice mild but strong enough to break the spell. "It's getting dark, and it's getting chilly. Are you going to let us in, or are you waiting for my nipples to get hard?"

Her attack, and I mean attack, at humor was totally her … totally Casey. Though I barely knew her, I could feel it. I loved this. She was brazen enough to follow and confront me, unarmed and alone. She was brave enough to be a part of Tony's crew and go face to face with the Pergasans. But most of all, she was not afraid to be herself, not afraid to speak her mind. And hopefully, not too guarded or shy to convey her innermost thoughts and feelings.

My reply had to answer hers. "We're in the middle of a war, Casey," I countered, with the utmost air of false conviction. "The thought never crossed my mind."

"You have heard of the Baby Boom, right?" She sensuously interjected.

"Sorry, ma'am, that happened after the war."

"Hmm … maybe we'll pretend that we won," she fired back, reaching for the door handle, letting herself in with a delicate wisp of feminine mischievousness … her words resonating in my mind like canyon echoes at sunset. This was going to be interesting … very interesting.

The first thing I noticed as Casey entered my secret sanctuary was that she was one of those people that had the gift of immediately filling a room with their presence. For me, this had been a cold, dark, lonely hideaway from a world gone mad. I had sequestered myself in this abyss of alcohol and dead memories. As I turned on a small corner light, the room seemed a bit brighter than it ever had been before. Instead of stark and shadowy, it took on a warmth and glow that seemed to radiate directly from her. The glow not only filled the room ... it also filled me. This had been a day of death and terror, yet that sick, lingering feeling of extreme violence and horrific loss was somehow slowly melting away like an ice cream cone at Coney Island. What was churning away at my scattered mind just a few moments ago now seemed discarded and lost in the dark caves of mental antiquity. I felt a strange sense of relief and contentment. What was outside was truly outside, almost in another universe. What was inside, here and now, in this insignificant fortress of what had long been a prison of shadow and fear, was hope, light, and life. She, like my lost wife Athena, was the feminine lightning rod that shot electricity and sensuality into a man's soul, never forfeiting strength and intelligence. Casey was dangerous yet gracious, and always a mystery. She moved around the room like a warrior ballerina taking inventory in a fine crystal shop, checking out everything, curious and refreshingly relaxed. Even in this cluttered and confined environment, her movements were smooth and graceful, almost choreographed. She seemed to know the place, almost like she'd been here before. Her thoughts seemed present yet evasive, while mine raced aimlessly in desperation, trying to read into hers. In my house, she would now have to takeover as bartender and host. She would have to break the ice and pour the first drink. And that she did.

"Nice place, Nate," she said, blowing dust off some innocuous item on a tattered shelf ... "Didn't know we had the same decorator."

"Simple but chic," I replied, "Keeps me humble."

Still cautiously gliding around the room, she gently added, "If I knew I was coming, I'd have baked you a cake."

Nice return from the visiting team, I thought. Now it was my turn to dig deeper into the secret world of my mysterious fleeing angel.

"Somehow, Case, you don't strike me as the Betty Crocker type."

"You should see my coupon collection," she said. The ice now fully broken, first drinks poured and quickly finished.

"Is that what you do when you're not slaying dragons?" I coyly replied, eagerly anticipating her next reaction.

"I only do dragons on Saturdays," she cheerfully responded, holding up her hand. "They're murder on nails, you know."

Having hit a home run on that one, I quickly regained my bartender and host status, pouring the both of us a real drink ... two tall Jack Daniel's ... sorry, no ice. She graciously accepted my liquid welcome mat and took a healthy sip. I realized that she and whisky were no strangers to each other. Having surveyed the evening's digs to her satisfaction, Casey's focus shifted suddenly back to me. I felt her internal spotlight, hot and revealing, exposing me like a bad day in the tabloids.

"When you're through sizing me up, Nathan, I'll thank you for the drink. Until then you can quit digging and put away the shovel. I'll let you know when you're there."

"Am I that transparent?" I asked.

"*Salud,*" she said, holding up her glass ... decimating the last remnants of the real round one. She turned the spotlight off, and the humorous warrior ballerina returned.

"So what do you do for fun around here?" she asked, reaching out to touch one of the Smart Girls. "Friends of yours?"

"Good friends," I replied, not knowing whether to laugh or run for the door.

"Uh-huh," she said, quickly retracting her hand. God only knows what she was thinking at that point. She soon replaced her hand on one of the composite goddess's breasts and gently squeezed. "Did you ask if these were real?"

"A gentleman would never do that."

"They tend to lie, you know."

"I hadn't noticed," I replied, thoroughly enjoying the moment.

Casey grinned girlishly. "Just as well ... they are cute, though. I do see the advantages. No monthly friend, no PMS, they won't spend your money, and hey, if you're losing the argument ... just hit the switch."

"You truly are an enlightened woman, Casey."

"Me, the enlightened one ... look at you, Nate!" she laughingly countered. "Five beautiful women and no one to give you grief if you can't get the job done!" She paused for a second to collect her thoughts. I figured Casey had probably heard of the Smart Girls before. They fascinated her. "So just how smart are these girls of yours, Nathan?" she seductively asked.

"You really want to see?"

"I really want to see."

"All right," I said, quickly addressing the one blonde robotic angel, knowing full well she was completely powered down.

"Athena," I ordered, "Kiss Casey." Casey's eyes suddenly grew wide; I had finally caught her off guard. "Kiss her on the lips ... with passion."

Casey jumped back, an expression of shock and laughter overtaking her, "Whoa, cowboy!"

"You're not afraid of a little plastic doll now, are you, Case?"

"It's what makes that little plastic doll tick that gives me the creeps, Doctor Franken-Love."

"Just don't make her mad."

"I'll leave you in charge of the *Stepford Honeys,* dear. I like my girls an even ninety-eight five."

"Oh, you can check her temperature any way you like."

"You'd just love that, wouldn't you?"

"After a while, plastic and CPUs only go so far ... even in my world."

"So is that what you do all day, Nate? Sit around here playing doctor with your oversized Barbie dolls?"

"Beats team sports."

"I'll bet you play a lot of those, too."

"Beats solitaire."

"I'm not even going there," she delicately remarked. I could feel her really warming up.

"Ou ... who let the dogs out, sistah!" I soulfully feigned. Casey *was* hitting this one out of the park!

"Let's see, four brunettes, one blonde. No redheads?"

"I don't like redheads. And besides, with one blonde in the house ... it gives the brunettes something to talk about."

"So much for equal opportunity," Casey sharply quipped.

"Between you and me, the blonde still has more fun," I replied. Quickly remembering that Casey herself had beautiful, dark auburn hair I realized I had just treated myself to a true Sagittarian interlude, foot in mouth and all. But I don't even think she heard me. I could feel the mood in the room change as if someone had suddenly cut the lights. Casey reached behind the blonde mechanical mistress and found the sole connection between my frail bridge of fantasy and reality. It drew her away from my witty banter and into a deep emotional vortex. What she found was simply a photograph.

Holding the dusty wood frame in one hand and putting the other on the cold cheek of the blonde robotress, she softly asked, "Was Athena your wife?"

"What makes you think that?" I queried, a little uncomfortable and leery of the moment.

"You look at her differently than the others. You're constantly glancing in her direction, almost like you're begging for her attention, seeking her approval."

"Old habits," I said sadly. "I never could take my eyes off her."

"Is she ...?"

"Yeah, first viral wave ... It was quick."

"I'm sorry, Nathan. You miss her, don't you?"

"When she was alive, she walked and slept beside me. Now she lives deep inside my soul. When I die ... she will be my last thought."

Now I was drawn into my own emotional vortex. Though I kept Athena close and thought about her every second, the realities of my daily existence took her farther and farther away from me. There was a growing void between what was and what is. I wanted Athena's soul in a box that I could open at random, that I could crawl into, to swim in the very essence of the greatest love I had ever known. But that wasn't to be, and I knew it. The only thing I could do was watch as the sweet memories of my past joined a setting sun methodically sinking onto its final horizon, its radiant colors of life and love slowly merging into the solid black of eternal night, no star to guide ... no kiss goodbye.

And what of Casey? She was now a part of my new reality, my new daily existence. I had feelings for her, as I still did for Athena. Though the feelings were different, they were strong, and getting stronger by the moment. There was that peculiar rush one feels when confronted with the entrance of a mysterious member of the opposite sex running through your backyard, visible, yet unknown. The elation of that first meeting; you want more ... the present, the conversation ... the possibilities, the night still evolving and young.

Was I wrong for wanting a taste from this mental candy store, or had solitude and madness finally corrupted my organized emotional closet, throwing my clean, perfectly folded thoughts into a dirty room of confusion and anarchy? What was ... was, what is ... is. The past is gone and what lies on the other side will only reveal itself when we show a ticket to get in. The reality of now is survival. And survival in this new reality is three-dimensional ... like chess on *Star Trek*. But you don't have to be Mr. Spock to figure this one out. Instinct and intelligence will show the way. For now, feelings and memories of the past must take their rightful place on the dusty shelf of life, to be taken down occasionally and enjoyed, then promptly put back in their cloistered sanctuary once they have served their sentimental purpose.

Casey quietly walked over. Gently taking my hand, she kissed me. Soft, warm, and human, nothing could have prepared me for what I felt inside. Words now became like colored speckles adorning the top of Auntie What's-her-name's chocolate cupcakes ... sweet and fun, but not important. I was back in the now, with the warm taste and feel of a woman on my lips, generating a path straight to my heart and beyond. I wanted more. But I needed to know more. I needed to know the origins of this unearthly, leather-clad warrior-angel. I didn't want to know all her secrets ... I just wanted to know her.

"I think we should sit down, Case. What kind of music do you like?" I politely asked.

"Anything but polka, you start playing that crap, you might as well just take me home," she replied, laying her body sideways on a tragically tattered, overused loveseat.

I was glad to see there was still humor circulating in the room. Though I appreciated the closeness Casey and I had just shared, there was still the issue of her and her past. I knew none of us were brought to the present reality by the choo-choo train to Fun Town. Something deep down inside told me Casey might not be as tough as she appeared. But we were in a good space as long as we proceeded slowly ... and had another drink. I poured a repeat of the first round and handed Casey her glass. As she took the first sip, she casually unzipped the top portion of her leather suit. Wearing nothing underneath, she seemed completely comfortable a little more exposed than usual. She fanned herself lightly, and I caught the faint trace of soft perfume ... not bad for a post-apocalyptic warrior chick.

"So who is Casey?" I inquisitively asked, still desperately trying to pull the magnets out of my bloodshot eyes.

"I ... was a varsity cheerleader, valedictorian of my graduating class, and all-state in women's track and volleyball. I was training for the Olympics when the turtlenecks hit us."

"Well, that explains a few things."

"Like how I smoked you in town?"

"Hey, I gave you a head start."

"I was running at half speed."

"We might be on for a rematch, girl," I said, knowing full well my next question would take us in a completely different direction.

"How about your family, Case ... anyone still alive?"

"You were going to play some music, Nathan?"

"I find it much nicer listening to your voice without any background noise," I replied.

"You're a sweet guy, Nate," she warmly responded.

The lack of music didn't really matter. It actually did seem to be better that way. No audio distraction to distort the honesty of the moment. But I was getting mixed signals now. Once again, she was bartender and host. She continued on ... but she was hitting hard ground.

"Just me, my father he..." she paused, and the world stopped. I hoped we hadn't gone too far back. Casey's strength may have rested on her ability to block out personal memories of the past, but I had to know, I needed to know. I was a cynic turned romantic, but I could feel a change in the weather. Whatever convoluted sense of logic the universe had sent our way to dictate the fate of our lives didn't matter any more. We were together here and now. And though I had never believed in random chance, astrology, or fortune cookies, there was a reason for this. This was meant to be, and I was not about to let it go without a fight. What I first took as sadness I quickly realized was Casey's entrance into clear thought. This may have been the first time that she actually went back that deep with another person. She finished her drink and slowly put down her glass. For a moment, she looked me straight in the eye. Her gaze strayed to a place that only she knew. With a mixture of emotion and fortitude, she spoke, reflecting bravely on the past.

"He held on for a couple of weeks. He was the strong one, ex-marine sharpshooter, weapons expert, hunter, you name it. If it involved a gun, he did it."

"Is that a shared gene?" I asked. My fleeing angel, reluctantly revealing her secret life to a robot-banging, booze-pouring complete stranger ... I was honored.

"Is now," she responded in a somewhat icy tone.

I decided to stop digging, at least for the moment, and rescue us with another drink. Taking Casey's glass and making the short pilgrimage to my pathetic excuse of a bar, I felt immersed in a strange and unexpected silence. I tried to find a creative, witty way to fill the gap ... fix the moment. But in reality, everything was fine. Casey showed up with her own toolbox, reminding me that sometimes it didn't really matter what the job was ... just that a woman could get it done better.

NOTHING NEEDED TO BE FIXED ... I JUST NEEDED TO LISTEN

Casey returned from her brief hiatus. She seemed to approach the future not as a warrior willing to take on anything for the sake of survival, but as a loving woman, a person still questioning why her loved ones were gone ... and why she was still alive, fighting with the strongest of personal wills, yet desperately hiding the most broken of hearts.

As I gave Casey her drink, I couldn't help but find myself once again seeking the present path in her smiling green eyes. But for the first time since we made spatial contact, I could not find it. Instead, I found it in her voice. I suddenly realized that the eyes weren't always the gateway to the soul. Screw traditional euphemisms and romantic legend. The body was the true gateway ... all of it. And like a map or great recipe, if you didn't know how to read it, you'd end up lost ... or with a real crummy batch of cookies.

Casey continued, holding me a willing prisoner ... captive in her true-life story.

"I always had a clear vision of the future, Nate. Or at least I thought I did. My parents taught me that, and their parents taught them. They were Sicilian, very proud, very traditional. They didn't take crap from anybody, but they never dealt it either. They were very loving and wise. People picked up on that and loved them back, and truly respected them. My father had an interesting credo. He used to say, 'Never kill anything that can't kill you first.' I used to mess with him and ask, 'Okay Dad, so then why do you still eat chicken?' And his answer would always be 'I didn't kill the bird.' I still haven't quite deciphered the meaning of all that yet. But even as a trained military assassin, he still respected life. When he could, he gave people a chance ... he gave them a choice. That's why I loved him so much."

Casey paused. Whatever sacred ground she was walking on in the back of her mind suddenly took her farther away. She had arrived at the crossroads. The intersection of her past life and future fate now merged in her lost eyes. Now I, the intrepid traveler, got what I came for. But would the prize be as sweet as I had hoped? Or had I wasted good booze and the chance for a potential girlfriend just to satisfy my insipid, voyeuristic curiosity?

"My father lay there on the floor ... drowning in his own blood, his arteries and veins expanding and exploding from the Pergasan virus. I had to make the choice for him, Nate. No one could do anything ... he didn't stand a chance. I did what needed to be done."

It took a second to register. The tone of her voice and power of her words had, like her eyes, held me spellbound.

"Are you saying what I think you're saying?" I asked hesitantly, knowing full well the answer. Casey had personally carried out the most devastating act of love one could ever imagine. I could only guess what it had done to her.

Casey didn't reply. She simply looked me in the eyes. That was all I needed. Quickly downing the rest of her drink she sat up and threw her hair back. Sounding like a Texas cowgirl on a Saturday night she suddenly howled, "*Uno más, Capitan!* Don't you know you all's got a thirsty girl over here?"

She slowly let out a faint sigh and looked away. As she sensuously slumped back, her beautiful auburn hair rested gently on her face. It was obvious that the memory of her father's death had a strong effect on her. Once again Dorothy was being chased. But this time it wasn't the Tin Man or an evil alien in hot pursuit. It was Casey herself. A mirror reflection of her own mind, hurt and exposed, dusty sheet pulled from the looking-glass ... nowhere to hide.

Though I was thoroughly caught up in the moment and not quite refreshed from my faux nap earlier that day, I quickly finished my drink. I knew Casey wasn't keeping score, but I was. A juvenile habit of mine, but she could have easily been the girl of my dreams, and I was not about to let the girl of my dreams drink me under the table ... even though she probably could. We had both reached a new plateau together, and in every respect I had to keep up with her, lest I miss an important junction and stray off the evening's path.

Once again making the pilgrimage to my fermented den of pleasure, I heard Casey's voice. She had returned from her walk in the sacred graveyard of memories. Her tone was clear and thoughtful. Though I had my back to her, I could feel the smile returning to her eyes. Once again, she buried the dead and brought life back to my humble abode of shadows and fear.

"We've both suffered great loss, Nathan, but we're still here ... still alive. I'm not religious, but I do believe in the spirit, the soul. We're alive for a reason. I don't know what that reason is, but I'm glad I'm here with you, Nate. I'm glad we have Tony and Gina and General Lee and Danny. I'm glad we all still have hope. That's important."

Casey's words struck a chord deep down inside of me. Was it time? Was I there? Were we there? Casey said she'd tell me when. I had stopped digging, and Casey had willingly shared the pain of her deepest thoughts with me, revealing in detail the secret map to her present state. We must be close. I decided to play it safe for the moment. I trusted her. I knew she was driving this bus and I was the honored solo passenger. She would know the right time and place to stop. I would savor the ride, and prepare for our destination with great expectation. I finished pouring round four and headed back to my angelic guest, immediately returning to the warmth and familiarity of her smiling green eyes. They had become my new safe haven. I wanted to stay there forever.

Once again, she broke the spell. "What are you thinking, Nathan? I mean *really* thinking. Are you thinking about the little girl, survival, another drink ... maybe having sex with me?"

"A little of everything, I guess," I answered thoughtfully, returning to my seat. Amused but *not* surprised by her forwardness. "I'm really hoping Tony and his crew will be safe tonight. They did a lot of damage out there today. We're bound to get a visit from the fun police soon."

"Don't worry about Tony; he's got our people and Henderson's."

"Henderson. Yeah Tony told me about him."

"He's a heavy dude, and he comes with lots of iron."

"I hope so, Case. I really do. That's reassuring and all, but in the back of my mind I'm praying that our fate won't be decided on the battlefield. If it is ... we are all history."

"Don't tell Tony that," Casey replied, in a soft warning tone.

"He knows. He's just giving us hope, and at least a chance to fight and die with dignity," I said, as Casey slowly stood up.

Though we had been sitting in separate chairs, it didn't feel like there had been any distance between us. The space quickly disappeared as Casey came over and sat down on the thick velour arm of my torn and dated throne. She put her drink down on a nearby table and seductively wrapped her arms around my shoulders and neck.

"Whatever happened to old age?" she playfully asked, kitten-like and warm.

"Well, look at it this way: We won't have to worry about wrinkles or gray hair."

"Or menopause," she added, getting closer by the moment.

"That wasn't on my list," I coolly replied.

Casey slid comfortably into my lap, kissing me gently for a moment. "In that case, we'd better make good use of our equipment now, while it still works."

Reaching over for her drink, she spilled the glass and its remaining contents on my tattered oriental rug.

"Oops, I didn't need that anyway," she exclaimed lightly, amused at her sensual clumsiness. Repositioning herself back into my lap and once again holding me close, she warmly whispered in my ear, "I hope your girlfriends won't get jealous."

"They won't see a thing," I whispered back as I reached around and turned out the last remaining light.

The darkness blanketing my shadowy sanctuary became a warm and comforting host. The night itself, once a time of loneliness and fear, was now a safe haven of bliss and peace ... the first peace I'd felt in a long, long time.

THE SUMMIT

My night with Casey was some of the best sex I'd ever had. She evoked passion where there was none, and brought warmth to a soul quickly cooling from the somber face of its present reality. She was all woman, but her sense of self was as strong as any man

I had ever encountered. She was a warrior, a leather-and-lace angel with the heart of a lion.

If Casey was the queen in Tony's quest for the union of our two worlds, he was decisively in control of the board. But Casey pulled her own strings, controlled her own destiny, and chose her own path ... perhaps choosing some of ours. And be it dice or cards, Casey ran the table. Tony respected that ... and so did I.

That morning we were to meet with Tony in town. He and his turtle-hunting cronies had taken over a crumbling luxury hotel, which was to be the venue for the summit. This was where the future of mankind was to be questioned, negotiated, theorized, and decided. They had taken the little girl there too, for more evaluation and care.

The events of the previous day would be a topic of discussion as well. We had taken out not only several Pergasan fighters, but also one of their major ground-based bad boys. This meant they'd eventually be back ... with attitude. This meeting of very important resistance leaders would have to be quick. If all of them were to be taken out at once, it would quite possibly be the knockout punch in man's surreal fight for his endangered future. Some time during the night the General Lee appeared outside my temporary den of love.

Casey was nonchalant. "We probably weren't alone. Someone was watching out for us."

Mid-morning, we headed into town, driving *Dukes of Hazzard*-style. I'm not a big fan of alien invasion, but hey, no cops ... no tickets!

As we pulled up to the hotel, we saw Tony outside talking to one of his soldiers. General Lee gave us the once-over, making sure we didn't put any new dents or scratches on his metal mistress. Once reasonably satisfied, he gave us a warm smile of approval. Tony soon approached us, a playful, suspicious grin his welcome mat!

"You didn't keep her out all night, did ya?" he asked, knowing full well which horse had pulled the cart.

"Why, sir," I pleaded. "My intentions were completely honorable."

Tony quickly gave Casey a *curious* look. Satisfied with his quirky brush of humor, he said, "It wasn't your intentions I was worried about, Nate. Anyway, being that you're still in one piece, let's take a tour of the mansion. It's open house today, free coffee and donuts."

"Whoo-hoo," I replied childishly. "Can I get mine with pretty colored sprinkles?"

Tony shook his head and gave *me* a curious look..

AND THEN FOR A QUICK SECOND
BERRIES CAME TO MIND
I COULDN'T FIGURE OUT WHY
OH WELL
IT PROBABLY WASN'T IMPORTANT ANYWAY ... RIGHT?

We entered the building through the front door. The hotel looked like it had been a Hilton or a Hyatt at one time. It was hard to tell. The outside signage was shattered and the building looked like it had been a battleground. The structure was heavily fortified and guarded by resistance fighters, all armed and on high alert, their eyes meeting mine for a quick sizing-up, and then returning to the never-ending task of perimeter security.

Some of them I recognized from our previous encounter out in the field, others I had never seen before. This was the largest collection of live humanity I had witnessed in one place since the original alien attack. So many people from so many different places and walks of life, yet all with the same distinct look in their eyes ... a mixture of horror, pain, and disbelief, hauntingly framed with the gaunt glare of survival and revenge.

What set Tony apart from the rest of them was that he seemed to thrive in this nightmarish carousel we were all unwillingly tethered to. He acted like a rebellious teenager cheerfully joy riding in his parent's car: tearing up the road, yet proceeding with awareness and caution. There was a minute swagger in his step, and a swirling nest of hornets surrounded his ego, buzzing "Bring it on!" From the outside, he seemed larger than life, but there was a sense of unseen vulnerability only your deepest instincts could chart. Maybe this was all a show? Theatrical wizardry by the master himself, a smoke-and-mirrors production expertly staged to convince his people that there was still a reason to smile, still room for hope. Maybe his soul was so torn from previous events that he wasn't afraid to die. We all had lives and stories before this. I wondered what was his. Though I knew a bit about him, I wondered where he truly came from.

What gave him the insane ability to laugh and make light of the very forces that at any second could strike us down right where we stood? And what would occur if, God forbid, that moment actually happened?

Of course, any good magician has an assistant, and his buddy General Lee was the perfect foil. Lee was definitely an enigma. An incorrigible second banana with a big carnival-esque smile ... and even bigger guns! They were two very different people from completely different backgrounds. But like peanut butter and jelly, together they made the perfect sandwich.

I was looking forward to the summit that afternoon. I hoped to learn more about Tony and Lee, and I was fascinated by the prospect that I could possibly be witness to the earliest plans of humanity's reconstruction ... and to the eventual downfall of the Pergasan invaders.

We walked through the main lobby and out back to the conference rooms. Tony guided us into what appeared to have been the main ballroom. It literally looked like it had been hit by a bomb. Big pieces of chandelier, plate glass, and lumber were piled into every corner of the room. There was a strong smell of rotting wood and who knows what else. Most of the windows were shattered, and in one area of the room, the ceiling had been blown out, exposing the floor above. Pieces of sheet rock and trim dangled like bats in a cave, and an eerie breeze sailed through the room like an invisible voyeur. I could only imagine the benign, mundane events once played out here, hundreds, maybe thousands of times ... over and over again within these shattered, ghostly walls. Weddings, holiday parties, retirements, and graduations, all celebrated in the soft warm rain of the all-but-dried-up human condition … I was getting depressed real fast!

At that moment, I felt a pressing need for levity. "Like what you've done with the place," I chimed.

"Maid's year off," Tony quickly replied. "But they've got a killer continental breakfast."

"Nice," I said, my mind switching gears for a minute, nostalgically recalling the days of vacations and romantic getaways with Athena. "You pick out the wallpaper too?" I added, effectively returning to reality

"Actually, Lee chose the decor. We call it *Aliens Hate Us Chic.*"

"I'll call you guys next time I redecorate," I said, catching one of Tony's subtle looks out of the corner of my eye.

Gina and Casey soon entered the room. As they approached, Gina glanced Tony's way, and for a brief second the electricity level went off the scale. I felt an exclusive kinship with Tony and Gina now that Casey and I had shared the ultimate connection. The four of us in some strange way completed the circle of this world. Tony, Gina, and Casey were opening their deepest and most intimate doors to me. I had no idea why. The answers to that question would have to wait.

The room was set up conference-style. There were three long tables formed into a U shape, and a smaller table with maps and plans at the open end. Warmly smiling, Casey approached. Reaching out and taking my right arm, she guided me toward a corner of the room with a pile of large green wooden boxes. Finding a crowbar, she pried the top off a box. Reaching into the soft tan packing material, she happily emerged with an army-issue M16 rifle.

"Don't say I never gave you anything, Nathan," she seductively said, one hand giving me the gun, the other slowly perusing my most intimate of places. Grabbing the gun back she threw it down and pinned me against the wall, her body grinding and molding into mine like hot lava on the Hawaiian shore.

"Get a room!" Tony cried. "Jeez, man. Kids nowadays … they can't wait for anything, you know!"

Tony finished his exaggerated rant and looked at Gina like a distraught nanny. Gina smiled and gave Tony another one of her bedroom looks, and for a brief, wonderful moment ...

EVERYONE IN THE ROOM LAUGHED!

Laughter, starting slowly, suddenly gaining momentum and warmth, filled the ghost-like room with concentrated life, and then faded away quietly like the last drops of a warm summer rain. This unexpected moment of humor and unity was the undisputable resurrection of our human spirits. It personified our inner strength and total commitment to dignity and survival. Our souls were still intact, a little scarred and torn but still there. The Pergasans brought the fight to us. Now we would bring it to them. They were the ones that took the wrong turn off the freeway at four in the morning. They were in the wrong yard playing with the wrong kids. They were in the wrong place at the right time. Yes, we would bring the fight to them! We would fight to regain our planet. We would fight to ensure the survival of our species. We would tear down the walls of bondage and genocide and take back what was rightfully ours. And we would laugh.

The laughter soon dissipated into the reality of the moment. Lieutenant Fox, the young female soldier from the previous day's battlefield entered the room, followed by General Henderson flanked by his elite posse, dressed in a smooth mixture of Mobster Chic and Special Forces. This was a group I would not want to run into in a dark alley ... or even on a sunny day at the beach!
GOOD THING THEY WERE ON OUR SIDE!

General Henderson was the epitome of a seasoned warrior. Tall, gray, chiseled, and alert, he filled the room with an aura of authority and strength. Though the general and his people were living the vagabond life like the rest of us, his uniform was crisp and well maintained. He still wore his stars, all four of them. A warm flash of recognition shot between Henderson and Tony as they shook hands. The new future of mankind was beginning, and I was here to witness it! General Henderson's entrance was rock star personified. Though the colorful Captain Tony sported his tattered American flag, Henderson and company had a flag of their own. Its design was simple: two hands clutching a bolt of lightning superimposed over a single five-pointed star, the star symbolizing the one unified state of man. The hands and lightning meant solidarity and power, a simple visual underscoring a complex and deadly situation. Man had been stripped back to his basic elements, and that's how he would fight ... with the help of a few of the general's toys. The last remaining examples of mankind's inhumanity to itself would now be righteously pressed into action against an enemy larger and more powerful than ever imagined.

AT THE TABLE:

GENERAL TOMMY "TOM-TOM" HENDERSON, ARMY AIR FORCE (RET.)
CAPTAIN TONY, NORTH LEAGUE SOFTBALL (RET.)
NATHAN THOMAS COLE, INTERN
LIEUTENANT KATRINA FOX, HOT ARMY CHICK FROM THE BATTLEFIELD
SASHA CONRAD, SECOND ALLIANCE (SOUTH BAY CHAPTER)
CORPORAL BOBBY TYLER, ARMY NATIONAL GUARD
ARTHUR "ARTIE" WEST, MARINES SPECIAL OPS

AND A SUPPORTING CAST AND CREW OF HUMANITY'S LAST AND BEST!
(At least in this neck of the woods)

After a brief love fest of hugs, handshakes, and good will, it was time to begin writing a new declaration of independence. As the main players seated themselves at the head table, with General Henderson dead center, the room became suspiciously quiet. Though the task at hand was serious, I felt calm in the eye of the storm. Though we were here to plan the fight for our lives, I felt compassion and warmth. I held Casey's hand as she stood beside me, and feasted in the short silence of the moment. It was electric and unexpected. I could have died right then and there, but we were here to live ... and live was what we were going to do! As the silence faded into a sea of anticipation, General Henderson stood up.

"I want to start by personally thanking all of the group leaders, commanders, and their brave people for making the dangerous journey here. You came at great risk. You are mankind's last hope, and I stand humbled and proud in your presence."

Once again, I felt a flood of humanity circulating throughout the room. The seasoned, soft-spoken warrior-god struck an impressive chord in his captive audience. They responded with sincerity and passion to his opening statement. There was even a glimmer of admiration in Captain Tony's eyes. That was huge. I'd seen Tony in battle, and I'd seen him deal with everything cast upon him, but this was the first time I'd ever seen him step out and acknowledge that he was not only bearing the weight of the world and his people, but that he gave credit to a potentially larger and higher power, albeit human. That was huge!

The general went on. "I'd like to personally thank Captain Tony and all of his people for the lovely accommodations. But next time, Tony, let's not forget the dessert bar, okay?" he joked, eliciting an enthusiastic round of laughter and applause. "Oh, and by the way ... do you have a last name?"

"No!" Tony replied sharply, like an impish child hiding a stolen bag of candy, giving the desperate group one more reason for a stolen moment of treasured comic relief. But it was obviously time to dispense with the pleasantries and get down to the business at hand. The general's body language stiffened and his voice, though still soft, took on a more commanding tone.

"It's been almost a year since the Pergasan occupation began," he said boldly. "I think we have made great strides in our quest for survival and reunification. But the road ahead will be difficult. We must make the impossible possible, and show God and the universe that we will not be taken down ... not by anybody, or anything. The Pergasans have brought the fight to Earth. Now it's time for Earth to fight back. The purpose of our being here today is urgent and clear. We must prepare the blueprints for the destruction of the alien plague that has infected our planet, a plague that has threatened all our futures!"

ARGHHHHHHHHHHHHHHHHHHHHOHHHYEAHHH
HHHHHHHHHHHHHHHHHHHHHHHHHHHHHHHHHHH
HHHHHHHHHHHHHHHHHHHHHHHHHHHHHHHHHHH
HHHHHHHYEAHHHHHHHHHHHHHHHHHHHHHHAR
GHHHHHHHHHHHHHHHHHHHHHHHH!!!

THE CROWD GOES CRAZY
ELVIS IS IN THE BUILDING
THE MARINES HAVE LANDED
AND SO HAVE THE BEATLES
YES, THE FREAKING BEATLES!!!

The general has just inducted himself into the Post-Apocalyptic Human Hall of Fame. These people, this block of depleted humanity, crammed into the tattered, rotting remnants of a once grand ballroom, rose majestically in spirit and adulation. Clapping, cheering, whistling ... some even crying from the effects of an emotional deficit incurred not by their own reckless spending, but from the lawless greed and hate of an alien banker bent on draining every stone on earth of its very last drop of blood. The remaining captive audience, spilling out into the halls and even observing through gaping holes in the ceiling from the floors above, joined in the revelry, providing a deeply emotional reminder that we were *back.*

The general patiently waited for the end of the chorus of approval, observing not with arrogance but with understanding and compassion. Slowly, the excited crowd returned to their seats, and order in the universe was restored. Total silence took hold. A pin dropping would have shattered the creeping silence as the general once again bathed in the complete attention and loyal acceptance of his beleaguered yet hopeful followers.

"All right, we're going to start with what we already know," he said. "Almost a year ago a Pergasan probe entered our atmosphere, effectively disabling our entire power and communications infrastructure, rendering us basically defenseless. That probe was followed by an armada of carrier warships that somehow evaded detection by our most advanced tracking systems. Those ships dispersed an airborne pathogen, killing or seriously injuring about 82 percent of the earth's human population. Animal, insect, and other lower life forms were also affected. We discovered that the alien virus attached itself to the hemoglobin in the bloodstream, creating a molecular reaction that expanded the individual cells to hundreds of times their normal size, causing complete circulatory and physical implosion. The horrific nature of this virus, or whatever it was, remains a mystery. The attack itself was quick and devastating, yet as all of us in this room can bear witness, it did not infect everybody. As to why some were immune, we have no answers. Nor do we know the true reason or motivation for the Pergasan attack. What we do know is that they have implemented death squads in an attempt to kill the remaining human survivors. They have established base camps for their carrier ships and personnel at various locations across the globe, yet it appears that a good number of those ships have returned to the home planet. It seems that Earth's environment and Pergasan physiology are not a good fit, and that might be the one key element in our eventual success.

"The carrier ships themselves are equipped with everything the Pergasans need to survive and carry out their mission. They have food, weaponry, and all their basic essentials, as well as long-range fighter craft and troop transport vehicles. Because of their immense size they need a significant area to dock their ships and store supplies. It seems the Pergasans prefer larger airports and military bases due to their open space, storage facilities, and accessibility to major cities and arteries. They prefer coastal locations due to their physical inability to function effectively under higher temperatures. That's why they do most of their dirty work in the early morning and at night. Our water itself is toxic to them. Every drop they use needs to be specially treated and stored. They need large amounts to keep themselves hydrated and cool ... another disadvantage in our favor. The shell-shaped units on their backs are not a physical extremity but an extension of their body armor, shielding their hydraulic cooling units and breathing apparatus. Once the gear is stripped off, I can't imagine what they look like. They might even look like you, Tony."

Everybody laughed.

"That's pretty much the bulk of it. Now it's our time to make plans and move forward. It's time to fight, people. From this day on, in a cohesive and organized fashion, we will re-group, organize, mobilize, and fashion the strategies needed to retake our planet ... any questions?"

"General?"

"Yes, Sasha? For those of you who don't know her, this is Sasha Conrad. She's the leader of the Second Alliance, South Bay Chapter. Great soldiers ... what's on your mind?"

"Sir, if the attacking armada of carrier ships was using some form of invisibility screen to escape detection from our tracking systems, why didn't they shield the initial probe too?"

"A decoy," the general replied. "It's been theorized that whatever device they were using to cloak their ships would probably have been rendered useless and exposed them once they hit the upper atmosphere of the planet. They wanted a clean kill, no confrontation.

We were expecting a reply from the Luna-One project, so why not just send an innocuous probe right in through the front door? According to Luna-One, we would welcome them with open arms. The logic worked unfortunately."

"A question, sir."

"Colonel Tyler."

"Sir, the original Pergasan probe, the one that knocked out our power and communications, traveled a long, dangerous route to get here. What if it hadn't made it? Do you think the armada would have carried out the second viral part of the attack without the advantage of us being powerless and blind?"

"Chances are, yes, colonel. Engagement was unavoidable. It would have been a very different invasion, but it would have happened. The viral attack was well planned, and probably contingencies were well rehearsed and part of the basic protocol. Besides, they still had technical superiority over us and they'd invested too much and come too far to just turn around and go home. What I don't think they counted on was this many survivors. Their mission seemed to be to take us all out in one fell swoop. That didn't go according to plan. In order to fulfill whatever agenda it is that they have, they now need to backtrack. That has put them in a very uncomfortable position, because they're having a hard time acclimating to this planet. For the remaining personnel on the ships that haven't gone back, they're fighting sickness, disease, and a slow dwindling of their indigenous supplies. In my opinion, it's created a unique stalemate. That will fit into our attack strategy. We'll go over that later, anyone else?"

"I've got a question, general."

"Lieutenant Fox."

"We know that the Pergasans have let up on jamming our communications and they are using them now to track us. But is it true that they're voice-printing field commanders, and actually drafting humans into service to hunt down and assassinate them?"

"Right now, it's unclear, lieutenant. Rumor has it that certain Pergasans have the ability to communicate telepathically with humans. It's been speculated the Pergasans have infiltrated the human ranks, guaranteeing them their lives and promising them a place in the new world order, sparing anyone willing to join the Pergasan cause. The membership fee is infiltrating and killing anyone on the side of the resistance, with big rewards bestowed upon those killing their leaders. That's you, Tony."

"So much for the free breakfast," Tony chuckled, looking like someone just stole his bike.

Without warning, the general's attention suddenly focused directly on me. It wasn't necessarily hostile, but it made the hairs on the back of my neck stand straight up. Tony must have told him about me earlier; for this was the first time he acknowledged my presence. He seemed to know exactly who I was.

"Mr. Cole," he began. "Captain Tony has informed me that you were on the design team of the Luna-Two probe, the one presumably destroyed shortly after entering the A-73 system. You were also involved with CPU and data transmission systems, I believe."

"I was, sir."

"Was there an investigation into why the probe was lost?"

"There was, general. Unfortunately the findings of the investigation raised more questions than answers."

"What was the function of that craft?" he asked inquisitively.

"Luna-Two was a more advanced version of Luna-One, sir. It was faster and had a telecommunications and response craft designed to gather and relay information, nothing more."

"Luna-Two served no other purpose?"

"Not that I am aware of, sir."

"Were you aware that Luna-One carried living organisms from this planet in both a state of cryogenic freeze and suspended animation?"

"That project team came years before me, general. I believe that information was then and still is classified."

"I had a close friend that chaired the top-secret committee that sanctioned the research and construction of the Luna-One probe, Mr. Cole. I can tell you right now, that craft contained living organisms."

"I've heard stories, sir, but I have never seen proof."

"Do you think, Mr. Cole, that your predecessors understood the dangers of introducing a foreign body into an alien environment?"

"I understand the question, general, but how does this relate to me?"

"I wasn't implying anything, Nathan, especially in regards to you. I was merely wondering how a friendship probe could elicit such a violent and tragic response, especially from a race as advanced and technologically superior as the Pergasans, a race that in no possible way could ever have a sustainable future on this planet. Yet they're here, and they're killing us ... killing us with impunity and no sense of remorse whatsoever. I've given a lifetime of military service. I know war, Mr. Cole, I understand war. But I know nothing about this situation except for the fact that we are on the verge of extinction. That I do know. Yet I do not understand why."

"Neither do I, general. If I get more answers, you will be the first to know."

"Relax, Mr. Cole," the general calmly said, flashing a faint reassuring smile. "We're all on the same team, son. We're all just looking for the same answers."

He refocused his attention back on his captive audience. I was relieved to be out of the hot spotlight of his searing gaze and probing questions. I suddenly realized that while I was on the stand, Henderson and I *were* the Super Bowl, sans beer, commercials, and trips to the can ... everybody was tuned in, wow!

General Henderson stood up. Scanning the room and gazing down the halls, he seemed to be making a concerted effort to establish eye contact with everyone, reaffirming that in this army, privates and generals all ate at the same table.

"All right, everybody," he said with sincerity. "I want to break this party up for now. I'd like to meet privately with all the commanders and their division leaders. For the rest of you ... it's been a pleasure. I say once more I am honored to stand in your presence, and I'll be honored to fight by your side. When we meet again, history will be rewritten. Once again the winds of war will fill our sails, guiding us out of night and back into the safe harbors of day, Godspeed."

With that, the General made his exit out a side door and into an adjacent room already prepared for his meeting with the commanders. From across the room, Tony flashed me the hang-ten sign. He too disappeared into the command den along with Danny, Gina, and Casey, leaving my frail ego hanging in the balance like the odd kid out that didn't get picked to play ball that afternoon. C'mon, I'm not a commander, I'm not a division leader, I'm not technically even a fighter yet ... I'm still an intern. But I felt my rightful place was in that room with them, by their sides, mapping out the future for all mankind, a warrior amongst warriors ... a hero amongst heroes. Oh well, the intern would just have to wait.

The meeting only took about two hours. Obviously some of the strategy had been thought out beforehand. When Tony and crew emerged, I made a subtle effort to read their faces. I was looking for confidence and reassurance. Tony seemed mellow and somewhat satisfied. Casey gave me a welcome kiss and we all stepped outside.

The basic plan seemed simple ... and shamelessly suicidal. At dawn, the general and his forces, Captain Tony and company, and the rest of the summit elite would converge on a location five miles outside of town. There they would regroup and begin the arduous trek fifty-two miles south to the Pergasan carrier base at San Francisco International Airport to engage the enemy head on. If they even got there in the first place ... given that the Pergasans knew where we were and had probably figured out we were coming.

This was where the line between futility and honor became seriously blurred, blurred by hope and desperation, revenge and reality. The human warriors had planes, tanks, guns, and a genuine will to survive. Their opponent had advanced weaponry and technology, and a seemingly insatiable hate for all things

human. The line in the sand would be drawn, awaiting the waves of destiny to roll in and decree a sovereign victor.

AND SO IT WENT

As the afternoon passed and the summit dispersed, disparity became strategy. Faith became detail, and hope morphed into the common thread of the unbreakable human spirit.

For the moment, we would all part. General Henderson and his people began the trip back to their secret lair, leaving all of us with hope in our hearts, ideas in our heads ... AND A S---LOAD OF NEW TOYS.

THE AFTERNOON WAS YOUNG ... AND FULL OF POSSIBILITIES!

THE SKY IS ON FIRE!

"Red skies at night,
A sailor's delight ...
Red skies at dawn,
... Sailors be warned."
—Traditional

RED SKIES AT NOON ...

DEATH COMES SOON

Tony seemed happy. We were all happy. In theory, the summit had been a big success. But the reality of that success would reveal itself at another time ... another place. For now, we reveled in the spirit of hope, and the anticipation of a greater future. Outside of the smashed hotel, I was enjoying some fresh air and a new perspective on life in general. But slowly, it became apparent that something was very wrong. In the distance, the yellow sun turned a blood-orange red. Black plumes of smoke danced on the war-torn horizon. A sound rose in the distance. The ominous sound gradually became louder and subtly demonic.

FOR THE DEMONS WERE ALMOST UPON US!

I remember Tony calling them "tribes," the very flower of humanity at its worst. Man killing his own not for the sake of survival, but for power, greed, and mere thrill ... violent manifestations of a torn civilization clawing, chewing, gorging blind and drunk in the sadistic blood of its most basic instincts. The psychotic backlash of a world turned upside down.

Tony soon emerged from inside the tattered structure that had housed the summit of hope, his eyes intent on the approaching enemy in the distance, a look of knowledge, not bewilderment, on his face. As the sound grew louder, it became more identifiable. Motorcycles, cars, trucks, trailers, and heavy equipment were bearing down on us like angry wasps protecting their nest. They approached the edge of town with lightning speed, a loud convoy of death flexing its arrogant muscles before going in for the kill. The lead dancer in this chorus line of doom roared past us on a large Harley. Surprisingly, she was a woman, a chiseled caricature of the proverbial Amazon warrior queen. Her dark skin and tall, muscular frame glistened in the sun. She wore no helmet or sunglasses. Her hair was long, straight, and dirty blonde. If I thought that Gina and Casey were the ultimate warrior women, I had just been visually upgraded. And though her beauty was obvious, I was off on the idea of banging a woman that I wouldn't want to meet in a dark alley ... and besides, I had Casey. Surveying the impending war zone, she stared Tony down like an angry bull facing its impending matador.

Tony responded with a simple phrase. "If looks could kill," he murmured.

"Just your type, Lover," Gina quipped.

"Bad blood," Casey added

"Who are they?" I asked.

"They call themselves Huns," Tony replied unemotionally

"How do you know?"

"Some things you just know, Nate. I've heard of these cats but I've never seen 'em. I was hoping they were just a myth. Some wicked people, man ... it's even rumored they're in bed with the Pergasans. "

"So much for solidarity," I half-heartedly joked, knowing full well that this was where the humor train made its final stop.

"We're fighting two wars now," Tony responded, reaching for his radio. "Gina, get the guns ... Danny, you out there?"

"Got you, alaka'i," Danny answered.

"We've got company, my man. I want you and your guys in sniper positions, rooftops and upper floors, only where it's safe, fire into the middle of the street. We'll take ground cover and close range. I don't want anybody caught in the crossfire. And see if you can raise General Henderson ... get us some backup, they shouldn't be too far out!"

"We'll work it, bro ... hey Tone?"

"Go ahead."

"What about the women and kids, man?"

"If they shoot at you—" Tony stopped abruptly, an uncharacteristic look of sadness and vulnerability in his eyes.

"Understood," Danny quietly replied through the radio.

"One more thing, brother, we need to get some scouts out on a perimeter check. I don't want us to get flanked. I need know if there's anyone else out there."

"This is it, Tony. They're bringing everyone in through the front door. Apparently Blondie's got a big set of *cojones* on her as well."

"I'll take your word on that one, brother. Good work, Danny."

"See ya at the movies, Tone."

"Peace, bro."

As the angry bull and her lost herd sped by, Gina returned, handing Tony a loaded M16 rifle and a chrome-plated .45. Once again, reality was taking a sick and unexpected twist. This was a whole new chapter in my surreal existence. I had stayed sequestered and ignorant for so many months in my makeshift memorial cocoon, self-medicating and dancing in the shadows

of denial, hiding from the greatest personal tragedy of mankind by means of alcohol, plastic women, and faded memories. It became clear to me now that the Pergasans weren't the only enemy as I gazed into the death stares of the Huns, all with the same look of hunger, malice, and hatred.

At the end of the main drag, they stopped and regrouped. It was a serious showdown and nobody was about to leave the dance. Once again, my attention turned to Tony.

"What are they waiting for? Why didn't they just come in blazing?" I asked.

"They're sizing us up, getting the lay of the land ... probably trying to establish a kill zone. I don't think they've been through here before."

"Let's hope it's their last time," I said, realizing I was beginning to sweat profusely.

"That's gonna be up to us," Tony replied.

"How many do you think there are?"

"A hundred at least, not countin' the kids. But I'll bet there's more out there."

"Kids ... that's flipping crazy."

"These are crazy times, Nate ... crazy times," Tony said, once again clicking on his radio and simultaneously addressing everyone within earshot. "All right everybody, listen up!" he ordered. "They're gonna make a pass, they're gonna hit hard, real hard. You hit 'em back, understand? Hit them hard; don't give 'em a second chance. Danny, you and I will focus on the leader, she's gotta go down quick. Remember the legend of the scorpion, my man."

"Kill the head and burn the body ... lest the tail rise and claim vengeance," Danny recited.

"Damn straight, brother. That's one body I wanna see on the spit tonight!"

"Such a waste," Casey sighed, giving Tony a playful peck on the cheek.

"She pique your interest?" Tony coyly remarked, knowing full well Casey flew freely on both sides of the cage.

"Hey, I heard that," Danny squawked. "And it's getting me hot, hot, hot!"

"Business before pleasure, ladies, we've gotta stay alive before we have fun!" Tony commanded, making a last check of his weapons and surveying the area. The feeling was tight and tense, yet everybody remained relatively calm and seemed to know exactly what to do.

"Where do you want us, Tony?" Gina asked.

"I want the three of you at ground level with me. Gina, Casey, keep an eye on Nathan. He has a habit of getting himself in trouble," Tony quipped, an almost brotherly sense of emotion replacing his previous commanding tone… though his face and eyes were alive with adrenaline.

With the spectacle of the Huns' power parade down Main Street concluded, I could hear the urgent activity of Tony's soldiers preparing for the ultimate showdown. There was the distinct sound of guns being loaded and footsteps clambering for cover. Suddenly things took a dramatic turn. The post-apocalyptic terrorists began splitting up forces, some staying out for a frontal attack, others breaking off, circling behind the buildings on both sides of the street.

Sensing new activity on the Huns' side of town, Tony suddenly refocused on the lethal intruders. "Damn," he quietly muttered under his breath.

"What is it?" Casey asked.

"They're splitting up," Tony cautiously answered, reaching for his radio. "They're tryin' to surround us … Mobile Ronnie, you got your ears on?"

"I see it, Tone," Ronnie replied. "You remember Middletown?"

"I remember it well, my friend."

"We got the back door on this one, brother. Just take care of what's in front of you."

"I'll put in a good word for you at the front office."

"That'd be nice … if we had one," Ronnie said, signing off on a semi-ironic note.

Tony put down his radio. "All right, you guys, find cover." He paused. "It's goin' down now."

Having split their forces, the Huns began their main assault … thundering down the middle of the street and behind the shattered buildings.

I FELT A SUDDEN RUSH
OF HOT ANXIETY
AND ICY FEAR
A JOLT
OF ELECTRIC EXCITEMENT
A RUSHHHHHHHHHHHHHHHH
LIKE I HAD NEVER FELT
BEFORE

As Tony yelled for everyone to take cover, he did an odd and unexpected thing … he just stood there, out in the open. As the thundering onslaught neared, he raised his M16 and began firing wildly into the oncoming wave of death. Several shots rang out in his direction, one hitting him in the arm as Gina ran up behind him, pulling him into the building as a hail of bullets shredded the structure around them.

"Are you crazy?" she yelled with concern and passion. "You could've gotten yourself killed!"

"They just piss me off," Tony replied, like an angry schoolboy who had just had his lunch stolen.

The radio suddenly came to life. It was Danny. "Hey, Tone!" he jokingly raved, "Next time you decide to stand out there and shake hands, ask for a donation, okay?"

"If I do that, I'm keepin' the money, brother!" Tony replied.

"Flipping crazy," were Danny's parting words as the battle began to rage.

Gunfire crackled from the rooftops and rang through the midday mayhem as bikes and assorted vehicles roared through the streets, answering back with their own arsenal of toxic diplomacy. Mobile Ronnie's ground crew kicked in as gunfire erupted behind us. *This is what war is like,* I thought. *But why are we fighting amongst ourselves?* I'm sure Tony and company had asked themselves that very same question many times before.

EITHER WAY ... IT WAS ON!

Casey and I hunkered down behind a long steel dumpster on the right side of the hotel stairs, close to the entrance. Tony was inside, as was Gina, occasionally ducking outside to return fire. It was hard to tell the exact numbers of the opposition, and at that moment it felt like we were in a scene from *The Magnificent Seven.* The enemy seemed to be everywhere. But the Huns were exposed and taking some devastating hits, their motorcycles and ragged vehicles providing little or no protection from Tony's experienced marksmen.

It had barely been a year since the initial Pergasan invasion. Barely a year since the Garden of Eden turned into the cesspool of Armageddon. Perhaps the Huns themselves had fortuitously become too organized, too powerful, too soon. Extricating blood and sustenance from a bleeding world that they themselves were a part of, blind to the fact that they were not the only strength humanity had left, and that the power of morality and hope, though futile at times seemed to have a small advantage ... at least for a while longer.

The Huns' advance through town was swift and impressive. One had to appreciate their tenacity under fire. They protected their leader well, surrounding her on both sides with large trucks, lobbing grenades at the ground crews while she fired at Danny's snipers. For the moment at least, she seemed to forget about Tony, the girls, and myself. I wondered why they were really here, and whether there were other reasons more specific than just a simple attack on the Summit.

The Huns fought hard, but they could not match the firepower and skill of Tony's elite tribe. They took horrific losses on their first pass. Wrecked machines and bodies began to pile up on the narrow main drag, making a second pass back extremely dangerous. Tony was frustrated that he couldn't get the bull, having been literally pinned down by grenades and gunfire. Still he remained composed and focused, seemingly content with the fact that the Huns were beginning to be significantly thinned out.

Heading back in the direction of their original entrance, the Huns could clearly see General Henderson's support troops steaming in their direction, sealing their fate. Their choice was between facing tanks, trained troops, a war seasoned general and fifty-caliber machine guns, or a second round of M16s, handguns, a semi-mad Hawaiian with crazy snipers, some real cute chicks, and a former softball player turned warrior named Captain Tony ... they opted for the latter.

As they made their turn to attempt the perilous trip back through Tony's gauntlet, Danny's snipers opened fire on the large trucks protecting the Scorpion Queen, successfully shredding their tires and rims, making them worthless for battle. The warrior and her remaining cult began their last run.

It was clearly obvious that Tony wanted to take out the blonde Amazon himself. Maybe she represented the very thing that he stood against with every fiber of his body and soul ... the destruction of man. Maybe he didn't like her hair color. Maybe he just wanted her Harley. Maybe it was all of the above. No matter, she was his present task, one that he would take on with extreme prejudice. He was facing what he had alluded to earlier as one of his greatest fears: the Tribes. The Huns were the consummate example of *"Kill Junkies,"* and just plain bad neighbors to boot. Tony was a negotiator for the new regime. He wanted peace, understanding that his secretary of state might have to be the end of a sawed-off shotgun. Diplomacy and justice would have to be quick, lest the diplomat perish under the idealism of blind compassion ... something some of us still had. Our own personal righteousness was a potential monkey wrench in the gears of survival.

As the blonde warrior came around on her final pass, it was once again the angry bull and the adept matador poised for the last act of something that seemed already prophetically scrawled in the diary of cosmic fate. The taste of blood was on the menu.

The Amazonian leader shot down the street like a desperate pinball trying to rack up points. She and her cronies shot at everything in sight as they jetted past Tony and his ground-based marauders. Tony fired at her and missed, the ricocheting bullets hitting one of the Huns square in the chest. The unwitting target careened through a large plate glass window.

"Lucky shot!" Tony yelled out with a smile. But the smile would not last, for the angry bull turned her bike straight at Tony, showering him with bullets and lots of bad love. As she barreled down on him, he raised his M16. It jammed, and for the first time since I had met him, I saw Tony at the mercy of the gods ... and the universe.

Barely thirty feet away she suddenly lunged back like Kennedy in Dallas. The gods, the universe, and Danny had picked up where Tony left off. Aiming his high-powered rifle at the warrior queen, Tony's favorite Hawaiian squeezed off a shot, piercing her chest above the left breast, tearing her from her bike and slamming her to the ground.

Their herd dramatically thinned out, their leader shot and incapacitated on the ground. The Huns retreated as quickly as they had emerged, leaving their dead and dying lying amidst the twisted metal and burning wreckage.

Tony approached his shattered nemesis, who was injured and helpless in the street. Tony himself was bleeding slightly from his left arm. Though mortally wounded, the Amazon's eyes were still ablaze with malice and hate as she focused on Tony.

THE UNIVERSE SUDDENLY STOPPED ... AND IT WAS ONLY THOSE TWO

Tony wasted no time as he approached the bleeding scorpion. There was no gratuitous moment of reckoning between the living and the soon-to-be-dead. No somber, overplayed burying of the hatchet as the two warriors that fate had paired up in an obscure theater of the damned squared off for their final act. Standing over her, Tony leveled his .45 at her head.

Clicking back the chamber he asked her in a calm voice, "Did they get to you?"

The wounded bull stared quietly at the matador.

"DID THEY GET TO YOU!?" he shouted.

The wounded bull slowly reached into her vest and presented a live hand grenade. "Eat this, Captain Tony," she said in a low, harsh voice. "EAT THIS!"

"Grenade!!!" Tony yelled as he raced for cover, scampering quickly over the hood of a wrecked car as the Amazon went up in a futile puff of smoke and blood.

Not since the horrific Pergasan attack on the young mother trying to protect her daughter had I seen a human body ravaged so completely by violence. Gina and Casey ran over to Tony to see if he was okay.

"You guys all right?" Tony asked, getting up from the ground and brushing himself off.

"Nothing a day at the spa won't help," Gina replied, shaking her head, ridding herself of shredded wood and debris, "So much for my good hair day."

"At least you're not on your period," Casey chimed in, wiping Tony's arm and wrapping it with a bandana. "It's just a graze, Tone, but we've got to get it cleaned."

"That's it," Tony said, with a mixture of pain and exhaustion. "I gotta find another line of work. Where's Danny? Where's your dad, Gina?"

"They're probably off chasing the Huns, Tony. You know those two can never leave well enough alone."

"Great," Tony sighed. "All right, Case ... you know what to do with these weapons. Coordinate with the team leaders and get everything ready for tonight. Get Doc Smiley out here, too. You and Danny do a call-in, check for casualties. I'm takin' five."

Picking up the fallen leader's still-running chopper, Tony thoughtfully mused, "I guess every new garden of humanity has its weeds..." Maybe he really did want the bike!

Tony got on the warrior queen's Harley. I approached him, and so did Gina. He gunned the engine. Over the deafening roar of America's finest machine ever, I asked him, "Are you all right ... can you ride?"

"Just a flesh wound," he said, his cocky demeanor still intact, even though a subtle change in the mischievous armor of his eyes and voice struck me like a flat note at the Sunday opera. Something or someone in the band was off, and the entire production was going down with the *Pinafore*. Someone had to step up, recreate the magic, and remind us that this horrific reality we were all living was merely a single transfer away from a bus ride back to salvation.

THE MAN ON THE HARLEY WAS NOT OUR SALVATION ... HE WAS OUR TRANSFER

If Tony went down, even in spirit, what would become of us? We were the cold, used machinery left out in the field to rust with the rain and rot with time. Why? Because of change, we were archaic. Not archaic because of uselessness or age, but because we were replaceable ... the replacements for us coming out of a violent, unnatural order. A glitch in the universal balance of whatever kept things balanced ... if there ever was any such whatever to begin with. Tony rode the wind and slayed the evil dragons, while we were stuck in the junkyard of humanity, desperately waiting to be rescued, refueled, shined up, and allowed to run freely once again. Tony had to prevail, lest we all perish.

I closed the door to my wandering thoughts and met Tony's eyes once again. He spoke as I attempted to turn down my own inner volume, and tune in to his words.

"Just a flesh wound. Yeah, I've always wanted to say that," he said. A weak attempt at humor but unexpectedly strained. He seemed a little irritated and off base, the Huns' malicious attack probably raging through his brain like a Texas tornado in a trailer park. None of us saw that one coming. We were all so preoccupied with the Pergasans that we momentarily turned away from the inevitable reemergence of human nature. No matter how bad the circumstances, the simple fact that our own species, our own flesh and blood, would even think of selling us out to the very evil that would eventually turn and kill them too was a vile and insane thought. It was sickening, and brought up the question that deep in the back of our minds spun survival and confusion into a runaway train of uncertainty and despair. For now we all silently wondered ...

WHO DO WE TRUST?

Gina appeared, calmly circling Tony's bike, stepping in front of it as if to block his passage out. "Where are you going?" she asked, a playful sense of schoolgirl vixen radiating in her voice.

"I'm gettin' away from it all," Tony replied.

"Want some company?"

"Hey, gas, grass or—"

"You are incorrigible!" Gina blurted as she hopped on his bike.

Tony looked back at me. "You ride, Nate?" he asked.

"Yeah," I said, not quite remembering how long it had been, but honored that he was asking.

"Find something that runs and let's go," he boldly offered.

It appeared I had just made it to Tony's A–list. *Right on,* I thought. I saw a chopper that looked halfway descent and hit the starter. It turned over immediately. I was stoked ... it was time to hit the road.

Tony's invite was cool. I felt like I was being let into the innermost of inner circles. He didn't even invite Danny, his closest and most trusted of friends. Maybe Tony wasn't really a warrior. Maybe he wasn't the quintessential Hollywood superhero we all hoped and dreamed he was.

***MAYBE HE WAS JUST AN ORDINARY GUY
FACING EXTRAORDINARY CIRCUMSTANCES
SAYING "SCREW THIS
IF I DON'T DO IT ...
WHO WILL?"***

"To the last I grapple with thee..."
—Herman Melville/Khan

The Huns' brutal attack was playing in my head like a Saturday-afternoon double feature. It was a surreal mix of gratuitous violence and some of the craziest visuals ever brought to the big screen. I wondered if Ebert and Roeper would give it two thumbs up, or pan the Huns for lousy costumes and equally bad acting. Who cares? I'm rambling.

As we left town, I felt a strange, unexpected sense of liberation. The past two days had been a never-ending loop of blood, horror, and death. Suddenly all that felt years behind me. Maybe it was the sheer exhilaration of riding the bike, that great feeling of power, freedom, and unlimited destiny. Cruising with Tony felt like a scene from *Easy Rider.* I could hear the voiceover now. *Captain Tony, his beautiful girl Gina, and his faithful sidekick ...whoever, out to find America.* It was a nice distraction; I hoped this feeling would last, at least for a while.

Tony seemed to know where he was going. We roared through suburbs and open country into a thickly wooded forest. We pulled off the main road into what looked like an old national park, the asphalt quickly morphing into a smooth dirt path. We rode on for about ten more minutes, and then stopped beside a beautiful, clear-running stream.

As we shut down the bikes, I was taken aback by the stark contrast between the loud, powerful Harleys and the haunting solace of the quiet, gentle forest. The physical sensation of riding the formidable two-wheeled rocket was replaced by the mystical spirituality of our towering redwood hosts. For a moment, I felt frozen in time, plugged in and profoundly connected to my new environment. For a brief second, I heard Athena's voice. I felt her touch my arm and whisper in my ear. I turned to find her just as a giant black crow flew directly overhead, making its presence obvious.

I turned back to Tony and Gina, fully expecting them to be running around half naked by now. But they were still on the bike, both looking directly at me. For a brief moment our separate universes collided, at least in my mind. I felt the connection I had so desperately been hoping for was suddenly there, and I had finally crossed over into the private and secret sanctuary of Tony and company ... I was in the club for real. I felt warm and fully vested in their presence. *I hope it's not temporary* I thought, for at that moment Tony and Gina were looking straight through me. They must have sensed my mind was racing. The looks on their faces conveyed amusement and friendship.

"You act like you've never seen a tree before, Nate," Tony laughingly said.

"Too much *Star Trek*, killer, you gotta get out more," Gina added, sharing Tony's glee at catching me in a weak moment.

We all had a good laugh, and for once I think we were really feeling good. Gina and Tony got off the bike and playfully embraced, whispering and kissing like giddy teenagers at the drive-in snack bar. I didn't feel left out, but I wondered why Tony asked me to come with them. Maybe he felt he owed me, but I couldn't figure out why. He needed to be with Gina alone. Had Tony even been here before? I wasn't really sure. But the place itself seemed to mean something to him. There seemed to be a secret reason for the three of us to be there. Maybe he wanted us to see him out of the theater of war ... just a normal guy, no aliens or machine guns, no pain or death. Maybe for a few stolen hours, he wanted us all to be out of it.

For me at least, the summit, and the ensuing attack by the Huns, raised more questions than answers. True, the weapons and information exchanged were important and useful, and we all left the table with a great sense of purpose and hope. But it seemed to me we were still trying to kill the dragon with a flyswatter. And we had made the dragon angry. We had to leave, and soon. Much too much had happened; the Pergasans were certainly on their way to get us. The question was when. And where would they come from?

MAYBE THIS WAS TONY'S WAY OF SAYING GOODBYE

As my thoughts began to stray from uncertainty and back onto the surreal beauty of my present surroundings, Tony and Gina sat down about ten feet away from the stream. They both seemed incredibly relaxed, letting themselves melt into the garden of fluorescent dragonflies and looming green giants. Tony pulled a joint from his vest pocket. Lighting the joint and taking a generous toke, he handed it to Gina.

"It's hard to believe where we've been, what we've just done. And now ... now we're here," Tony said.

"Where is here?" I quietly asked.

"Here is anywhere you want it to be, Nate," he replied, taking another smooth hit off his herbal friend and holding it out for me to enjoy. I walked over to him and Gina. Taking my own sweet taste of Mother Nature, I began to relax a little more.

Tony continued. "Take a load off, bro. Check your guns and your mind at the door ... we're off the clock."

As I sat down next to Tony, Gina suddenly stood up. Handing the joint back to him, she stripped down to her panties and slipped into the cool clear water. I should have been a little surprised, but I wasn't. We were all family now. I watched as she gently swept the rushing water through her hair and over her face, seductively splashing her arms and breasts, moving her hands slowly down her snakelike body and caressing her slender torso. It was an art-school moment, playfully and seductively meant to benefit the two people who would appreciate it the most.

She then sank into the water. Anchoring herself between two rocks, she let the water lift her body and flow freely over it. It was as if she was letting nature make love to her. I envisioned both Gina and Casey in the water. It was almost too much ... I took another hit. The weed was kicking in and this vision of Gina had me seriously missing Casey. But she had to stay back and get those new guns ready for battle. Duty called.

After a minute or two, Gina rose from her soft-porn playground and joined us back on the shore.

"How's the water?" Tony asked, smiling like a man who'd just inherited the Playboy Mansion.

"Cold," Gina replied, her voice moderately trembling.

"I can see that," Tony remarked, still beaming. "Goosebumps," he mischievously added.

Tony's remark was an obvious reference to Gina's firm, wet nipples.

Flashing a girlish smile and playfully flipping him off, she quickly slid back into her black leather vest. This was her way of showing the two of us who was really in charge. We had another good laugh.

ALL WAS WELL ... AT LEAST FOR THAT MOMENT

This was the second time Tony had unselfishly opened the door for me, the door leading directly into the intimate world of his mysterious women. He and Gina were opening their bodies and souls without second thoughts or reservations. Why me? Had he let Danny or any of his other brothers this close? Maybe this scene had been played out a hundred times before and this was my simple introduction to the new order of things.

Maybe in their world, this is how it was, a new, free society. Tony had said earlier that the rules now were that there were no rules, except survival, of course. Maybe they were the new hippies, carrying automatic weapons instead of peace signs ... but still crusading for peace and love in the only way they knew how.

Maybe Gina just needed a bath and didn't care ... it had been a rough couple of days.

At that point I decided to stop questioning and start enjoying my new life and friends. Who knew how long it was going to last? Though I was honored to be there with them, I decided to remove myself, at least temporarily, from the picture. It seemed right to leave Tony and Gina alone to privately explore their thoughts and feelings during this short, rare departure from our lurid reality. I too would benefit from my own self-exploration here in the sanctuary of God's outdoor cathedral. But Tony wouldn't hear of it. He said there was still danger and we had to stay close, within eyesight of each other. Gina agreed. I went off to the water's edge. Clearing a small area, I lay down. The stream's flowing rhythm was hypnotic and peaceful.

I was soon half asleep, completely aware of my surroundings, yet physically disconnected from my mortal bondage. As I slipped further into semi-conscious bliss, I slowly became aware of Tony and Gina's voices. Their clarity of tone and familiar warmth befriended my innermost thoughts and became one with my lonely soul. I drifted onto a new level of conscious neutrality and spiritual comfort. I heard every word they said and did not fight to tune them out. Instead, I let them join me at my table of drifting euphoria, as we shared a quiet afternoon of gentle flowing water ... and intimate conversation.

GINA'S SOFT VOICE OPENED THE DOOR

"Let's get out of here, Tony, I really mean it, as far away from here as possible."

"Won't work, Gina. We've already talked about this. Where would we go?"

"The desert, Tone. The Pergasans don't like the desert, they can't take the heat."

"You're forgetting one small detail."

"What's that?"

"The desert gets very cold at night. Besides, things are too dangerous now; we need to stay with the people that we know. You saw what happened with the Huns. They're just the tip of the iceberg, man. There's a lot more like 'em. Dangerous times, girl. It's all about solidarity and teamwork now. That's the only way we can even hope to survive."

"Then we'll take the people we know with us. Henderson, the Alliance, we can trust them. We'll all go together."

"They've got their own agenda man. Everything's a negotiation and if people don't agree, they're just gonna do what they want. Everybody's fragmented. We have got to organize, get stronger, and stay on the offensive. Besides, what if we were to run? Your father wouldn't have anything to blow up. That would just break his heart."

"Do you love me, Tony?"

"Huh?

"Do you love me?"

"Do I love you?"

"Don't be evasive, mister. I used to be a cop, remember?"

"Am I being interrogated, missy?"

"Do you love me!?"

"Do flies like …?"

"Answer the question, cowboy, yes, no, maybe, all of the above, none of the above, A, B, C, or D. Answer the question, my dear!"

"With all my heart, Gina."

"I'm taking that as a yes. I just wanted to hear it!" She kissed Tony.

"You know, when I was a kid, I used to come to a place just like this."

"With your father?"

"No, alone, my father and me … we weren't close. He wasn't around much. I basically just got in his way."

"I'm sorry."

"Don't be. I liked being alone. It made life a lot less complicated."

"Yeah, look how it turned out."

"Hey … nobody invited the turtlenecks."

"What happened to our world, Tone? What's going to happen to us?"

"I don't know, Gina, but we can't give up. We can't give in to fear and paranoia … monsters in the closet. We just can't."

"But there are monsters, Tony. They're out of the closet and they are killing us."

"I know, girl. I know," Tony reluctantly agreed.

"Look, I have something to tell you that's rather harsh, love. I didn't know when the right time or place would be and I don't want you to get upset."

"You don't love me anymore?"

"I'm afraid this one isn't funny, Tone … my father's dying."

"What?"

"Cancer, he was diagnosed shortly before the attack. They gave him a year. There's not much time left."

"Why didn't you tell me this earlier?"

"He didn't want you to know. There's nothing any of us can do. Listen, hon, my father wants to die on the battlefield, not in a hospital bed. He's a dignified man, and a proud warrior."

"Well, he'll probably get his wish."

"How do you want to die, Tony?"

"I don't know. Making love to a beautiful woman … you?"

"Well, not quite that. But there is one thing I am sure of."

"What's that?"

"I don't want to live without either one of you, let alone both. Make me a promise, Tony. Promise me one thing with all your heart and soul."

"What's that, Gina?"

"Promise me that we'll die together."

With those words, my invited guests left the table of half-sleep, silently disappearing into the tranquil, mysterious forest. The shallow running stream that had taken me to the outer realm of semi-conscious bliss now rose far beyond its assigned borders, caressing my body and taking me into the deep blue sea of well-deserved slumber as the last faint wisps of Tony and Gina sailed effortlessly into eternity. Would they too join the tragic ghosts of a world gone mad?

Suspended in the ambiguous fortress of shadow and dreams, I was suddenly awakened by the loud, rumbling sound of American ingenuity.

"Wake up, Sleeping Beauty. You're gonna miss the party … whoo-hoo!"

It was Tony and Gina. They were on their bike and ready to go.

"If you wanna stay here, we'll send the pumpkin around for you later," Tony jeered, obviously back in good form.

"That's Cinderella, doink!" I yelled, not knowing whether I should hug him or punch him.

"Shoot me," Tony replied, holding up his arms. "I'm a Roadrunner fan."

At that moment, I felt an emotion stirring deep down inside of me, like our afternoon in the woods had solidified and strengthened our newfound kinship. In a deluded way, I felt things were somewhat normal.

As we left the enchanted forest, the sun began to sink through
the whispering trees. A mystical haze danced in and out of
the delicate leaves, acknowledging nothing but its pale fragile
presence; delighted by its own rebellion against gravity …
Suspended magically by the invisible universe of the
untouchable …

Its door open to any soul wishing to enter.

"SO HIGH YOU CAN'T GET OVER IT …"

It was getting dark as we headed into camp. A running inner monologue of the afternoon's conversation between Tony and Gina gently played over and over again like a favorite song that embeds itself in your soul and promises never to leave. Gina's somewhat spontaneous water ballet refreshingly stirred my deepest thoughts with a warm, subtle sense of excitement and anticipation. My semi-conscious tour into the personal world of Tony and Gina had provided me with a secure and much needed feeling of love, friendship, and a great sense of belonging. But it also left me with a haunting sense of concern … one I could not immediately explain, but it played in the back of my mind like waves traversing sideways on the shore, like the sun shining at night … something just wasn't right. Either way, I couldn't wait to see Casey. The ride through the woods had opened up my soul, and taken me out of my den of darkness, shadows, and fear … I felt alive again and wanted to share that with her, I wanted to share everything with her. I was equally refreshed from my nap in nature's bed, and enjoying a delicious buzz courtesy of my oxygen-rich forest friends and Tony's weed. But nothing could have prepared me for the buzz yet to come. As we came into home plate, I could have sworn the fair was in town …

THERE REALLY WAS A PARTY!

Pulling into camp, I noticed a remarkable transformation from the previous night. Five M1A2 Abrams tanks, courtesy of General Henderson, had added their formidable presence to our arsenal, along with several large anti-aircraft guns and grenade launchers.

There were many new tents up. Outside one of them, I recognized the dark green crates of automatic rifles, Casey's favorite toys from the summit. I also noticed several Silent Giant generators and lots of new lighting, giving the militaristic base camp a circus-like atmosphere. But the sight that really surprised me was the elevated funeral pyres … lots of them, loaded with the bodies of our fallen comrades. There were also several piles of dead Pergasan soldiers, soaked in gasoline and diesel awaiting their fiery finale.

THIS WAS THE PARTY TONY WAS TALKING ABOUT

THE RITUAL WOULD SOON BEGIN!

Tony pulled his bike up next to mine. "We got everything but popcorn and cotton candy," he said, shutting off the engine.

"What about the waffle cones and corn dogs?" I asked.

"We're working on it," he answered sharply, stepping off the bike and giving Gina a kiss. "And you thought the county fair was a gas? Stick around; you might learn a few things!"

Off in the distance, I could see Casey playfully inspecting one of the tanks. She saw me watching her and blew me a kiss. There was a buzz of activity and anticipation in the air, like everybody knew something big was about to happen and they just couldn't wait. Amongst all this pain and death, there was a strong feeling of hope. It wasn't just about the fight ... it was about living, and these people wanted to live!

Danny appeared from one of the tents, flashing a big Hawaiian smile of friendship and extending his hand to Tony.

"How you doin', bro? How's the wound?"

"Good, my man," Tony replied, every bit as happy to see his comrade. "I see the general brought Christmas early ... he around?"

"No, man. They're diggin' in tonight, getting everything ready to move tomorrow."

"Good job on the barbies. Who's bringin' the marshmallows?"

"You know what, Tone? That's what gets me, man," Danny said, with a slight trace of angst. "I hate wasting good fuel on the Pergasans."

"Think of it as going to a good cause ... you ready to party?"

"Who you askin'?"

"Weedman got his magic bags?"

"Never leaves home without 'em."

"Cool ... oh, and tell him not to forget the pipes this time, I ain't spendin' all night rollin'."

"Right on, I gotta run, hoaloha. I got stuff to take care of before we light the candles

"Tell Spinner he better be in good form tonight. This might be our last shindig for a while. I want some good tunes."

"The brother is on it. What do you want him to open with?"

"Danny, my man ... there's only one song, bro ... 'PSYCHEDELIC SHACK'," Tony replied in an exaggerated whisper.

It had to be right, because tonight was an important night. It would be a night of unity and brotherhood, of hope for the future, of celebration and revenge. It would mark the beginning of the real fight, to be fought with no conscience or fear. Just the sweat, soul, blood, and ingenuity of those who refused to go down. The remnants of Earth's shattered core of humanity would rise and take back what was rightfully theirs.

And yes, tonight ... there would be lots of heavy drinking!

The scene was colorfully surreal, reminiscent of a major sporting event or a rock concert with hundreds, maybe even thousands, waiting for the main act. The fact that a great many of these people would be dead in a few days didn't seem to matter ... for tonight was the beginning!

My attention drifted next to a large canopy set up with two M1 tanks on each side, both decorated haphazardly with Christmas lights and American flags. Strobe lights flashed intermittently and there were several Silent Giant generators around the canopy. Up front and center underneath the psychedelic world of the canvas dome were a number of the dark green weapons and artillery boxes recovered from the summit. They were arranged to create a small stage. On the left side of the structure were several fifty-five gallon drums cut in half sitting on boulder beds, their steel bellies glowing with evening fire. Resting on improvised steel grates were several large pots of a gurgling stew I had never smelled or seen before. Tony explained that this was what they called "Road Chili." The ingredients, simply stated, were "Anything we picked up along the way." There was also lots of government cheese and canned grapefruit juice, go figure. Slowly, the intensity of the evening was elevating. The mood was festive and the feeling was not that different from attending a summer street fair or Saturday morning farmers market, just with lots of weed, funeral pyres, and smelly dead aliens. On the far right, beside one of the tanks, there stood a makeshift DJ booth loaded with old turntables, CD players, and milk crates full of albums and discs. Beat-up speakers with precarious wiring all around adorned the premises. The man Tony had referred to as *"Spinner"* stood patiently at his assigned post ... the last DJ standing, his body moving and gyrating to music that wasn't even playing. The essence of marijuana perfumed the atmosphere. It seemed Spinner had already started his own party. With his floppy-eared aviator cap, leather jacket, and light beard, he was the soul-brother version of a WWII bomber pilot flying very high ... without a plane!

This was indeed a rogue's gallery of colorful misfits and unsung heroes, and quite possibly mankind's last and only hope for planetary redemption.

BILLY BOB'S FOURTH OF JULY LAST-CHANCE USED PEOPLE BLOWOUT SALE OF THE YEAR!

That's right, folks! We got everything you'll ever need right here on a hundred acres of carnival tents and real live farm animals. We got every color and body style you could imagine. Yes sir, we got beer for the gents, soda for the ladies, and hot dogs and balloons for the kids! Boy howdy, this weekend only you can find warriors and cooks, tanks and planes, janitors and generals, cannons and pistols, and don't tell anyone I told ya this ... we even got a few lawyers thrown in! So come on down, come on down ... COME ON DOWN!

ALL RIGHTY THEN...

The combination of exhaustion, years of late-night used car ads, and Tony's excellent pot had left my mind spinning. There was only one cure for this: more weed, a bottle of Jack Daniel's, and Casey. But where was Casey ... and what about Tony? He and the girls seemed to have disappeared, leaving me halfway between here and back in the woods. To me, this was a celebration, a carnival of *angels* vs. *dragons* ... all with their own superpowers, all willing to die for what they sincerely believed in ... whatever those beliefs were. Time to party!

Suddenly, the sound of unrehearsed feedback filled the air, sharing space with the ever-increasing ambience of cannabis and who knows what.

As if by magic, Tony appeared on the makeshift stage, Casey and Gina on each side, a large tan cowboy hat with an equally large feather added to his normal attire. The crowd began to surround the stage. Wherever it was we were supposed to be at that moment ... we were there. Wherever it was that we were going, the tickets were torn. *The blood spilled from the previous days of carnage now filled the bowls of road chili, half-full glasses of Jack Daniel's and warm beer, and the eyes of the living, who symbolically joined with the souls of their lost brethren.*

Tony surveyed the crowd. Anticipating what was to come, they were amazingly subdued ... the calm before the storm. Tony opened up the doors ... and the crowd rushed in.

"HELLOOOOOWOAH-WOAH-WOAH-WOAH WOAHOOOOOOOOOOOOOOOOOOOOOOOOO OOOOOOOOOOOOOOOOOOOOOOOH ..."

"For those of you already on acid, I probably won't have to repeat that," Tony said.

The crowd reacted with love and energy. Tony now owned the room. The anticipation was over ... it was officially on! No turning back, not on *this* night.

He continued, the smooth, articulate orator of the damned addressing his loyal congregation as only he could. "Ladies and gentlemen, and everyone else ... welcome. We are here tonight to honor our brave dead, and celebrate the continuing demise of the Pergasans on this field, and in the skies above us." The crowd began to cheer and clap their hands. Tony paused for a moment, well aware of the emotions he was stirring up in his battle-weary but proud audience.

"Tomorrow ... tomorrow is the new dawn of resurrection for our world, and our people. Some of us here tonight won't live to see that new world. But your souls will be eternal, and your spirits will be beside us. I want to thank all of you in advance for the brave and unselfish commitment you have made to yourselves ... and to your brothers and sisters in arms. I'd come down there and give you all a big wet kiss on the lips, but I don't think Gina would like that. And besides, some of you all's breath is a little funky."

Once again, a warm and enthusiastic reaction emanated from the crowd. Tony realized his words and their mission signaled a the beginning of a heavy and dangerous journey, but a little humor seemed to soften the launch. This was a night of celebration and irony, of bearing witness to and participating voluntarily in one's own potential wake ... depending on the winds of fate. Tony knew everyone's feelings at that moment ... and he knew exactly where to go.

"So without further distraction or further adoooooooooo," he merrily continued, "Because I wanna get loaded tooooooooo ... we're gonna turn it over to your friend and mine, man of mystery, old records, CDs and eight tracks, a guy who claims he's still a virgin ... the one and only, the young, the lovely, my man in the booth ... Mr. Spinner Jones!"

THE CROWD BURST INTO
A FRENZIED STATE OF CELEBRATION
I WAS WAITING FOR THE MUSIC TO START
BUT TONY
HAD ONE MORE THING TO SAY TO THE CROWD
BEFORE THE RITUAL COULD BEGIN
"MR. OHANO," HE SHOUTED ... "LIGHT THE BARBIES!"

Tattered vehicles of all kinds started up their engines and began racing toward the elevated funeral pyres and sporadic heaps of dead Pergasan warriors. Tossing road flares and torches and even using flamethrowers, the honored and dishonored alike were lit. Flames quickly shot into the night sky, lighting up the surrounding venue like a wildfire in the Black Forest. The crowd's rush was intoxicating. The invisible riptide of human emotion rose with the flames, meeting the spirits and souls of the downed warriors. Anticipation and energy began to flow as Spinner's voice came across the PA system. Slow, warm, and soothing, the ultra-cool DJ put the crowd under his spell ... and got the groove thing going.

"Cool people ... cool down, cool down and listen ... SOMEBODY'S AT THE DOOOOOOOOOOR ..."

"… SO LOW YOU CAN'T GET UNDER IT."

Spinner Jones, the partying warrior, pantomimed the opening door of "Psychedelic Shack."

MASTERFULLY FOLLOWING
THE ORIGINAL RECORDING
THE DOOR OPENED …
IT WAS ON
IT WAS ON!

"LET ME TELL YOU ABOUT A PLACE I KNOW, TO GET IN, IT DON'T TAKE MUCH DOUGH …"

The blaring sounds of a classic Temptations song shot through the cool night as Captain Tony suddenly jumped off the stage and grabbed a rather trashed and string-less Fender guitar. Holding it up behind his head like Hendrix, he ran off into the dark like a crazy drunken sailor chasing an invisible siren. Gina and Casey stayed on stage, dancing like cage girls in a Philippine strip club. Tony came back with two beautiful red roses and gave one to each girl.

"I love both of you," he said over the blaring music, in a heartfelt and endearing voice.

"We love you too," they replied in unison. Casey bent down and kissed Tony deeply on the lips. It was a kiss that went on for quite some time. Gina looked on smiling. Eventually Tony pried himself away from Casey and repeated the process with Gina, and disappeared again into the smoky night.

A crowd gathered in front of Gina and Casey's stage and began doing what could only be described as "The line dance from hell." But it looked real fun. Suddenly the bright lights went off, and a myriad of rotating strobes turned the event into a screaming, dancing acid trip. The music went pure jungle … pure erotic. Drums pulsed like blood through a junkie's favorite vein. The line dance became seductive and ritualistic. The shadows of Gina and Casey on stage were snakelike and hypnotic. When the lights came back on, the two girls were grinding their bodies slowly on each other, sensuously making out.

Tony reappeared through the smoke and lights. The smile on his face as he gazed at the stage was pure Christmas morning ... Santa knowing that Tony had been a good boy all year.

ONCE AGAIN ... HE DISAPPEARED

With Tony gone, I felt alone in a strange and exciting void. My attention once again turned to the stage as Casey beckoned me to join her.

She knelt down and, in pure Hawaiian style, placed Tony's rose in my hair, resting it gently upon my right ear. She then kissed me and looked deep into my soul. I felt warm and safe, like the tanks, guns, and burning bodies around me had never existed. I felt an insane sense of playfulness.

"I feel like I'm kissing two girls at once," I quipped, referring to her and Gina's earlier performance on stage.

"It's fun, you should try it sometime," she replied joyfully, a sweet satisfaction in her voice, as if she had just eaten the most delicious chocolate truffle in the world. *The sensuous and playful nature of her words intensified my emotions, leaving me to gravitate toward my own inner peace as I danced off toward the invisible sun.*

As the party raged on, I felt my energy starting to wane. These guys were seasoned professionals. I was a rank amateur. Tony and the girls were off on some crazy adventure, and it was time for me to turn in. My consumption of what in our past world would have landed me in rehab for at least ten years was quickly catching up to me.

Making my way to my tent, I lay down on a historically aromatic cot, but couldn't quite turn off the brain tube. The remote was lost, and the on/off switch wasn't working. There was still so much to process. The party had been great, but somewhere along the line, I began to feel like we were putting the wake before the funeral. An hour later, I walked back out to the sleeping carnival, now a mere shadow of its former grandeur. The early fall atmosphere was crisp with the lingering essence of weed, fuel, and burning bodies. A few crazies were still running around in the distance. Out of the corner of my eye I could see Casey slipping into our tent.

Tony was standing on a small-elevated platform, quietly observing the gypsy carnival of life and death spread out before him ... a thoughtful expression on his face, a concerned look in his eyes. I approached slowly, not wanting to intrude.

"Surveying the wreckage?" I asked, maintaining a safe distance.

"Comes with the job, Tony replied in a low-key tone.

"Good benefits?"

"They suck, but I get lotsa vacation time. Hey, you should be sleepin', man. We're movin' out at dawn."

"What about you?"

"I don't sleep much anymore. I've learned to dream with my eyes open."

"Some nightmare."

"Tellin' me?" he replied in a soft, exasperated tone.

"This was a little dangerous, don't you think, Tony? Maybe we should have just hidden out," I asked, paranoid that our makeshift county fair might have attracted the Pergasans.

"Everything we do is dangerous, Nate. You can't lose your humanity 'cuz of a few bullies, they know we're out here. Henderson thinks they need to regroup before they attack again."

He looked at one of the ceremonial funeral pyres, now smoldering. "We're all gonna end up like that eventually," he quietly observed, his tone uncharacteristically sad.

"Don't tell me you're losing hope in mankind, captain," I replied, hoping to bring the old *"self-assured"* Tony back.

"Nope ... I just know who got the good side of the draft this year."

Tony continued to stare into the smoky distance, acknowledging my presence not with his eyes, but with his words.

"You know, when I was a kid, my old man wasn't around much, and my mom, she drank. So I used to go out into the woods and dream. I'd daydream for hours and hours and hours."

"What did you dream about?" I asked, watching him take a generous drag off one of his trademark short black cigars.

"I dreamt that I lived in this house with all my friends, and that they never left. They were always there by my side. The girls were pretty, the guys were fun, and we all talked and laughed about anything that came to our minds. Not a care in the world ... we didn't even have a clock. And you know what? As crazy and deluded as it sounds, I've kinda got that now ... in a crazy, deluded way of course."

"A true house of cards, considering the circumstances," I replied, sensing we were approaching some real deep waters. Why was I being the pragmatic one? I still had one hell of a buzz.

"I'm afraid I agree with you, Nate. We're all cruising on some temporary visas right now."

"What do you think about tomorrow ... the attack, do we even have a chance?"

"You a bettin' man?"

"Only if the cards are marked."

"Well, in this case, you'd be better off bettin' on the *Hindenburg* makin' a safe landing."

"Then why are we doing it?"

"It's our path, Nathan ... it's our path."

"What happened to the path of least resistance?" I asked.

"That went away the day the earth stood still bro," Tony shot back. "That was the day an innocent afternoon on the softball field became the most horrendous bloodbath I have ever seen in my life ... even to this day. And believe me, I have seen a few. The past we lost and the future we inherited ... it just doesn't make sense, I will never forget that afternoon ... never."

"We've all lost a lot, Tone."

"Brother, you don't know."

"Maybe some day you'll tell me. You know all about me. When do I get to pull the sheets on the real Captain Tony?"

"Tomorrow, Nate. Tomorrow, I promise. Now get yourself some sleep."

As Tony headed in the direction of his tent, his silhouette quietly disappeared into the slowly rising tulle fog. There was something disturbing about that vision. It was almost as if he was walking into eternity. As his physical presence disappeared, I felt a sudden sense of loneliness, like I had just lost my best friend. Perhaps Tony was right ... maybe I did need sleep.

As I returned to my tent I lay down next to Casey, understandably passed out from the night's festivities ... but I couldn't sleep. My mind was racing as scenes from the past couple of days flashed through my mind in a dizzy, maddening sense of random order. Like an insane game of sardonic word association I began to place Tony in the realm of historical conflict and classic confrontations, and then it hit me ... *Moby Dick.*

"All that most maddens and torments; all that stirs up the lees of things; all truth with malice in it; all that cracks the sinews and cakes the brain; all the subtle demonisms of life and thought; all evil to crazy Ahab, were visibly personified, and made practically assailable in Moby-Dick. He piled upon the whale's white hump the sum of all the general rage and hate felt by his whole race from Adam down; and then, as if his chest had been a mortar, he burst his hot heart's shell upon it."

—Herman Melville, *Moby Dick*

No one truly understood the Pergasans bloodlust for humanity, but one could easily see why they hated and pursued Tony. But what was I seeing here ... was there a connection or was I just spinning out? I mean, what was the true motivation of Ahab's' intense hatred for the great white whale he so vehemently stalked? Was the crazed captain simply doing what he thought right? Or was he hopelessly obsessed with the unrelenting commission of his own personal vendetta? Was his hate a strong statement made by a selfless victim drowning in his own tragic circumstance? Was Ahab hero or villain? Or did he fit comfortably in between, commander of an ambiguous wasteland of anarchy on the high seas?

And what of the hunted white whale *Moby Dick?* Was he not guided by the ultimate motivation to survive by any and all means possible? Was he not the sole guardian of his own future, entitled to preserve his endangered existence against a proven and deadly opponent?

So what fueled the Pergasans rage? It certainly couldn't have been money or blubber. Their motivation was raw and deep. They were the Ahabs of the universe. Hell-bent on revenge of some sort, or at least that's what it felt like. And you can bet they wanted Tony. He was their white whale. He taunted them, damaged them, and at times ... killed them. Not for the sake of the kill, but for the sake of his own survival ... and the survival of his own people

The questions of the present circumstance remained curiously unanswered. But the imminent collision of ideologies would ultimately prove fatal to some.

FOR ON THIS COOL, MISTY DAWN, THE AHABS FOUND THEIR GREAT WHITE WHALE ... AND THE HAUNTING DEEP BLUE SEA TURNED A BLOODY CRIMSON RED

This was the second time in two days that I had been yanked from the breast of well-deserved slumber and thrown into the tumultuous underworld of cataclysmic disaster. I could hear the footsteps, yelling, and total confusion of a horrific conflict arising from the ashes of darkness, consuming everyone and everything in sight. The former group vibe of confidence and hope had now transformed into the sounds of pure terror.

As I ran from my tent to witness the onslaught, I caught a glimpse of Tony gazing toward the sky. While everyone else desperately sought weapons, Tony remained calm and stoic, his eyes never moving from the shadowy, hovering aggressors ... Man vs. Alien ... the ultimate showdown.

A solider I had never seen before slowly approached Tony.

"What do they want?" the young man asked. "What are they waiting for?"

Tony's reply came from somewhere that sent a shiver down my spine. Was the last bastion of man's hope now going down with the house of cards built on the shifting sands of blind faith and cruel denial? Was this an attack ... or an assassination? Tony had tried to warn me of this day, but he himself could not accept its inevitable outcome. This day stood for everything he was against, yet it was stronger than all of us ... and he knew it. He knew it ... and I knew it.

Tony's eyes never left the sky. "This has gotten very personal," he replied. "You know what they want? They want us to fear death, fear it ... before we feel it."

"Maybe they just want to talk," the young solider replied nervously, searching Tony's face for some kind of hope.

"These guys don't talk," Tony solemnly answered ... they just kill.

And with that statement, those few words uttered from the mouth of the former softball great now turned elite hero and transfer to our new salvation; I understood, I saw the light, I got it ... or at least I think I did.

TONY SAW DEATH COMING; MAYBE HE SAW IT EARLIER THIS EVENING ON THE SMALL ELEVATED PLATFORM OVERLOOKING THE SMOLDERING GYPSY CARNIVAL OF LIFE. OR PERHAPS ... PERHAPS HE SAW IT EARLIER, MUCH EARLIER. PERHAPS HE SAW IT THE DAY AN INNOCENT AFTERNOON ON THE SOFTBALL FIELD BECAME THE MOST HORRENDOUS BLOODBATH HE HAD EVER SEEN ... *THE DAY HE CHOSE NOT TO FEAR DEATH.*

The stage was now set for confrontation, but the odds were horribly one-sided. Gina and her father were silently climbing into one of the tanks General Henderson had provided, no longer illuminated by festive party lights but dark as the death they represented.

"I want you on one of the fifties, Case," Tony said, referring to one of the fifty-caliber anti-aircraft guns. "That's where you'll get your cleanest shot."

Without a word Casey ran about twenty yards to the nearest one and got on board, aiming its cool steel barrel skyward.

Suddenly it became frighteningly clear that we were all out in the open, exposed and vulnerable. It was then that Tony went into full gear, but the look in his eyes told a story I did not want to know. It wasn't the look of fear, just the look of truth. And if I read Tony right, blind justice was not on our side. It had all come down to this. There was no negotiation, no creative banter from lawyers or politicians. The polls were closed and there would be no vote for peace or war ... and no second chance.

"Nathan, you need to find cover," Tony barked. "Danny, raise General Henderson now!"

"I've been trying, bro," Danny replied, his voice concerned. "There's no one out there, Tone, just static."

Tony looked at Danny with a quiet understanding.

THERE WAS NO GENERAL HENDERSON
THERE WAS NO LIEUTENANT FOX
THERE WAS NO SASHA CONRAD
THERE WAS NO COLONEL TYLER
THERE WAS NO ARTHUR "ARTIE" WEST ...
THERE WAS ONLY US

Soon every large weapon had been manned, and every gun, missile, and grenade launcher had been distributed. A young solider handed Tony and me M16 rifles, and for a brief sickening moment ...

THERE WAS SILENCE
THE ONLY THING YOU COULD HEAR
WERE YOUR OWN MORTAL THOUGHTS
AS THEY WHISPERED QUIETLY
IN THE COOL SHADOWS
OF DAWN

A shot came from the hovering Pergasan predators. We were already surrounded. Casey got off the first rounds from her fifty-caliber, and it all broke loose.

Confusion and death were poured by the gallon as the ruthless Pergasan attack carved and tore through what was once a celebration of great hope and future dreams. As the house of cards slowly began to fall, Casey was hit. Her body flew through the air, mercilessly slamming onto the cold morning ground. For a second … it all went black.

The next thing I knew, Tony was running toward Casey's lifeless body, ambivalent to the shower of laser bullets strafing the twisted landscape. The Pergasan fighter that hit Casey was sweeping down on Tony like an angry hornet, relentlessly pursuing its target with deadly intent. As in the field with the young girl and mother almost two days earlier, the terror in me remained, but the fear left my body. I ran toward Tony and Casey, firing upward round after round from the M16 until the magazine was empty, praying in vain that one bullet would pierce the hull of the Pergasan craft and slay the soulless beast at its controls. I threw the gun away and suddenly found myself face down on the ground, something heavy resting on top of me. I heard Danny's voice … *no,* brother … no!"

I didn't see Tony get hit, but I could feel his presence fading. Getting up, I could see he was on his knees, not moving. His left side was pierced and bleeding from the Pergasan laser bullets, the wounds partially cauterized from the intense heat of the projectiles. A crimson pool of Tony's waning life grew slowly beside him. His were eyes glazed but never left Casey's lifeless body, and his breathing was slow and stressed. There was no hint of cognoscente expression on his face, but I knew his mind was in overdrive, aware of his ensuing fate yet silently mourning one of his own … quiet last moments of his life being tossed and shuffled faster than a deck of cards in a Vegas casino.

The stench of death and burning diesel permeated the scene like a blanket. A slow, sickening choreography of the living, the dead, and the soon-to-be dead, was playing out on a stage the

Pergasans had helped create. As quickly as it had started, the aliens broke off their bloody attack and were gone. A haunting silence stalked the deadly dawn. Time stood frozen, and if you believed, you could almost feel the spirits of the fallen heroes ... alone and confused, not quite understanding that they had just crossed the bridge between mortality and the beyond.

Casey was gone, and Tony hadn't been there. Though she had not died in vain, she died quick and alone. Not in the arms of the man who loved her as much as his cherished Gina, but on the cold, harsh ground of an unforgiving battlefield of pain and broken dreams.

The radios whispered dead static as Danny turned away from me, disappearing into a spiritual silence that made him almost invisible. The silence permeated every vascular cavity of my mind and soul. Time was now flowing backward in a blood-red river of chilling disbelief. Did that really happen? I stood frozen, locked in a void of conscious terror and unconscious confusion. Where was I a minute ago? Where was I now? Where were Tony and Casey? They must be back at the party. Yeah, the party, there is a party, right? I'm not sure. It can't be over, it can't be, we've got so much to do ... so much to do tomorrow. Tomorrow's the beginning! This isn't tomorrow, is it? ***Tony and Casey, get up please ... no more fooling around. Get up, dammit, get up ... c'mon guys, stop messing around ... get up! Please ... get up!***

Doc Smiley approached Tony, who was still kneeling beside Casey, his eyes frozen in time.

"Tony," Doc said.

Tony slowly raised his left hand into the air, a simple gesture but one understood by both. Doc backed away and like Danny, he too quietly disappeared into the night. Gina came over and gently touched Tony, letting him know she was near, allowing him another moment to grieve. She was the only one that didn't seem to have changed. Everywhere around me, people's eyes were glazed and lost. Their faces framed a picture of shock and disparity, a complete antithesis from the glow of confidence and hope shown only a few hours earlier. But Gina's face remained calm and soft. Her eyes radiated with compassion and understanding. She carefully helped Tony to his feet and guided him toward their tattered white tent. The life was draining out of Tony's eyes as they drew near but he managed one last sharp gaze.

"It's all yours, Nathan," he said in a weak voice. "Now you're the hero."

That was the last of his strength, his head and eyes slowly fell back. Every moment of his life was now a struggle.

Gina gave me a brief look, an unspoken expression that solidified the heartbreaking fact that it was all over. The dream had died and now there was nothing left ... *nothing.*

She then beckoned me to follow. As we entered the tent I returned to the moment of Athena's death, now compounded by the loss of Casey, and soon, Tony. My body felt lifeless and without soul, my mind without purpose or direction. I could not be Tony's hero. He was the hero. I was just the guy he met two days ago. The guy he made feel like a hero. Now I would fade back into obscurity, for without him, there was no hope.

It was obvious to Gina that Tony loved Casey as much as he loved her, and she forgave him for that. But alas, a man cannot serve two mistresses ... he can only die with them.

Helping Tony lie down, Gina removed Tony's rose from her hair and placed it in his right hand, helping him to grasp it.

"My soul to yours," she softly whispered.

He was slipping away fast and Gina knew that in mortal life, they only had moments left. I suddenly remembered their prophetic talk in the woods. Tony wanted to die making love to a beautiful woman. That was not possible, but at least he would be in the presence of one. As Gina slowly unbuttoned her blood-stained silk blouse, Tony managed a weak smile. *"Nice try, kid,"* he said.

Those would be Tony's last words. He would go out a lover and a hero, but sadly incomplete of his own life's personal mission.

As the final sigh of life left Tony's shattered body, Gina's rose fell solemnly to the ground. His head turned slowly to one side. His eyes remained open, Gina's gentle weeping image forever locked in their final gaze, a memorial not to the man himself, but to a woman whom he loved. I felt Gina's heart and soul grow heavy. She had fought with every fiber of her mortal existence to avoid this moment, yet she knew it was inevitable. Tears streamed down her soft cheeks. The woman warrior that had fought so hard for life and the lives of others had, like Tony, reached the end of her forlorn journey.

Though she was a beautiful woman and a formidable warrior, without Tony, there was no reason to be a warrior … and no need to be a woman.

Gina had asked Tony to promise her they would die together. But that was no longer possible. Tony could no longer promise, but she could fulfill. As it had been from the start, Gina's sensitivities and instincts were the guiding force in whatever decisions needed to be made. She had always been in touch with her inner self, and trusted the deepest voices of her soul.

On a crate nightstand, she found the sharp Kunai throwing knife her father had given her years before. Though ineffective in any practical engagement against a Pergasan, it still represented the power of a small piece of steel in the hand of a mortal human. Gina kissed Tony and held him, tearfully speaking her last words to an audience that lay scattered on the morning wind … hopefully waiting for her on the other side.

"SLEEP MY LOVE TONY.
NO MORE PAIN,
NO MORE DEATH …
NO MORE WAR."

Gina gave me one last goodbye glance as she slowly slid the knife down the inside of her arm. As her warm blood gently drained, it bathed Tony's earthbound rose with the final quiet moments ... of *Gina's* life.

I made no attempt to keep General Lee from entering the tattered white tent. The screams of pain and agony, the sound of a father losing his only child, would have at one time raised the hairs on the back of my neck and sent a cold chill down my spine. Now it just felt normal. This is what our world had become, and there was no turning back. My lost heroes were now simply a footnote in history's coldest chapter, souls lost in the dawn of humanities new ice age.

Exiting the tent, I looked in the eyes of the little girl whose unexpected entrance into my life propelled me into the world of an extraordinary group of people; I could only tell her goodbye ... and good luck. It was time for me to return to my house of shadows and frozen angels, for I was now and forever ... out of the club.

This was not the epic ending we had wanted or expected. Ahab got his white whale, leaving the rest of us with nothing but an empty field of cold blood, and a heart full of broken dreams. The morning came on ... cold and slow.

The sun that was to rise on the new dawn of man now silently lit the still dawn of death. The speed and efficiency of the supposedly wounded Pergasans' early morning attack paid tribute to their single-minded obsession with eradicating humankind forever. The walk back to my house of frozen angels was more like a hypnotic death march through a dark tunnel. My senses were in suspended animation, my thoughts confused and lost in the broken abyss of hopelessness. The last time I had passed through my front door, Casey escorted me in life ... now she walked with me in death. The front room was dark, but there was no reason to turn on the light. For the light of life itself had gone out, and every relevant thought or emotion I had went with it ... all of them except sorrow. But this was sorrow and emptiness on a level I had never experienced before, even when Athena died. This burned and tore like hungry pack dogs in a wildfire, dissipating the very last remnants of my existence, casting cold shadows across the once-warm house of my soul.

I COULD STILL HEAR THEIR VOICES
FEEL THEIR TOUCH
THIS HAD JUST HAPPENED
THEIR BODIES WERE STILL WARM
KNEELING DOWN
I PICKED UP THE EMPTY GLASS
LEFT BEHIND
BY MY MURDERED
LOST ANGEL

Casey's life, like the forgotten contents of the spilled glass, had evaporated into the cold morning, quietly slipping away without even a whisper ... bravely joining the lost warriors of eternity.

Filling Casey's glass from the same bottle we had shared a short time earlier, I sat down and drank ... and waited. I could still feel her near, still hear her voice. I could not believe that she was gone. The sun continued to rise. As the house slowly got lighter, I realized I was not the only being in the room. I don't know when they got in, or how long they had been there, but four Pergasan warriors stood silently, menacingly, only a few feet away from me.

The emotionless, demonic alien beasts were carrying M16 rifles ... *human* weapons. They did not react or even acknowledge my presence, even though I was quietly staring them down, mentally begging them to take me out of my present misery. Their complete and undivided attention was focused on my five plastic playmates. And then, almost as if it had been repeatedly rehearsed to perfection, they aimed their weapons at my silent mechanical mistresses ... and opened fire.

Some of the bullets absorbed into their poly-composite skin like they were never even hit. Others sheared and dismembered the angelic technical goddesses like chainsaws at a beer-fueled lumberjack barbeque. For me, time had slipped into a psychotic nightmare of comic-book murder and mechanical mayhem. I flashed on the thought that my alien friends truly enjoyed using our own weapons against us. Did they get a sadistic pleasure out of all of this? Were they even capable of feeling pleasure? Did they feel anything at all outside of their voracious hatred for everything human? Was there a message I was missing? They were certainly putting a lot of time and effort into all of this. Strangely enough, they were focusing all of their attention on the girls ... and none of it on me. When the carnage was over, when they had completed their misguided assault against the unarmed warrior-goddess army of five, they left. They just *left*, leaving me alone and companionless ... to pick up the pieces.

I'M EXHAUSTED

I feel an aching sense of loss. That unmistakable hollow feeling you get when you lose a close friend or lover. I feel like I have just ended a great journey, and can't remember where I'd been.

With the exception of a few species of birds that inhabit the island, I know of no other animal life here. I know for sure there are no other humans. Yet I feel like I have just been touched, held, and loved by many.

The sun once again stands quiet vigil over my fleeting daytime shadows, but sheds no light onto the mysterious darkness. Still, I'm getting closer ... I can feel it. The walls and bridges of my questionable realities here, once blurred and uncertain, have been falling down like rocks off a cliff, revealing what I instinctively feel will be my inevitable solo truth. That truth, so aloof and taunting, dancing seductively and secretly through the very essence of my soul, is running out of music ... and lies. What eventually will reveal itself will be certainty. Clarity will return, but where will that leave me? Maybe this traveling circus of revolving daydreams and haunting nightmares was meant to protect me, shield me from myself and the possible wreckage I have left behind. I will continue to search ... and wait.

But for now I have the morning, a beacon fire, and my personal solace ...
For now, that is all I need.

Afterthoughts …

"A Previous conversation between Tony and Nate."

I caught a glimpse of Tony out of the corner of my eye. He was standing alone, staring thoughtfully into one of the crumbling funeral pyres. He was physically within reach, but mentally, he was miles outside the city limits. As was becoming standard operating procedure in such instances, I approached with curiosity and caution, careful not to disturb him.

"Is this a private conversation or can anyone join in? I calmly asked.

"Pull up a stool, pour yourself a drink," Tony casually replied.

"Great party, we gotta do this more often," I said. "What are you thinking about, man?"

"I'm not thinkin' … I'm apologizin'."

"Apologizing for what?"

"For the way I was." Tony spoke slowly, but gradually picked up speed and intensity as he went. "Sorry for the way we all were, so immersed in our own everyday tasks and petty lives that we literally became immune to life itself. Instead of going forward with our humanity, we stepped away from it. All the things that we thought would bring us closer together only took us farther away. We just let it happen, becoming a programmed society of white mice running for the cheese and mortgaging our lives with the intelligence and forethought of a second-grader with a Tootsie Pop. And look at us now, Nate. In some ways we're still the same, but our selfish actions aren't about fighting for the closest parking space at Walmart anymore. Now it's about making it through the night, living to see the next sunrise … it's all in perspective now."

"It's not about society, Tone. It's just who we are."

"You think so? Yeah, maybe you're right. I just wish I could turn back time, if for only one minute … kiss my wife, play ball in the sun, hear the kids, and smell the sweet, sweet grass of home. But it'll never happen, brother. It's just a dream, man … just a dream."

"I'm sorry, Tone. I'm sorry for all of us."

"It's not your fault. What do you dream about, Nate? What goes on inside that crazy head of yours?"

"The night before I met you guys, I had this freaky dream. It was so bloody real ... I mean I'm still feeling it."

"I've had those," Tony sighed. "Now they've all just morphed into one continuous nightmare. Go on, bro, share the wealth."

"I dreamt I was on this faraway *island.* I didn't know how long I'd been there, or how I even got there in the first place. I was just there."

"Where was this island?"

"I don't know, man ... somewhere beyond Tahiti."

"Any exotic hotties runnin' around, you know, all dolled up with the coconut shells ... or better yet, without 'em?"

"That's just the thing, Tone. I know I was alone ... yet at different times I could feel the presence of people. Not just random strangers, but people I knew. I could smell them, taste them, feel them, Tony. But they were never there, yet they *were* ... they were there."

"What were they doing, bro?"

"I can't remember ... I just don't know. The only thing I recall was a boat ... I think I found a boat."

"A boat?"

"I found her beached on an inlet. She was beautiful, but she was trashed."

"Maybe that's how you got there. Maybe it was your boat ... maybe you wrecked. You know, you can be quite impulsive at times, Nate."

"Yeah, but the boat ..."

"What about the boat?"

"There was something on it, something I found ... something that owned my soul and wouldn't let me go. But the island itself seemed to create its *own* truth. I couldn't be sure about anything."

"That's a trip, Nate. But it was only a dream, brother."

"Yeah, I know, Tony. It was only a dream."

BatPeople

Chapter Seven

"The irony of just cause and escaping persecution is not exclusive to any one planet or race of beings. It is universal." —Unknown

"When the Turbine Flower blooms its last and final breath of life on this planet, it will be then and only then, that we reveal our true selves and purpose. As the hybrid cousins of a dead race, created from the seed of necessity, nurtured and fed in the historical shadows of secrecy and patience we will rise to complete our task, claiming Earth as our new home and conquered dominion."

Today is a new day. Today is a day of acceptance and understanding. I will accept the plan the gods and universe have put forth. And I will attempt to understand my purpose on this island. I will let go of confusion and fear, and graciously open wide the doors of my new reality ... I will go with the flow.

She appears like a ghost ship out of the English fog ... a mysterious gypsy from an unknown world making a guest appearance on my little island, one more impromptu session of sanity check, Nathan. Okay, all marbles in the bag ... and she's still here. Are sanity checks valid while you are sleeping? For surely I am dreaming! She is beautiful, tanned, exotic, and young. Her hair is long and dark. Sensuously nestled in it is the most beautiful white flower I have ever seen. The girl and the flower are a mystery, one of many that I have encountered on this alien rock I call home.

One more mystery to add to the collection: She's come from the southeast part of the island. Though my hold on reality has been on serious trial since I awoke in this tropical nightmare, there is one thing I know for sure: that part of the island is impassable on foot, due to thick vegetation.

Yet here she is. She looks curious, almost startled to see me. Maybe I come as a surprise to her. I want to yell out to her. I want to ask her name, ask where she's from ... are there more like her on the island? But the bird of opportunity doesn't always fly in the direction we want, or at the time we desire ... and so the moment is lost.

As she turns to run in the direction from whence she came, I experience a moment of hesitation. But I cannot hesitate, I must follow. Like so many of the women in my life, I feel compelled to know her secrets, not as a man desiring a woman, but as a man desiring knowledge. Her flight might be a byproduct of shyness and fear, of unfamiliarity with the stranger before her. But if there are others on this island, maybe they can answer the questions that elude me. Maybe they can tell me where we are and how long I have been here. Maybe they can tell me how I got here, or if I have always been here and that my strange, haunting dreams have simply been dreams and nothing more. I'll try not to frighten her. I'll follow from a distance.

She seems to know the way. She has found an entrance into the dense vegetation, and with the moves of an exotic living scalpel, she effortlessly maneuvers the path toward her mysterious destination. She knows I am behind her, yet the urgency of her flight seems greatly diminished, almost as if she now has me exactly where she wants me. Oh God, am I once again being stupid, aimlessly chasing ghosts just to end up as lost and confused as I was when I started?

THE CHASE

It feels like we are in a rain forest. The air is cool on my skin and permeated with the scent of exotic vegetation. The ground is soft, and the lush, subtle vines sweep across me like hanging silk. The landscape is at times dark and foreboding ... yet strangely inviting. I feel an odd sense of security, though I am in a world I have never experienced, a world as alien as Mount Everest or the Grand Canyon. We run for what seems like hours. The rain forest has given way to an open field bathed in angelic sunlight. Almost as far as the eye can see, there are rolling hills and fields of the most beautiful white flowers I have ever seen in my life ... the same flowers that adorn the hair of my exotic fleeing gypsy.

She stops, standing alone in the middle of a field. She turns ... her eyes beckoning me to follow. Perhaps she feels I am falling behind, or just plain giving up. Once again, she is off, and once again I am chasing Dorothy across the alien landscape ... across a sea of beauty to an island in the sun, a world unexplored or perhaps to the Emerald City itself, where the great and all-powerful Oz awaits my arrival. If by chance I catch my Dorothy, perhaps she will have the answers to the mystery of my presence here on Terra-Donna ... or wherever I am!

OVER THE RIVER AND THROUGH THE WOODS

The landscape is now in a constant flux. Fields of beautiful flowers quickly turn into forests of darkness and mystery, which in turn morph into rolling hills and back to the lush rain forest that began our journey ... and still we run!"

We run to the edge of forever, until there is no place left to run, to the end of the enchanted forest ... and straight into the mysterious world of the fleeing island gypsy.

IT'S AS IF DREAMS
HAVE BECOME REALITY

AND REALITY
A DREAM …
WE ARE HERE

THE VILLAGE

There are people, structures, animals, and yes … flowers. My presence here is barely acknowledged. I am not a mysterious stranger unwittingly happening upon a secret clan … I am merely tolerated. Their level of curiosity is low, as if they knew I was coming, or they simply knew who I was. They look at me with subtle recognition and little wonder. I, on the other hand, view them as wondrous, to say the least. They are of all races and ages, yet their eyes and skin color are exactly the same, almost as if in some molecular context they are connected. Their skin is dark and evenly tanned, their eyes a bronze-amber glaze, giving surreal beauty to even the least attractive of the group.

The village itself is a strange sight. Classic thatch huts are intermixed with steel structures. The architecture and materials used are rudimentary at best … but out of context for this destination. I have never seen this place before. Aside from the usual coconut trees and Paradise Berries, there are pineapples, mangos, passion fruit, exotic apples, and many more fruits and vegetables not indigenous to the island. And there is more. They have chickens, goats, sheep, and pigs. The ground level and surrounding hills are saturated with the beautiful white flowers I had seen before. Their sweet essence is reminiscent of pungent plumeria on a crisp Maui morning. I am not only intoxicated by their lovely aroma, but by their simple beauty. They speak a secret language to each other … and to me. They catch the wind with the grace of a ballerina, slowly bobbing and swaying to their own cosmic concerto.

"Turbine flowers," she says in a soft, angelic voice. The mystery gypsy now stands before me. "They only bloom on this island, and nowhere else in the world," she explains. She seems to have forgotten the long chase just concluded.

"You speak as well as you run," I reply, "Thankfully not as fast, but equally as graceful."

"Thank you," she warmly says, basking in the glow of a compliment. "That is very nice of you, Nathan."

"You know my name ... how?"

"My name's Jade." She replies, kicking my question to the curb with aloof charm. "Come, let me show you my village. I'm sure that you have many questions. Just be patient, Nathan ... be patient."

"Do I have a choice?" I ask, looking straight at her. Her eyes and smile give me the answer ... words are not necessary.

I follow her to a secluded part of the village where there are only a few thatch huts. We walk toward one dwelling that has a large, smoldering fire pit a few feet in front of the entrance. Multitudes of the beautiful white flowers cover the hut's sides and the sloping hill behind. We enter quietly and encounter a man of great years, with an air of great wisdom. He wears a simple hide loincloth and traditional American Indian beads and feathers. His skin is the same dark tone as Jade's, but I cannot yet see his eyes. He sits silently in a lotus position, deep in meditation. He senses our presence and slowly acknowledges us. As with the rest of his mysterious clan, his eyes have the same bronze-amber glaze. But they are not focused on Jade and I. Instead, they seem to be reaching across the universe and far beyond. His facial features are humble and wise, but there is a stern tone in his very essence, as if he holds the secrets of all those near him ... including me.

"This is Pomare. He is the senior elder and the oldest on the island. He is also a shaman," Jade explains.

His eyes meet Jade's for a brief moment. I sense a strong bond between Jade and the mysterious shaman, something I feel but cannot explain.

"How old is he?" I cautiously ask.

Before Jade can answer, the aged shaman speaks. He joins the dialogue in a language I do not recognize. Jade is now translator ... and I am confused, and secretly fascinated. Jade's strange world seems to slowly be opening itself to me ... this is going to be interesting.

"He says it is not polite for a man to brag of his years," Jade explains. "He says on the island, age is revered. He does nothing for himself except eat, sleep, and meditate. The villagers take care of the rest of his needs."

He definitely wouldn't dig L.A. I'm thinking, but something is telling me to keep my smart mouth shut; this isn't the time or place ... whatever this place is. He continues as Jade follows.

"He says you have many secrets. They trouble you. Though you acknowledge their existence, you cannot grasp their significance."

"He's good. Does he take insurance," I tease, knowing full well I may have opened up the wrong door ... oh well.

"He says your sarcasm is real, but not as real or as strong as your fear, the fear you run from so desperately yet hold so close."

"I wish I knew what it is that I'm afraid of."

"Those answers will come," she translated. "They will come sooner than you think."

Jade's mediation places vagueness on the shaman's advice. I have no assurance that her translations of his words are literal. I have yet to discover her agenda ... if there is one. I have not forgotten how she casually walked into my camp, or how she led me here. Still, this interaction is interesting, though I am not getting any solid answers. The dialogue is intriguing.

"Your shaman says my answers will come sooner than I think. Is this a premonition?"

"No, Nathan, a reality."

"Reality is one thing I do not trust."

"He says this is because your future has been altered by a powerful event. Like a winding river, your course has been changed. It no longer flows to the sea. Instead, it wanders in limbo."

"And how do I get back to the sea?"

"You must first find your path. The moon will be your guide, but Pomare cautions ... the moon lies."

"Anything else I need to know?"

"He says you must spend the day's light with me and learn. Then return at day's end for the *Ritual of the Moon.* Then, and only then, will the answers you seek shower your soul like warm evening rain."

"Nothing like a nice warm shower at the end of the day," I quip, noticing that the great wise one, still in his lotus position, has lit up a long pipe of something exotic and pungent. As he exhales the first hit of his mystery weed, he slowly turns away from the two of us.

"We will leave now," Jade says.

Exiting the shaman's hut I am once again struck by the beauty of the village and its surroundings. But I am silently troubled by the elder's words. I have been plagued by an odd feeling of uncertainty and doubt ever since arriving here. Jade is certainly a mystery, as is the village. But who is he, and how does he know my innermost thoughts and feelings so well? And how did Jade know my name? Who is Jade, and who are these people? Where did they come from?

Even out here on this island in the middle of God knows where, they seem foreign, real foreign ... out of this world foreign! And what is the Ritual of the Moon? I hope it's not some blood-sucking, mescaline-soaked, dance-naked, get-hairy, howl-at-the-midnight-sun kind of deal ... though I wouldn't mind seeing Jade naked. You can forget the rest ... my college days are long over. But what are their plans for me?

"Are you all right, Nathan?" Jade asks, once again sultry and warm. "You're awfully quiet."

"I guess I'm not used to having my mind read and my fortune told all at one sitting," I reply, hoping Jade will sense my frustration and just tell me a bit of truth.

"Pomare's wise, but he does tend to exaggerate."

"Maybe that warm evening rain will do me some good."

"Did I mention he's quite poetic too?" she lightly adds, not giving one inch of satisfaction.

"You speak good English, Jade, a little too good. What about Pomare?"

"He speaks many languages, including English, but he chooses to communicate and live life according to the old ways."

"What are the old ways?"

"They are the ways of our forefathers, the first people that came to this island."

"And when was that."

"I don't know."

"There must be records of your people, where they originally came from … how long they have been here."

"That is kept with the shamans. It has never been written. It is passed down by the senior elders."

"Pray they all don't get wiped out by a hurricane."

"It's the way it has always been."

"So how old is Pomare?"

"Nobody knows. But legend has it he was one of the original people to inhabit the island."

"That would make him how many hundreds of years old?"

"Good genes, I guess."

"So how old are you, Jade, if you don't mind my asking?"

"I don't mind you asking, Nathan, but does it really matter?"

"I guess not. As long as you don't turn into a 400-year-old, blood-sucking, dust-farting vampire, I'm cool."

"I can assure you I won't do that, Nathan."

"Good, 'cuz I don't see any garlic growing around here."

"It's not vampires you have to worry about," Jade replies cryptically, once again going into stealth mode.

"What do you mean by that?" I ask inquisitively.

Walking a little ahead, she simply says, "Forget about it. Come on, I've got something to show you."

"Can't wait to see what's next," I reply cynically.

Jade leads the way as we walk through the village to our as-yet-unknown destination. I'm beginning to notice small details about the village and its people that I didn't catch my first time through. Unlike Jade, most of the villagers move very slowly. Though they aren't necessarily looking down, they seem to make a concerted effort not to look directly into the sun. Instead, they look away, or fix their gaze on close or inanimate objects. This gives their body language an eerie quality, and what I originally mistook for lack of interest now seems to be something else altogether.

They stay close to structures and at times duck into them quickly, without provocation, only to emerge moments later to return to their previous tasks.

There is little if any interaction and communication among them. Their eyes seem to do most of the talking. These people seem like zombies, though their frozen ballet is captivating and hypnotic. Their mysterious ways are puzzling. I hear the voices of children but I cannot see them. They are not the voices of children at play, but more like schoolyard Gregorian chant, or romper-room mantra.

There is a strange blend of architectural styles and building materials used on the various structures in and around the village, suggesting that at one or more times they had been visited. But where are those visitors now? Did they just come and go? Did something else happen to them ... something sinister?

We exit the village and enter what appears to be jungle. Jade slows down and comes back to stand with me.

"So where are you taking me?" I ask, desperately hoping that this time I'll get an answer that makes some kind of sense.

"We are going to the Temple of Dreams," she replies with childlike giddiness in her voice, as if she was taking me to her own secret place.

"Temple of Dreams?"

"It is where I have discovered the worlds beyond this island. It's a place that takes me away, far away, to places I'd like to ..." For a brief moment Jade stops in her tracks. Her tone changes from excited expectation to haunting sadness. "It takes me away to places I will never get a chance to visit in reality."

"Who knows, Jade? Maybe someday we'll all be found."

"You don't understand, Nathan," she quietly says. "We can never leave this island."

"You make it sound like we're all prisoners here."

"In a way, we are."

"Why, Jade? Why can't we leave?"

"I'm sorry, Nathan. I've said too much, we'll talk later. Come on, we're almost there."

At this point, I am more curious about the Temple of Dreams than I am about Jade's continuous monologue of mystery and unanswered questions. As we break out of the jungle and into a small clearing, I know exactly what it feels like to be Indiana Jones. Before me stands a large, ancient structure, very recognizable from my early school days.

"That's a freaking Mayan temple," I exclaim excitedly. My choice of words was not worthy of my astonishment.

"That's what you call it," Jade coyly remarks. "This one is quite different."

"How ... oh, forget it I'll find out later, right?"

"Let's go," Jade says, disregarding my frustrated attempt at humor.

She approaches the building and pulls out two oddly shaped stones from the base of the structure. "Follow me and be very quiet," she says, as if we are being watched.

Going to the opposite side of the building, Jade places the two stones into carved notches that have seven mysterious symbols chiseled around them. As she slowly removes the pieces, the sound of grinding stone fills the air. A small entrance appears.

"This is sacred ground," Jade says reverently. "Entrance into this temple is reserved for shamans and senior elders only. No one else may enter."

"So how did you get the keys?"

"I followed Pomare one day. I watched how he got in. I think he knows that I come here."

"What's inside?"

"You'll find out," she says, leading the way. "Watch your head. It's kind of dark; I'll light some candles when we get in."

After walking through a dark, narrow hallway, my senses tell me that we have entered a large chamber. The lack of adequate light heightens my non-visual senses. I am overwhelmed by the dank, musty smell of antiquity.

"Okay, Nathan. Just stay where you are," Jade commands. She slowly begins to light strategically placed candles around the large room. From the shadows, I begin to see the cascading walls and vaulted ceilings of the stone shrine we have just entered.

Once again Jade finds two stones and places them carefully into slots. As the now-familiar sound of grinding stone echoes, a remarkable transformation occurs. The ceiling begins to open up. The chamber fills with light. For the first time I can see why Jade called this her Temple of Dreams.

Books ... hundreds of them, thousands of them, everywhere, it is an impressive and daunting sight. This jungle temple is perhaps the most incredible library I have ever seen. I am beginning to wonder where I truly am, and if any of this is real. There is a moment of silence as I study my new surroundings ... and Jade studies me. Perhaps she is proud. Like taking your buddies to your garage and showing them the hot rod you worked on all winter. Or maybe she was just looking for appreciation ... appreciation that she had shared something so deep and secret to her that I got the only invitation.

Jade does not break the silence. She must want those first words to come from me, to hear the swelling of true wonder and emotion that only unexpected discovery can conjure up, for she has created this moment. Judging by the lack of life in her village, this opportunity doesn't arise often.

"This is amazing, Jade, where did you get all these books? Where did they come from?"

"Mainly from sailors and lost explorers, they'd trade them for food and supplies. We'd give them fresh water and fruit, and guide the lost ones to safety. The ancient volumes were brought here by our forefathers."

"So you do know where we are?"

"The elders do, but they keep that to themselves."

One more secret the old guys aren't willing to share. Oh well. At this point it really doesn't matter. I am in historical and intellectual heaven. Jade might magically know my name, pulling it out of the hat like a bad Vegas card trick, but she does not know me from

Adam. Come to think of it, I don't know *myself* from Adam. But one thing I still know for sure: I love reading ... and I love books. This was also my Temple of Dreams. As a child I had embraced books and wrapped myself within their wondrous pages, never wanting to leave my cocoon of leather and text. They were my salvation, the vehicle of all my hopes and fantasies. They were my education. They were my friends, and one of my strongest memories of growing up.

Looking closer at the books, I make a startling discovery for myself. "Most of these appear to be first editions, Jade!" She already knows.

It is time to dig in. "Let's see, what have we here? Ooh, this is a good one. *Frankenstein,* 1818, by Anonymous, hmm, Oh yes, *Frankenstein,* 1831, Shelley. My mistake, you *do* have some second editions."

Jade doesn't respond. I continue.

"Moby-Dick, 1851, by Melville, Condon, 1959, *Manchurian Candidate,* I liked the movie better. *The Adventures of Tom Sawyer,* 1876, published by Chatto and Windus, England ... England, now *that* I did not know. *The Romance of the Forest,* 1791, Anonymous ... don't tell anyone, but it was Ann Radcliffe. Virgil's *Aeneid,* first century BC, now there's an oldie but a goodie ... and of course, who can forget, everybody's favorite, *Mein Kampf,* Adolf Hitler, *volksausgabe* edition, blue cover, 1926. Do you realize how much these books are worth, Jade?"

"Value, Nathan, is not like beauty. It is not always in the eye of the beholder, but rather in the heart of the one that truly desires. One who desires knowledge and the beauty of antiquity does not sell it, but instead holds it close and protects it. It can be shared but must never be let go."

"Those are beautiful words."

"They are my father's. He taught me that learning as much as possible in one's lifetime is the reason why we are here. And that the sharing of knowledge is divine. He taught me language and how to read when I was a child. When I found this place, it all made sense."

"Your mother, where is she?"

"She died when I was young ... very young."

"I'm sorry," I reply, realizing that the conversation is now turning away from books and island history ... and is getting real personal.

"It's all right; I never knew her. It doesn't hurt. We don't feel loss for what we never really had. What about you, Nathan?" Jade asks in a curious and nurturing tone. "Is there a special woman in your life?"

"Do you believe in ghosts?"

"What kind of ghosts?"

"How about the kind that leaves their taste on your lips and their scent in the room even though they were never really there to begin with?"

"Who is she?"

"Someone I once knew, someone I loved very much .... and every time I experience her, I can swear it's real, like she's kissed me, made love to me, called out my name ... but I just can't hold on to her. She comes and goes, a recurring dream that I just can't seem to remember."

"Ghosts are like people, Nathan. If you want to find them, you must go to where they are. If you desire a flower growing high in a tree, you must climb that tree to possess it."

"You mean I have to dream to find her?"

"If that is where she hides, that is where you must go ... if that is where she really is."

"You mean she might be somewhere else?"

"She's *your* ghost, Nathan."

Jade's reaction is puzzling. It's almost like she knows something and is trying to lead me to the answer, or she knows I know and am just not aware of it. We continue talking about whatever comes to mind, eventually hitting the innocuous plateau of talking about absolutely nothing of relevance. We become tired after a long while.

Jade is slowly falling asleep. It is late afternoon, and already it has been a very long day. Putting my arm around her, I can feel the temptation of late-afternoon slumber overtake me ... as Jade snuggles close, my confusion turns to compassion.

Maybe she's waiting for the right time to raise her veil of secrecy. After all, timing is everything. Perhaps she feels that too much too soon will drive me away. Since we reached the village, she has shown no fear of me. Is this *trust*? Maybe she actually wants me to stay. That would be nice. *But would her people accept me as one of their own?*

Or would I linger in the shadows of prejudice, precariously dangling on an anxious thread of desperate love and lost hope? I can feel her heartbeat and smell the exotic perfume of the mysterious white flower in her hair. The strangeness of the village and the ancient shaman's words take a back seat to the present moment. Could I be falling in love? No, that's impossible, something always holds me back. That's not how I roll. But nothing on this island is what it appears to be anyway. So why should I be any different? *I don't even know how long I have been here. Do I really know who I am anymore?*

THE DREAM

Jade's kiss is tender, her skin is sweet. She accepts me ... all of me. We are one. The books are on fire. History is slowly dissolving, as if it never existed. The only proof left is the smoldering ashes gasping their last breath of life. Time now stands still as the ashes are scattered off the bridge of yesterday ...

THE YEAR IS ZERO
THE MONTH IS ZERO
THE DAY IS ZERO
THE TIME ...
IS ZERO

History restarts in the Temple of Dreams. The past is dead and the world is new again. *No more pain, no more death ... no more war.* No racism or hate, no religion or greed, no landlords of shame ... no aliens or monsters. Jade and I walk naked in the

Garden of Eden, free from the snakes of temptation and the apples of fate ... paradise found. Beautiful white flowers dance gracefully to mysterious breezes that whisper our names and caress our bodies with ethereal sensuality and touch, warming our souls as we laugh carelessly at nothing, and kiss with passion and erotic fire that burns to the very core.

But the skies are growing dark and the garden turns cold. The sun hides behind ominous clouds of warning. The ashes of time have deceived us, and the selfish moon, lying in wait, hoping to steal the night, has lied once again. What lies beyond the darkness stirs restlessly, awaiting inevitable release.

Fear brings trepidation and uncertainty ... releasing our innermost demons. Every dream can become a nightmare, and every nightmare can be a frightening reality. I can hear them. At first, they growl in a frenzied state. They are not animal, they are not human ... but they are real. The garden is gone, and the mysterious predators are upon us. Jade and I are not alone. They are coming ... coming for us. This world of dark uncertainty is now turning backward. There is no gravity, and the clouds cry blood.

THEY ARE HERE!

GHOSTS
IN THE DARK
EYES
EVERYWHERE
SOUND
IN THE SHADOWS
PANIC
IN THE AIR
BREATH
ON MY BACK
BLOOD
ON THE FLOOR
TEETH
IN THE BONE

DEATH
AT THE DOOR …

NATHAN!
NATHAN!
WAKE UP!
WAKE UP!
NATHAN, PLEASE!
WAKE UP, NATHAN!!!
…WHAT?!

"Wake up, Nathan. It's getting dark … we've got to go, we've got to go now!"

Jade seems panicked and frightened. My sleeping angel's eyes are now wide with concern and terror. This is a new Jade, a Jade I have not yet experienced, a terrified child confronting her strongest fear. A strange wind rises and howls through the shadowy temple. It feels warm and smells of blood.

"Follow me, Nathan, now!" Jade yells. As we exit through the dark hallway, mysterious sounds emanate from the surrounding jungle. Leaves crunch and twigs snap as someone or something runs wildly through them … sounds of animal bloodlust such as I have never heard before echo savagely from the dense foliage. The creatures' growl and snarl like hungry beasts out for a kill. We are at the mercy of whatever surrounds us as dusk unmercifully consumes the comfort and safety of daylight. We are in the grip of a terrifying nightmare, awake and exposed.

"Follow me and don't look back!" Jade warns. Once again, I am chasing Dorothy. But it is not me she runs from. Is she running from fear, or from relentless pursuers of which only she has intimate knowledge of?

"What happens if I stop?" I breathlessly ask.

"You will die!" Jade answers without hesitation.

I'M AT MY LIMIT
I'M AT THE END
I'VE GOT NO MORE
I AM GOING TO DIE …

I AM GOING TO DIE

And still I run!

The howling wind consumes me. I can feel their hot breath searing my back, their sharp teeth tearing my flesh. This is how it ends. I will never live to solve the great mystery surrounding my tropical island exile. I will never live to climb the tree, pick my flower ... or find my ghost.

Still I run ...

THEY'VE STOPPED!

As quickly as it started, the terror is over. We are out of the jungle and apparently out of danger, at least for the moment. The air is quiet, the trees still, and the mood heavy and uncertain. I am in a strange vortex of relief and contradiction, where absolute fear and disturbing reality have found a common ground and the universe itself seems up for grabs!

"Are you all right?" Jade asks.

"I'll let you know when I catch up to myself," I reply cautiously, thankful to be in one piece.

"Don't worry, they won't leave the jungle. They can't."

"Are they prisoners too?" I ask, fully expecting another mystery answer.

"Something like that. Let's get back ... it's getting dark."

Jade won't explain what just happened. But I guess we are safe for now. I am in a state of mental and physical confusion; hot, disoriented, and scared to death! As we head back to the village, she calmly tells me about the Ritual of the Moon. It seems quite simple, even a little primitive. Where some cultures worshipped the sun, the villagers here have chosen to worship the moon. I don't quite fully understand everything she says, but she implies that the villagers are connected to their "midnight sun" in some physiological way. The evening is when they eat and socialize. It's a fascinating premise, though a little reminiscent of the Dark Ages.

It could explain one or two things though. The bronze-amber eyes they all have, iridescent like nocturnal animals, seem to have a *soul* of their own. Add to that the fact that the villagers didn't spend much time out in the daylight, or wander too far from their huts. Still, it does not explain their dark, evenly tanned skin ... but what else is new?

Approaching the village, I smell food and hear the voices of many more people than I had encountered when I first arrived. Their communication is much livelier than what I had witnessed earlier in the day. Young villagers bring us trays of beautiful, fresh fruits and cooked meats. I am given a silver cup containing perhaps the most delicious beverage I have ever had in my life. Jade explains that it is a traditional elixir made from the turbine flower. I ask her for the recipe. She nervously laughs.

As the curtain of night drops, slowly swallowing the backlight of day, the vibe gets heavy again. Perhaps I am not used to so much good food, or the subtle trancelike effects of the delicious turbine flower elixirs ... but I am definitely feeling something. There seems to be a subtle transformation within the mysterious clan themselves. Now only torches, raging campfires, and shades of moon glow provide light for the village and its people as they steadily grow more active. I hear the sound of drums, and intermittent high-pitched noises I have never heard before.

I'm beginning to feel an unfamiliar rush, almost as if there were two of me inhabiting the same body, one trying to reach in to find the answers to so many mysterious and unanswered questions, and one desperately trying to break out of its physical and spiritual prison. My head feels hot and my eyes even hotter as the nearly full moon burns liquid pathways into my brain ... something is definitely happening ...

SOMETHING IS CHANGING

What is this? Who are these people? They are not human. They have wings, claws, fangs, and eyes as red as a bordello nightlight. The trance-induced momentum now suspends them above ground for long periods of time; some of them are even flying.

Their shadowy forms dance upon the night sky with precision and elegance. Jade approaches, her face and body are different. But I can still tell she is a woman, though now only half-human. She is followed by the shaman elder ... now complete in his own physical transformation.

Jade is looking at me, though her eyes are not the same. I realize that she is not like the rest ... but she is powerless to act on her own free will, for she herself is a prisoner.

"I'm sorry, Nathan," Jade says sadly, ***"But this is the way it has to be ... the way it has always been.*** In a few moments I will not be able to speak to you. Please believe me, Nathan, you are in my heart. You always will be. You have given me something that I will never be able to give back to you. I'm sorry ... I truly am."

"I don't understand. What is happening? Am I hallucinating?"

"No, Nathan," she replies quietly. "You are not hallucinating. You're seeing the real truth for the very first time ... we owe you that much."

"Owe me?"

Jade turns and addresses Pomare, who is standing by her side. "I think you should tell him, father." Sadness caresses her gentle voice.

"As you may have already guessed, we are different, Mr. Cole," he somberly intones, speaking in perfect English. *"We are not from this island.* As a matter of fact, we are not indigenous to this earth, even though we have been here for centuries. What you see before you is the result of advanced DNA manipulation that, for a time, made it possible for us to acclimate and survive on this planet.

"Thousands of years ago, there were many more of us. We left our home to escape prejudice and persecution, only to find it rampant and thriving here. It was then that we realized we had traded one bad apple for another, and that we would never be fully accepted into human culture. We had been cast out, only to once again become outcasts. We decided to colonize this planet and make it our own. We infiltrated culture and tradition. We blurred the line between your history and ours. At times we faced anarchy and power struggles within our own ranks. Ideological differences and mismanagement caused divisions and rifts, especially between the leaders. We began to splinter off, sometimes losing sight of our own goals. Though at times we were seriously off track from our original plans, we held on and somehow managed to work together. Progress was at times slow, and very unpredictable.

"We made a mistake with the so-called *'Black Plague,'* but that was just an experiment. Many of the great civilizations you claim as lost were not … they were taken. Some of your own mythology and religious icons are based on our earthbound forefathers. Over the centuries, we have lived in many forms. Constantly evolving, becoming more and more human and growing stronger by virtue of our own science and genetics. Many of your most notorious leaders, mass murders, spiritual revolutionaries, and even scientists have been members of our race. The ruthless nature of humanity made it easy for us to fit in. As mankind became more sophisticated, no longer muddling in the murky depths of ignorance and superstition, our need for absolute anonymity was threatened. We protected it only with great effort.

"As our physiology evolved, our ways did too. Our basic adaptation to human culture and environment was in itself genius. The model for this bold mode of planetary gene-hopping came from years of research and pioneering scientists who had themselves been on furlough to alien planets. This was by no means an exact science. We morphed our DNA with that of humans to survive. We never show our true forms to anyone outside our own genetic circle.

"We would eventually use the turbine flower, beautiful yet toxic to humans, to complete our clandestine takeover. Though we faltered along the way, we prevailed. But perseverance and science were not enough to balance the genetic manipulation that eventually turned on us, leaving us vulnerable to human disease. Once the bloodline of our genetic engineers died off we slowly reverted back to our original form, standing here before you. To escape humanity's wrath, we fled to the most secret corners of Earth, far away from human contamination and plague. But the damage had already been done. Our genetic codes had been compromised and we began to die off in great numbers. We believe that we are the last colony left, and that the turbine flower, which itself is a transplant from our home planet, is keeping us alive. We will never see it blossom to fulfill our dreams of colonization ... for we learned too late that the only place on the planet where the flowers will actually grow and flourish is on this island. And for those unfortunate enough to find us, Mr. Cole, this island becomes their final destination. You, like them, are a threat to our very existence ... *that is why you must die.*"

His words cut through me like a razor through paper. If this is true, if this is no hallucination, no mescaline-fueled weekend with the boys in the Arizona desert, it's quite ironic. These beautiful flowers, that so sensuously adorned Jade's hair and brought beauty and warmth to this exotic village, will be the implement of my final demise. But the shaman's next words are even more puzzling. It's understandable that the elders would know great secrets about their own history and culture, but he seems to reach directly into my own mind, exposing my greatest fears and confusions, as if he were the one that put them there in the first place.

"This island is a museum, Mr. Cole. The realities you have experienced here are in themselves their own realities. It is not up to you to extrapolate their true meaning, only to understand that your destiny is no longer yours ... you threw that away a long time ago."

Jade is slowly fading away into the fog she originally emerged from. The shaman's voice grows cold and very distant. I feel sleepy and light as if my body were being released from the trappings of its own mortal bonds. Am I dying, or am I just reemerging from another spell of island fever? I can still feel the rain forest, though everything around me is dark and unfamiliar. Am I still chasing Dorothy? Or did I miss the Emerald City only to land in the purgatory of my own past? I can see a light, yes a light ... warm, bright, and yellow. I will run

to it. ***I will break the mystery of the dark and follow the truth that surely*** **this** ***light will reveal …***

AND STILL I RUN

Reflections
"Far Away"

Here you come
A midnight ghost again
Whisper softly
Shake your chains
Make your call
Pale white host again
Here we go, far away

What'd you say?
Well, it's so quiet here
Can a kiss
Save a life?
We can't wait
We just might die right here
Take my hand
Close your eyes
As they see
And sing of nothing else
Crystal tears
Violet smiles
Far away
I feel such comfort here
Almost free
Hold on tight

Alone, in the silence … of the night
I burn, as a fire … with no light
I wander, through the shadows … of your heart
And sleep, in the silence … of the dark

Girl, you call, and madness takes a bow
Like an actor, on a stage
One last kiss, and we'll be on our way
Holding hands, through the rain
Far away

The Proper Order of Rage

Book Two

"Here you come, a midnight ghost again ..."

Comfortably nestled within the warm, familiar blankets of one's own personal experience lay the memories of youth and passion. And though these memories remain strong, their clarity and detail can sometimes become cloudy and distant ... in the churning vortex of time and age.

A RAINY AFTERNOON ... SUMMER 1995

That much I was sure of. Month, week, day, forget about it. That information went down with the ship. On this particular rainy afternoon, I was doing one of my favorite things in the whole wide world: cruising Thrift Store Alley. Thrift Store Alley was a little side street off Main in Redwood City, California. Not only was it chock full of antique stores and second-hand treasure troves, but it was also home to a very colorful, almost dangerous cast of street characters. It wasn't a rogue's gallery of prostitutes, drug dealers, or addicts. No, it was more of a quiet ballet of the homeless and lost. Some worked their surroundings with precision and finesse, like they were meant to be there and always had been. They ruled the streets with arrogance rivaling that of Wall Street moguls and heads of state. Masters of negotiation and survival, they cut through their impoverished existence like a surgeon's blade through warm butter. And then there were the "shufflers," men and women who wore their tattered existence and shattered souls like a mink coat on the beach, slowly picking through the dumpsters of hope. No matter where you looked or how fast you walked, the obvious desperation of their situation was indelibly etched in your mind ... at least for that moment. And if your eyes made contact with theirs, you were immediately rewarded. That reward was remembering that you had people at home that loved you, and that your only problematic negotiation of the afternoon was Burger King or McDonald's, Whopper or Big Mac, chocolate shake or vanilla ... large fries or small.

I had a strange fascination with these people. This discarded group of dirty and homeless humanity still ate, slept, bled, and dreamt like the rest of us. But what did they dream about? Did they dream just like we did? We dream about being millionaires, rock stars, super models, and superheroes. We dream about a bigger house, bigger car, and even bigger bank accounts. We dream about more than what we have. And no matter what we end up with, we always dream for more. Did these people dream like we did? Or were their dreams hopelessly mired in the harbor of loss and despair? Perhaps the ugly truth was that in a world of skyscrapers and diamonds, they were the discarded leaves from the tree of humanity, forever blown around on the dirty streets of life until they crumbled into nothingness. We didn't care about their dreams. How could we? We didn't care about *them*.

But I knew they dreamt, and I cared. I longed to look into their secret world and for just one moment, stand in their shoes, wear their clothes, and touch their souls through the eyes of their mysterious slumber. One day, mankind will awaken from the drunken stupor of his self-obsession and discover the thin, almost microscopic, spiritual line between the haves and have-nots. Until then, we will never truly be a brotherhood of man. Until then, we can only dream what it's like to be on the other side. Balance will never be achieved as long as so many spend their days hungry and their nights cold.

On this rainy, deep-in-thought afternoon, I was on two specific missions. The first: I would spend ten dollars on sweaters and coats, and like a Robin Hood of the Nineties, distribute them among the poor and destitute souls of Thrift Store Alley ... my colorful sanctuary for God's lost sheep.

THAT WAS MY HUMANITARIAN MISSION

My selfish mission, mission number two, was to feed the dragon. To give in to the addiction I had so fondly come to know and love as being a vinyl junkie, scientific name, *Old Record Whore.* Everyone, including myself, owned at least one CD player at that time. But CD players lacked soul, and I was a soul man. There was something warm and reassuring about the spin of an old platter. Yeah, you didn't pick up the sound of squeaking chairs or joints being lit, but you got something out of it. There was something magically cool about reaching for that bulky cardboard sleeve with the torn plastic wrapper. Something sexy about picking the record out of its protective safe haven, exposing it to all of the world, and slowly introducing it to the welcoming clutch of a long, skinny spindle. With all that came a subtle anticipation and secret pleasure in picking out *"your song,"* carefully placing the needle in the right groove, making sure not to scratch or harm your rotating friend.

YEOWWWW!
(Feels good, don't it?)

Since the early days of CDs, people had been chucking away their old vinyl friends like rice at a Catholic wedding ... and I loved 'em for it!

Dear God,

Thank you for the gifts I am about to receive at Thrift Village.

Amen,
Nathan

Thrift Village was a big store, with a big used record section. I could spend the whole day in there, gratuitously suspended in people's discarded history and chipped furniture. It was my home away from home. Game on!

I WAS IN A BEATLES MOOD

Maybe I had dreamt about them the night before, I don't remember. But I was definitely searching for the Fab Four. From my secure perch in vinyl heaven, I was, for a scant moment, distracted by someone or something outside the Village's large front window, a sunlit corridor projecting movies from the street of lost and found dreams. But the urgency of my quest quickly returned. Minutes passed but who noticed? I was higher than a kite, flying intensely after the euphoria of the possible discovery of Atlantis, or maybe just a frayed, scratched first pressing of *Meet The Beatles.* Either way, they were both worth the hunt and I was the hunter slash intrepid explorer fearlessly seeking out my treasured and elusive booty!

AND THEN IT HAPPENED

When lightening strikes, it doesn't call first. It strikes with stealth, precision, and no remorse. If it doesn't kill, it scars and changes lives. The general perception of lightning is that it comes from the sky in the form of electricity. But the true nature of lightning is much different. It comes in many forms. And on this rainy afternoon of humanitarian gestures and vinyl madness, lightning came to me in its most potent and seductive form ... woman.

In between joy and pain lay the netherworld of contentment. In vinyl heaven, I was content, happy to be muddling through the massive bins of cardboard and torn plastic. But when a warm, gentle hand touched my shoulder and I turned to stare into the gypsy-blue eyes and sunshine smile of Athena, contentment became instant history. Joy was my new destination.

Suddenly, my senses were overwhelmed by the numbing electricity of the classic female element. I felt a strange, narcotic wisp of a warm and familiar presence. My senses caught the unmistakable scent of a woman long lost in the dark hallways of memory and time.

"Hi," Athena said. Her was voice soft and vulnerable, a little unsure but generously filled with recognition and sincerity.

"Hi," I replied. My heart and soul melting like a chocolate bar on a radiator. I too was now vulnerable, yet safe in the familiarity of Athena's angelic presence.

"Is there a word for moments like this?" she embarrassedly asked.

For a second, my mind went blank, coherent thoughts suddenly becoming the enemy. Then lightning struck once more.

"Pizza!" I exclaimed, congratulating myself for my fast recovery and quick wit. We both nervously laughed. Order in the universe was restored. She *knew* I loved pizza.

Athena hugged me for what felt like an eternity. She kissed me once to test the water. She deemed it safe to swim and dove back in, straight into my soul, back through the gaping hole she herself had put there years ago. Time froze as I closed the gate behind her, making Athena my spiritual prisoner. My dark, hollow existence filled with light and warmth once again. This was where we were supposed to be, where we should have been the whole time, where we would now stay forever.

"I missed you so much," she said.

"Missed you too," I replied, warming up to the comfortable sanctuary of our shared history.

"Where have you been?' I asked.

"Around," Athena said. Her gypsy-blue eyes and soft touch keeping the universe at her beckon call. It wasn't fair, but I bought this ticket years ago. And as I would soon discover ... the ride was not over yet.

"I've been keeping tabs on you," Athena said playfully.

"Ah, you found out I won the lottery," I countered, not quite knowing the full range of her statement but still trying to be funny.

"I'll bet you don't have ten bucks in your wallet, mister" she laughingly stated.

"Whatcha wanna bet?" I asked softly.

Athena's warm hands caressed my neck and cheeks, her soft lips and breath danced upon my ears, and the words she spoke at that very moment were the only words that I could hear or comprehend.

"My body," She whispered without hesitation.

The train had now left the station, and I understood the great advantage of knowing your opponent intimately.

I reached for my wallet, but Athena intercepted me. She gingerly slipped a hand into my back pocket, her eyes never leaving mine, her playful smile letting me know in advance that mischief was afoot. She took her time, slowly opening up the billfold and reaching in to feel up a few of my favorite dead presidents. Her gaze soulfully connected with mine as she slowly felt the paper without counting. She closed the wallet up and slid it casually down the front of her jeans.

"Wanna count my change, too?" I suggestively asked.

Her electric blue eyes slid down to my front pockets and back up to my own eyes. She looked around and spotted a pair of men's boxer shorts on a rack nearby.

Seductively retrieving them, she quietly said, "I was gonna try these on. Tell me if they fit?" Slapping the shorts over her right shoulder, she shot me the ultimate come-hither look. She proceeded toward the dressing rooms and entered a stall, closing the door slowly, never looking back. A small, feminine hand reappeared from behind the door and a delicate finger beckoned me to join her …

LIKE I SAID ... LIGHTNING STRIKES!

Athena's playful invitation for a romp in a public place both confused and excited me. It wasn't exactly her style. Athena was pure silk and roses. Perhaps she was unsure of my feelings for her and wanted to seal the deal quickly. Maybe she'd changed. Maybe she'd discovered sex could be a potent negotiating device when words failed. I sure hoped not. She was the girl next door. She was apple pie, drive-in movies, and long walks on the beach. She was my soul.

I'd like to say that I could remember every sweet detail of our brief reunion at Thrift Village that day, but the truth is I can't. But the power and the passion were still there. We found each other once again.

When it came to making love, Athena was in charge. It was a ritual, an experience to be thoroughly enjoyed but never taken lightly. We shared a physical and spiritual bond. We were solar twins illuminating the darkest corners of our sensuality. As the rain danced slowly on the fabricated steel roof of our commandeered bridal suite, I realized every sense of my body and soul had been awakened ... or reawakened. The communion was on. Athena's movements and body heat became mine, our heartbeats and breathing becoming one common rhythm ... our perspiration, a sea of divine sharing. With eyes closed, we saw and felt each clearer than we ever had before.

Once again ... we reached into our souls and staked claim to each other.

Maybe I wasn't meant to remember every detail of that blissful encounter. Maybe if I could remember the exact level of pleasure I experienced during those brief moments, I would be fated to seek that ecstasy for the rest of my life, forever chasing. It doesn't really matter, I was there ... and that I'll never forget.

When it was over, my elevated sense of manhood returned to its mortal state, the energy was drained from my body ... but I knew I was home. Home in the warm, protective world of Athena's gypsy-blue eyes, which guided me safely to port after too many years lost in a tumultuous sea of loneliness and confusion.

The rest of that day was emotional and full of nostalgia. A symphony of raindrops serenaded our afternoon of passion and remembrance. Every time we talked of the past or shared a sweet kiss, the doors to the future slowly opened wider and wider, like a restless siren tempting us to crash onto the rocks of our long, forbidden past.

I never found my Beatles album, but I did discover that the one great love of my life still loved me. This time, I would never let that love slip away ... for any reason.

The next week was a whirlwind dance of uncertainty and romance. The more we made love and talked, the closer we got. We both still felt an acute need to read each other's minds and feelings. Constant reassurance on all levels smoothed the waters of our emotional chaos. And though many questions remained, nothing could block the path of our historic passion. It seemed the train of fate was on a one way trip to the future ... *via our own collective past.*

THE M–WORD

Marriage to me was like an unknown alien spore. The very thought of it was exotic and dangerous, worthy of maintaining a safe distance. It's not that I didn't trust the institution of marriage; it was the long-term contract that had me a little scared. I had always been conflicted between being the consummate dreamer and the pragmatic pessimist. But with Athena, it was different. The thought of playing house with her for the rest of my life was warm and welcoming ... morning coffee, evening wine, and a white picket fence felt all right.

Everything about Athena worked, and worked well. Like a fine Swiss watch, but not quite a Rolex—too high-maintenance. She was elegant sophistication dressed in blue jeans and tennis shoes ... and occasionally, cowboy boots and a white hat. She could charm heads of state or swear like a truck driver. Her smile, delicately radiant, made the world hers with ease … her calling card … *electric blue eyes that could light the darkest of souls.* Her sandy blonde hair and slender body completed the earthbound goddess with calculated perfection. But it was her walk, and Athena's very essence that words could only struggle to describe.

For how can you describe something so angelic, so sensuous and beautiful that it could not possibly be of this radiant Earth? I stopped wrestling with that one years ago and gave myself over to appreciation, quietly feeding the vulnerability of my own desires. Those desires started years earlier.

I'd known Athena as far back as I could remember. Though she technically wasn't the girl next door, she was the girl on the next block. Athena was a mystery through grade school, and the unattainable, nubile cheerleader goddess in middle school. She seemed to have several incarnations through high school though, and just studying those variations made me keenly aware that I was obsessed with her.

Though I dated lots of other girls, I was fascinated with Athena. I had dreamt about her for years, dreams as sweet and vivid as one could ever imagine, but I never fell in love with her. Perhaps the jaded, untrusting state of mind I hold so close to this day sprang from a seed so innocently planted all those years ago. Even as a kid worshipping her from afar, she stuck a dagger of self-doubt through my very core. Though I revered her, I kept her at a safe distance. I held her close and shared our very first kiss every night in my dreams, but I hid from her like a scared vampire in the cruel reality of day. Through the years, we occasionally crossed paths, sharing classes and forgettable moments of small talk. But it wasn't until our junior year that she dropped the big one, the one I never saw coming … the one that would forever alter the course of our lives.

SHE INVITED ME TO THE SADIE HAWKINS DANCE!
(Whoo-hoo!)

Sometimes, if we're really, really lucky, life bestows upon us one of those magical moments that forever dance in the grand hall of our ordinary lives, moments that even the ongoing tsunami of life will never ever wash away. Moments that eternally shine, even after everything else has gone dark. Such a moment came in the fall of my junior year at San Mateo High School, specifically in the west end parking lot.

I was with my best friend, Carlo Roselli, and our buddy Artie. The conversation was simple, the question clear and precise: Hit the waves at San Gregorio, or walk a little farther north to the nude beach and pray for girls? The answer: neither. It was too cold and cloudy for surfing ... or naked girls. We needed a contingency plan, a coordinated effort to destroy the evil demons of post-lunch boredom. The day wouldn't stay boring for long.

"Incoming," Carlo said, his eyes beckoning Artie and I to turn around.

"Down boy," Artie said, patting me on the back like I was an eager puppy. "She's only a girl, man. You know, the opposite sex? She won't bite. But if she does, you thank her."

The immature ramblings of my two headbanger friends had recently become a pathetic constant in my life. Their teasing was an unfortunate byproduct of a sleepover at Artie's, my big mouth, and my unfamiliarity with something called beer-pong, a hundred times more powerful than truth serum, as I had discovered. They had cracked my secret emotional vault of *Athena*. And like crazed, hungry hyenas, they unmercifully picked the bones of my juvenile fantasies.

"And what makes you think she's gonna bite me?" I retorted, attempting desperately to maintain ice-cream cool in the midst of the mighty Sahara of post-pubescent Greek tragedy.

"Let's see," Carlo replied. "She's headed straight for us; she's staring at you like a homeless person outside a Wendy's dumpster, and yes, I believe the fangs are out!"

Artie couldn't stay out of the fun. "She wants your blood man, your *bloooood ... ahhhhhhh!*"

"Want some garlic, dude? It could save your life, you know," Carlo said, on a roll.

Funny thing was, Athena really did have fangs. A lot of people do ... cute little ones to say the least. Crazier than that, I thought they were really sexy, especially on a hot chick. Either way, fangs or no fangs, the meter was running and the moment of truth was about to pick me up and whisk me away to God knows where.

"Time for us to boogie on, boogeyman," Carlo said, with restrained psychopathic glee. "If she hurts ya, Artie's got a first aid kit in his car."

"Yeah, but all it's got in it is pot," Artie chimed.

"Exactly," was Carlo's last word as the two swam off into the sunset, leaving me exposed to incoming fire, alone without a sword to fight the four-headed, fire-breathing, bloodthirsty object of every obsessive thought and sexual fantasy I'd ever had since ... you know, ever since I started having them. I turned to face my destiny. My fate was in the hands of the gods; my dragon lay before me ... 5' 5", 110-pound ...

ATHENA

I prepared myself for impending doom. If the vampire siren wanted to drink my blood and steal my soul, she would have to fight for them. But as Athena got closer, my long-standing fear of contact with the sunshine goddess dissipated. And as she spoke her first words to me that afternoon, I found the ridiculous nature of my backward obsession dissipate. The dark dragon suddenly became an angel bathed in light. Her immediate presence put me at ease and warmed my tortured soul.

"Where are your friends going?" she nonchalantly asked. She made it abundantly clear that her feminine intuition had given the alert that we were all talking about her ... and that my "friends" had wisely decided to abandon ship before it hit the rocks.

"I think they're trying to find a bomb shelter with a wet bar," I replied, trying and failing for the second time that day to be witty.

"You're funny, Nate. You know, if you weren't so shy, you might make a good comedian. The world needs more laughter."

"I have my days," I calmly replied, feeling a miniscule amount of confidence returning. "I guess today I just got lucky."

"Well, you're about to get luckier," Athena replied, warmly smiling. "What are you doing Friday night?"

"Friday night?"

"Yes, Nathan. Friday night. You know, fifth night of the week? Unless your week starts on Sunday," she said.

"I uh ..."

"You're not afraid of me, are you, Nate?" she asked. Though the question was tough, she was anything but. Her gentle demeanor radiated like a thousand suns, and her electric gypsy-blue eyes shot lightning bolts through my soul. "Look, I know how you feel about me, Nathan. I've known for years. I'm not the enemy, Nate. I want to invite you to the dance Friday night."

"The dance?" I responded coyly, secretly agonizing that I had *not* been asked yet.

"The dance, Sadie Hawkins, you know? Girl asks boy? That way, things get done right!"

"Oh, that dance," I humbly acknowledged, knowing full well I was in the headlights and there was nowhere to run.

"Face it, Nathan. If I waited for you to ask me out, I'd be collecting social security by the time you did."

"Athena, I—"

"You've got your choice: a night of *Star Trek* reruns or a night with me. I know what you do when you're home alone."

"Hey, don't mess with Captain Kirk!"

"And don't mess with me, geekmaster. I've already bought the tickets. I'll pick you up at seven sharp. If you're not home, I will hunt you down and kill you."

"CIAO," SHE PLAYFULLY SAID
AND WITH THAT

MY NUBILE SUNSHINE GODDESS
KISSED ME
AND WALKED AWAY …
DISAPPEARING QUIETLY
INTO THE LAIR
OF FEMININE MYSTERY

THE WHEELS OF THE FUTURE WERE NOW SET IN FORWARD MOTION

That Friday night, Athena picked me up for the dance. In the car we started talking … and never stopped. At the dance, we didn't take the floor once. Instead, we huddled in a dark corner and continued our blissful conversation. As the night went on, we got closer, holding hands and sharing short kisses. I was amazed at how much experience we actually had with each other over the years, sometimes interacting and acknowledging each other's presence, sometimes not. The comfort of our long familiarity with each other was a definite plus. There was no uncertainty that evening. No first-date jitters or awkward silences. The night flowed gently on, slowly picking up speed, gently guiding us into the mind-numbing abyss of youthful lust and passion. We had both waited, not knowing the other waited too. Communication had empowered us … we would wait no longer.

WHEN THE DANCE WAS OVER
WE BOTH KNEW THE NIGHT
AND OUR FUTURE
HAD JUST BEGUN

I seemed to know what Athena was thinking, not because I could read her mind … but because I could read her feelings. They were like an open book to me, *pages scattered upon the wind, swept up in a hurricane of sexual and emotional surrender, purposely delivered to the doorstep of my soul.*

In my mind, I had always been her tortured solitary superhero, never able to reveal my true identity. She had been the bright star in the dark night sky, the only thing I dreamt of ... the angelic lighthouse shining hope for the last ship lost in the storm. I had been that ship, and finally ... Athena would bring me home.

C'MON ... HER PARENTS WERE OUT OF TOWN!

Athena's mom, dad, and sister were in Lake Tahoe, catching the season's first good snow. I'd always envisioned Athena as a little snow bunny. I would ride by their house in the winter and see them returning from many a frosty mountain adventure, Athena in her puffy white jacket and tan fur boots, blonde hair flowing beneath a white wool cap, her tender cheeks soft and flushed. This was but one of many images I had of Athena forever burned into my deepest thoughts and desires. Many times I had envisioned making love to her in a lost mountain cabin, wind howling outside, our bodies warm, naked, and intertwined inside. The dancing flames of a warm fire gently celebrating the joy of our perfect mortal union.

When we got to her house, she didn't ask me if I wanted to come in. Instead, she got out of the car, walked up to the front door, and opened it. Without entering, she turned back to me, looked straight into my eyes ... and waited. I didn't ask either. I got out of the car, walked up the sidewalk, and straight into the house. The house that had watched her grow from a shy child into a beautiful young woman. It was the fortress that had kept her in, and me out, letting only my imagination fuel my curiosity and angst for the fair maiden I had so worshipped from afar.

NOW
IT WOULD SHELTER HER NO MORE
INSTEAD
IT WOULD BEAR WITNESS TO MY ENTRANCE
IT WOULD ACCEPT WITHOUT NEGOTIATION
FOR THIS TIME
THE FORBIDDEN DOOR
HAD BEEN OPENED
BY THE FAIR YOUNG MAIDEN HERSELF

Athena closed the door behind me and all I felt was her gentle presence. From the moment the night had started, all we could do was talk, hold hands, and steal brief kisses. Now the page had been turned, and talk was a cumbersome liability. She quietly took my arm and led me upstairs.

**THOUGH THE HOUSE WAS DIMLY LIT,
I CAUGHT A BRIEF GLIMPSE OF HER
"ELECTRIC GYPSY-BLUE EYES ..."**

***THE MYSTERY OF THOSE EYES
HAD HAUNTED ME FOR SO LONG
NOW THEY GUIDED ME
TO THE GENTLE ABYSS
OF ATHENA'S SOUL ...
AND TO THE LAIR
OF HER ULTIMATE
PHYSICAL SURRENDER***

We silently reached the top of the stairs on our pilgrimage to Athena's bedroom. Though I knew we were alone, I felt the ghosts of Athena's family roaming the halls, doing everyday stuff and having everyday conversations. They were eating toast, washing their hair, doing laundry and watching television, mundane signatures of life we all take for granted. Yet I felt slighted, cheated, and angry that I had never been a part of those moments. I was an outsider, the spy never asked to come in from the cold ... until now.

Athena brought me in, but why had she waited so long? Did she not know how I felt about her all these years? Had my fascination for this nubile goddess deluded my sense of reality so far as to create a false sense of entitlement, allowing me to wallow in a cesspool of loathing and self-pity on the outside? Nice analysis, but this wasn't the time. Athena opened the door to her bedroom. As we entered, the ghosts in the hallway disappeared, and the house once again ... was quiet.

From that night on, we never looked at each other the same again. We'd been to the mountain and far beyond. And beyond the mountain, the rivers of ecstasy flowed free and the spirit was allowed to soar without fear or guilt. We had opened the gates of heaven, reached nirvana, and achieved total bliss. There was no turning back, and neither of us wanted to. This was the unfiltered essence of love, years in the making and well worth the wait. Each moment we were apart was an eternity, each moment together a physical and spiritual epiphany. I hoped this would last forever, and if forever would have us ... we would be eternally grateful.

That summer was our summer of love, and our senior year was a scholastic farewell to the innocent dreams of youth. Graduation would signal our first step into the dark mysterious catacombs of adulthood.

Prom night was an ironic carbon copy of the Sadie Hawkins dance, but this time we both knew exactly how the evening would end. After that, we would be free to face the brave new world together ... or so I had hoped.

That fall, I was set to attend San Francisco State, taking a plethora of computer tech and design courses. It was a slight commute but well worth it to stay at home, to stay close to Athena. What I would painfully find out later that summer was that Athena had applied for and received a scholarship to Oregon State, in some kind of advanced two-year horticulture program. When I first found out, I was crushed by the news. I felt angry and betrayed. My hurt began to drive an invisible wedge between Athena and myself. It began destroying me inside, and in turn it began destroying us. By the time August came and Athena left, there was no us.

THE GATES OF HEAVEN HAD CLOSED
NIRVANA WAS LOST
BLISS BECAME A POLAROID SHOT
EXILED TOO LONG
IN THE HOT SUN
ON SOMEBODY'S CRACKED DASHBOARD
ITS SENSUAL ENCHANTING COLORS
A SAD AND FADED MEMORY

OR SO I THOUGHT

Though our lives had changed dramatically between our brutal August goodbye and our joyous summer reunion at the thrift store years later, one thing was for sure ...

OUR STORY WASN'T OVER YET

We dated for five years after that, never spending one night apart. One cold December day in South Lake Tahoe, I swallowed the M–word like a cup of steaming hot alphabet soup ... and married my blue-eyed ski bunny. That was the moment I realized, that though the words are poetically linked in romantic context, wealth and love were at best distant cousins. For wealth was measured by entitlement and commodity. Love could not possibly be measured by such base standards. For love was magic, and magic could not be measured by how much of it you had, just that you had it was enough.

THE GATES OF HEAVEN REOPENED
NIRVANA WAS FOUND
BLISS BECAME THE COLORS
OF ATHENA'S FAVORITE FLORAL PRINT
... SENSUAL AND ENCHANTING

SO WHY AM I HERE? AND WHERE IS MY BEAUTIFUL WIFE ATHENA?

The Berries are sweet this morning, sweeter than usual. But my supply is getting low. I must find more. A storm is coming in from the west, not the usual southeast. This one feels different from the other storms I have weathered on the island. The air feels warmer, and has an ominous texture that envelopes my body like a soft, wet blanket. I need to move to higher ground, the same ground where the Paradise Berries grow in abundance. But my previous journeys have left me confused, sore, and scarred. The direct approach is steep, rocky, and treacherous. This time I will take a different less direct route. To do that, I will have to travel northwest on the beach until I reach the large inlet that cuts into the coastline and leads up to the higher elevations of the interior. Though I have seen the inlet from the upper regions, I have never explored it at ground level ... but something has been pulling at me to do so for quite some time.

The farther I travel, the worse the storm gets. I can feel it making peculiar love to the tropical landscape. The wind seems to howl and whisper, *you are mine ... I am coming for you!* The sky is growing darker and the soft, wet blanket has become cold and unforgiving. Savage ocean mist permeates my senses with salt and danger. I need to find shelter, and fast. I'm almost to the inlet; I can see it in the distance. It's farther than I thought. The waves are now hitting the rocks with violence and passion. They are taking over the shore like the troops at Normandy, with equal force, volition, and might. Just a little farther and I'm there.

The inlet is beautiful ... beautiful and more sheltered than I thought. Trees and vegetation are growing from the ascending, cathedral-like rocks. They cascade over me like a protective ghost, giving me a sense of security, structure, and peace. The storm is out there, and I am in here, anchored and steady in the calm waters of Terra-Donnas' majestic womb ...

AND SO IS THE BOAT

Somebody's boat, The *Electric Gypsy,* a large, beautiful sailboat with a cracked hull and shattered rudder. Who does this boat belong to? Are they still alive? Are they on the island too? Maybe they are the answer I have been seeking in my lost hours here. But where are they ... who are they?

The main quarters are beautiful but disheveled. She must have been in a terrible storm, much like the one right now ... the perfect storm, the one that not only takes you off course, but takes you away ... forever. She probably hit the rocks, but she got in. She's not seaworthy but she's still intact. *The GPS unit is still on ... it's still on! She couldn't have been here for too long. No bodies. Did they fall overboard?* Too many questions, I'll find the radio. If the transponder's functioning, the batteries are still good. Maybe I'll be rescued. But where is everybody?

WHERE IS EVERYBODY?

THERE ARE NO SUCH THINGS AS GHOSTS
SO WHY DO I FEEL THEM?
THERE IS NOBODY HERE
BUT THERE WAS
IF YOU WANT TO FIND THEM
YOU MUST GO TO WHERE THEY ARE
YOU CAN'T TURN BACK TIME
I NEVER SAID I WANTED TO

YOU'RE RUNNING …
SHUT UP!

This can't be déjà vu. It must be lack of sleep, or maybe lack of protein. Wait a minute, have I been here before … on *this* boat? Maybe they all just look the same. Yeah, that's it, all boats look the same. But that can't be right. Did the *Titanic* look like the flipping S.S. *Minnow*? No, scrap that thought. So why does this boat seem familiar? There is an odd sense of order and beauty in this discarded hulk. Notes and pictures scattered everywhere. Beautiful people … this one in particular. She's young, with radiant sandy blonde hair …

BEAUTIFUL EYES
BLUE EYES
THE EYES
YOU NAME A SHIP AFTER
ELECTRIC GYPSY-BLUE EYES

There's writing on the back of the picture …

"I'm sorry, Carlo. I'll always love you …"

Athena

My head feels hot. For a second, I thought I was on *my* boat. The lights are all off ... it's late. Why am I in Carlo's living room?

WE MUST HAVE GONE OUT DRINKING!

DAMN!
ATHENA'S GONNA BE PISSED
HOPE WE DIDN'T HAVE PLANS TONIGHT
SHI-T!

THIS HAPPENS EVERY TIME WE DROP BY THE CLUB AFTER WORK!
THAT JERK'S PROBABLY PASSED OUT
I'D BETTER CHECK ON HIM BEFORE I LEAVE
THAT'S WEIRD
MY GUNBAG'S HERE
WHAT'S IT DOING HERE?
THIS AIN'T RIGHT
CARLO'S DOOR IS AJAR
I CAN HEAR VOICES
HE MUST BE ON HIS CELL
WAIT A MINUTE
THAT'S A CHICK'S VOICE
DUMBASS DIDN'T PASS OUT
HE GOT LUCKY
THAT SON OF A BITCH GOT LUCKY!

MY HEAD IS SPINNING ... MAYBE IT'S THE ROOM

I SEE A REFLECTION
IN ATHENA'S FAVORITE PICTURE
ATHENA'S FLORAL PRINT
ATHENA'S FAVORITE PICTURE ...
ATHENA?

ATHENA?

I could see my reflection in the glass of Athena's favorite floral print, which hung directly above the headboard, the same one that we had in our house ... *in our bedroom!*

BUT THIS WAS CARLO'S APARTMENT
AND THEY
DIDN'T
SEE ME
AT LEAST FOR NOW

There would be no confrontation, no glorious spatter of emotion caused by the accidental discovery of the ultimate betrayal. No, the curtain would close on the final act here and now. There would be no conflict, no pathetic pleas for mercy or forgiveness, no excuses, and no last minute reprieve ... just resolution.

SALEM WAS RIGHT!

I remember now. I remember why I ran! I remember what I did. And worst of all, I can feel every sickening moment of it all over again ... my heart at the lowest point of human despair, my mind on fire, confused and unclear of the situation before me but certain of its deadly outcome.

I shot her first. I wanted to see the look in his eyes before he could no longer see. I wanted my anger to meet his fear in the ultimate last chapter ... the ultimate communication. He just froze and accepted his fate. He had no choice.

When it was all over, I sat on the edge of the bed. Holding Athena's hand, I stared at her body in limbo, hoping that she would wake up like nothing had happened and kiss me ... but she never did.

I WATCHED FOR A BRIEF ETERNITY AS
THE ROOM FILLED WITH BLOOD

A MACABRE SENSE OF IRONY
SUDDENLY GRABBED ME
WAS I SAYING GOODBYE?
OR WAS I LINGERING
LIKE A MURDEROUS PICASSO
ADMIRING HIS WORK
A MASTERPIECE OF BLOOD AND RAGE
A TEMPORARY SHRINE
TO THE ULTIMATE BETRAYAL
WAS I SAYING GOODBYE ...?

I heard sirens, it was time to go. I dropped the gun ... and fled.

THE STORM IS OVER
I'M EXHAUSTED
I NEED SLEEP
HERE COMES MY FRIEND
MY INTREPID SOLAR FRIEND ...

THE SUN

Reflections
"Paradise Berry"

Paradise Berry taste purple and sweet
Won't find 'em growin' on any ol' street
Just hangin' loose on an island lost
Don't give a worry about Stranger or frost

Paradise Berry don't wager or judge
Don't hold a debt and don't hold no grudge
Just show de movie when de lights go down
And you're de only horse in dis one horse town

Paradise Berry don't shake or swing
Never been fake, don't wear no bling
Don't carry phone and don't make no calls
Hold de soul prisoner when dey are no walls

Paradise Berry got much to say
But twelve lines of rhyme is enough today
Ol' solar friend he bring light to de eyes
'Cuz paradise juice rip through yo' disguise

Last Man in Paradise

Chapter Eight

"No berries this morning."

I think, to the best of my recollection, that there was one constant in my tropical island exile: the morning sun. He always seemed to rise in the same exact place, at the same exact time. His welcoming glow was always inviting and friendly. He was the only friend I seemed to have.

Never judgmental or critical, my flaring solar friend executed his daily rounds with heavenly precision. My friend the sun had his friends too ... the waves. He would spread himself upon them like butter on toast, and they would play. They danced where there was no music, they touched but never made contact, they whispered yet never spoke ... the perfect relationship, a union that wasn't. But today my heavenly friend looked different. He took on a wet crimson glow, an eerie cosmic warning that only he understood. What was he trying to tell me? How could I possibly decipher this stellar puzzle with no clues? I would have to wait, but for how long?

When would the prophetic secrets of the sky step out of their galactic shadows and let themselves be known? The future, if there was to be one, had once again taken me prisoner, handing down an unknown sentence for unspecified charges. Yes, once again, I would have to wait ... but I wouldn't have to wait long.

The first ships arrived late that morning. Like giant silver eagles gliding mystically across a turquoise sea of clouds and heavenly light, they met the earth with the grace of a delicate ballerina, and the foreboding presence of an angry lion. Angels and demons breaking bread and saying grace at the very same table ... was I to join in on the feast? Were these my saviors, sent by the powers that be to repeal my sentence of involuntary exile? Was it time for me to return to civilization? To retake my seat in a society I had so vehemently despised and mistrusted? Did I have a choice?

Maybe these weren't my saviors. Maybe these ships were what my crimson friend was trying to warn me about. Maybe the cosmic hangmen of karma and blind justice were here at last. Would I be tried and convicted, or merely let off with a slap on the wrist? Maybe all of mankind was on trial? Surely we deserved it. We were guilty of years of crimes against both our own humanity and the planet that had so unselfishly given us life. Maybe God wants to start all over again, and these are his interstellar erasers? I knew I would have my answer. But did I really want to know?

HIS NAME WAS BILL

"Bill" was an odd name for an alien who stood almost eight feet tall. Personally, I think he made the name up just to make things easier for me. His real name was probably something like ***"Klatuufunkymandiggerjones90210yourmamadontdance."*** We spoke, but didn't talk, just like the sun on the waves ... the perfect relationship.

I was hungry, very hungry, not having had my usual Paradise Berries that morning. So I hoped the conversation would be brief. Kind of an ironic situation actually: quite possibly man's first contact with an advanced alien intelligence ... and all I was thinking about was my stomach!

Bill was polite, warm, and refreshingly engaging. He even spoke English. I felt comfortable around him and was secretly looking forward to a new and lasting relationship.

"Hey, gang! I'd like you to meet my new alien friend, Bill!" Wow, what would they say back home?

SCREW THEM ... I HATED PEOPLE!

Humanity, in general, was a plague, an overpopulated Petri dish of worthless bacteria that could use a stiff shot of penicillin, everyday rats, mulling about their worldly maze for a single piece of rotting cheese ... worthless. I wonder if Bill knew this. Bill was quite articulate for an alien, and an excellent communicator. I liked Bill ... *I hoped he liked me.*

Bill told me about his home planet, where it was located in the universe and all about their ships and amazing alien culture. I was mesmerized by his descriptions of their art, social philosophy, architecture, and technology. I was sure we would be friends for a long, long time. He might even take me back to his home planet. Wow, what would they say back home ... screw them, worthless bacteria!

But then it happened ... just like that. The line went dead in the middle of what I thought was a wonderful conversation. Bill's warm, subtle demeanor suddenly turned bitter and cold. His calm telepathic voice slowly became terse and elevated. *Don't yell at me, turtle boy!* I thought, not knowing if he was at that moment reading my mind or not. His planet was dying, he said. His race slowly ravaged and massacred by a human plague unwittingly turned loose on an unknowing and vulnerable alien culture ... all under the guise of galactic unification and friendship.

The culprit was an unspectacular microbe, suspended in the miniature cryogenic chamber of a deep-space probe launched from Earth many years earlier. This earthborn microbe unexpectedly and mysteriously thrived and mutated in an alien environment, culminating in an unintended chain reaction of death and terror on an isolated planet, nestled in the darkest shadows of a cold and unforgiving universe.

ONE PLANETS PROBE IS ANOTHER PLANETS POISON!

No one was to blame for this tragic crime against the aliens, yet justice would be served. The human race was tried, convicted, and sentenced in a court of law never even witnessed by the accused, by a jury not of their peers, but of the victims themselves ... the ones still alive.

It had become dangerously clear that my new philosophically superior best friend and his buddies were here for nothing more than some good old fashioned home-cooked revenge, whippin' out a long-distance can of whoop-ass in the form of the complete annihilation of the human race. On my mammoth island paradise, I suddenly felt cornered, trapped in the headlights of a horrific Greek tragedy that had begun millions of light years away from my own back yard.

I thought of my family and friends. I wondered if Bill could see that. An unconscious clarity suddenly enveloped my mind. I found it strangely refreshing, and wondered if this was the "transcendental self," the euphoric state of total insight and bliss that all those yogis, monks, high priests, and acolytes spent their lives chasing. How funny, I'd never even given that stuff a second thought, yet here I was ... *transcendental.* I wondered if Bill was doing this. An advanced being such as himself who could travel light years across the universe and communicate telepathically in a language completely foreign to his own must have a few more tricks up his sleeve.

I thought of my many lost loves, and my beautiful wife Athena. Her sun-kissed hair, gypsy-blue eyes, and warm body suspended my senses in a radiant glow of inner peace and harmony. A new and strange feeling caressed my soul, hinting that maybe soon we would be together again ... joined eternally to forever make passionate love in the garden of plumeria and silk.

The irony of Bill's situation brought to mind that ...

EVEN IN FRIENDSHIP, THE ARROGANCE OF MAN PROVES DEADLY

Bill stopped his telepathic communicating. Silence permeated a strange and uncomfortable rip in the universe. My newfound clarity slowly began to fade. I said goodbye to my family, my friends ... *I said goodbye to Athena.* I kissed her soft, sweet lips and watched as her warm gypsy gaze joined the angelic mist of a million lost yesterdays, scattering amongst the dead leaves of memory and time.

I told Bill I was sorry. Sorry for his people and his beautiful culture, doomed to extinction by the inept and arrogant hand of man. I think Bill was sorry, too.

I REMEMBERED AGAIN
THAT I WAS HUNGRY
NOT HAVING HAD MY USUAL
PARADISE BERRIES
THAT MORNING
AND SUDDENLY I REALIZED ...
IT REALLY DIDN'T MATTER

On this day, my intrepid solar friend made his vertical ascent into the turquoise heavens, and then began his methodic descent into the nocturnal abyss.

BUT ON THIS DAY HE NEVER QUITE MADE IT, HE JUST WENT DARK.

AND I NO LONGER ...

WAS HUNGRY.

A Note From Bud

Contemporary science fiction has, more often than not, fed us the notion that a race with the supreme technology and motivation can traverse effortlessly across untold millions of light years to achieve their superlative goals ... whether they be peace, conquest, or destruction.

SUCH IS NOT THE CASE

For those with the most advanced technology and refined skills tend to fall victim to their own egos and agendas, creating a false wall of security for themselves, ultimately blazing a trail to their own demise at a high cost for everyone involved.

We have already learned this on Earth, where all we had to traverse were rivers, oceans, and sky ...

ONLY TO ARRIVE AT THE SAME CONCLUSION!!!

About the Author

Bud Higgins, a direct descendant of writer and poet Robert Lewis Stevenson, lives in Northern California wine country where he works as an artist and writer. In his spare time, he works on a four-hundred-acre wild animal preserve with cheetahs, monkeys, giraffes, and white rhinos. This is his first book.